PRAISE FOR THE SEER SERIES

"The strong female heroine will appeal to teen readers, and adults and teens alike may also enjoy the themes of corruption and religion, absolute human power, and government as God. . . . Dekker's debut is worth choosing."

PUBLISHERS WEEKLY on *The Choosing*

"The story vacillates between the sweetness of a tender coming-of-age romance and moments that almost resemble a Dean Koontz thriller. . . . At times frightening but often beautiful, [*The Choosing*] will leave readers eager for the next book of this new series."

SERENA CHASE, *USA Today*

"[*The Choosing*] is an amazing debut novel full of heart, drama, and complex believable characters . . . with a detailed plot and gripping truths that pierced my heart."

THE BOOK CLUB NETWORK INC.

"A swiftly moving plot puts readers in the center of the action, and the well-described setting adds to the experience. Deeper themes of value and worth will appeal to both young adult and adult readers."

ROMANTIC TIMES on *The Choosing*

"Whatever expectations you have of debut author Rachelle Dekker, go ahead and put them aside. Rachelle, daughter to bestselling author Ted Dekker, is carving out a space of her own. Her debut novel, *The Choosing*, is a rich statement about the author's future and her impact on Christian fiction."

FAMILY FICTION

"Ripe for discussion, [*The Choosing*] may inspire some readers to open up about the social pressures that they feel both in and out of their faith community. Expect it to appeal to dystopian fans of all ages."

FOREWORD REVIEWS

"Readers will find Dekker's storyline somewhat akin to her father's works in terms of action, adventure, and unpredictability. *The Choosing*, though, explores more the inner workings of her characters and how they feel about their lot in life. I look forward to more dystopian titles from Dekker in the near future."

BOOKREPORTER.COM

"*The Choosing* is an inspiring tale that reaches deep into the hearts of men and women, showing both the love and the darkness that can lurk within."

FRESH FICTION

"Marrying the themes of the popular Kiera Cass Selection novels with the action danger of *The Hunger Games*,

Dekker asserts a strong imaginative voice that had me gulping down sentences and events as quickly as they were relayed on [the] page."

"[*The Choosing*] is part adventure, part romance, part mystery, and it works. The writing is wonderful. It flows in such a way that it keeps the reader turning page after page . . . more than likely long into the night to find out what happens!"

"In her stunning debut novel, Rachelle Dekker plunges readers into a unique yet familiar-feeling dystopian society, where one girl's longing for acceptance, identity, and purpose becomes a mind-bending, pulse-pounding journey that'll [leave] you breathless and reeling. A superb story!"

"This intense dystopian read was reminiscent of the Divergent series. Christian themes of God's love and forgiveness are woven throughout [*The Calling*]."

"[Dekker's] strong storytelling voice and ability to convey her ideas comes through nicely in this book."

SHE WILL RISK

EVERYTHING

TO LEAD THEM

OUT OF

DARKNESS

THE RETURNING

RACHELLE DEKKER

TYNDALE HOUSE PUBLISHERS, INC., CAROL STREAM, ILLINOIS

Visit Tyndale online at www.tyndale.com.

Visit Rachelle Dekker's website at www.rachelledekker.com.

TYNDALE and Tyndale's quill logo are registered trademarks of Tyndale House Publishers, Inc.

The Returning

Designed by Dean H. Renninger

The Returning is a work of fiction. Where real people, events, establishments, organizations, or locales appear, they are used fictitiously. All other elements of the novel are drawn from the author's imagination.

Library of Congress Cataloging-in-Publication Data
Names: Dekker, Rachelle, author.
Title: The returning / Rachelle Dekker.
Description: Carol Stream, Illinois : Tyndale House Publishers, Inc., [2016] | Series: A Seer novel
Identifiers: LCCN 2016028466| ISBN 9781496402288 (hardcover) | ISBN 9781496402295 (softcover)
Subjects: | GSAFD: Christian fiction.
Classification: LCC PS3604.E378 R48 2016 | DDC 813/.6—dc23 LC record available at https://lccn.loc.gov/2016028466

Printed in the United States of America

22 21 20 19 18 17 16
7   6   5   4   3   2   1

For Chelise
May you never forget that the light living inside you
outshines the darkness living inside the world.

Do you know whom I see behind this thick glass?

A distorted image I call me.

But do I really know the person behind the mask, the body, the facade?

For you see, all I've ever known is how to attempt to be perfect

And when I fail, my mirror gets darker until all I see is filth.

Disappointment.

We all live in tainted glass that consumes us.

But do we have to?

What if I decided to wipe my mirror clean?

Pull a lamp string to bring in light.

Forgive myself for my mistakes . . . what happens then?

What if I chose to shatter my mirror altogether,

Believe in my beauty and worth and step beyond the

Fragmented glass

I'd have to live in a world with flawless glass,

Where I never hated myself, never hated others.

Wouldn't that be a world?

KARA DEKKER

CAST OF CHARACTERS

THE SEVEN

Sage Avery, *daughter of Dalen and Cece, original Trylin residents*

Kane Brant, *son of Ramses and Lesley*

Kennedy Brant, *daughter of Remko and Carrington*

Lucy Carson, *daughter of Selena Carson*

Timmons Gilford, *husband of Eleanor Lane*

Willis Lane, *son of Authority member Enderson Lane and brother of Eleanor*

Davis Tollen, *son of Wire and Kate*

SEERS

Remko Brant

Carrington Hale Brant

Elise Brant, *daughter of Remko and Carrington*

Graham "Wire" Tollen

Kate Tollen

Smith, *former City Watch lieutenant*

AUTHORITY CITY RESIDENTS

Jesse Cropper, *Authority President*

Dr. Roth Reynard, aka "the Scientist"

Nicolas Horner, *Authority army commander*

Sam Miller, *City Watch guard controlled by Genesis*

Franklin, *City Watch guard*

YEAR
2278

1 Trylin City sat against the monstrous mountain that served as its protecting spine. What was once a myth was now a functioning sanctuary for all those called to live outside the Authority City. Tall and majestic, the mountain's rocky peak shielded the city from sight and offered healthy soil at its roots, fresh spring water from its depths, indestructible stone for the walls, and a constant sense of security.

The morning was in full swing through the city streets, excitement swimming through the air. Everyone knew what today represented.

Carrington sat on her bed, the windows pulled closed. She wanted a moment to herself before the rest of the day dragged her into its depths.

A small cardboard box sat to her right. Folded paper filled its insides—letters and reminders of her past. Secrets she kept from everyone, even Remko. She glanced down at the unfolded letter she held between her fingers. It trembled as her eyes drank in the words once more.

November 12, 2260

My dearest Elise,

My heart is heavy today. Sometimes I fear that it will weigh me down with such ferociousness that I will never be able to walk again. I know that letting this pain cripple me hurts all those around me, but I can't seem to see through the darkness long enough to take hold of the light. I can see the hopelessness in your father's eyes. He has no idea how to help me; I hope he knows that I don't blame him for that. How could he possibly rescue me from this?

If I'm being honest, I'm not sure I want to be rescued. Would I even deserve to be happy after what I've done to you? Aaron sits with me often and tells me to remember and trust in the power that holds you. A power that cannot be threatened, that cannot be harmed, and at moments I feel that power as well. It allows me small moments of peace, but then I think of the power holding you close and I wish it were me. I find myself envious of the power and then angry that I've lost you and then shame because I let you be taken.

Do you hate me for that? You must. Are you suffering because I failed you as a mother? I have to stop my mind from wandering too far down the dark road that brings visions of what terrible things could be happening to you. If I go too far down that path, I will surely not survive.

Today is worse because today you turn two years old. I wonder if you're talking yet. What have you learned to say? I imagine you walking about, your legs finally growing strong enough to keep you steady, your mind full of questions about the world around you. Who is watching you grow? Who is teaching you?

It should be me.

Please forgive me for not being there. Please forgive me, for I will never forgive myself.

Your mother

Carrington clenched her eyes tightly to capture her tears and hold them back. She knew rereading these letters only brought pain, but after all these years of suffering it somehow felt comforting as well. More often than she'd like to admit, she'd steal away, pull out all the letters she'd written to her lost daughter, and read them, hoping, for just a moment, to be reconnected with her.

Carrington could hear the excitement building outside. The music had started. Voices of jubilation filled the air, and children's laughter echoed against the mountain, thrilling anticipation pulsing against the city walls. For weeks people had been preparing for today. For years they had been dreaming about this moment.

The prophecy was unfolding, and the time had come for them to send out the chosen Seven who would bring about the Awakening. The ones who would cross the wilderness back to the Authority City and finally bring the evil regime to its knees.

She whisked away the few tears that had escaped down her cheeks and folded the letter back into the box. She replaced the lid and moved to store it deep within her closet.

Moving to stand in front of the mirror, Carrington surveyed herself. She was dressed in plain tan slacks, a white button-down shirt, and her favorite navy cargo jacket. Her hair was pulled back and secured at the nape of her neck, showing her face clearly. Looking at herself, she noticed how time had changed her skin. There were lines in places that had once been smooth, wrinkles where the skin had been tight, and discoloring where it had been clear.

The physical changes didn't bother her usually, but now she found herself struggling to pull her mind away from the differences as she stared at her reflection. Not because she wished she looked different; more because it meant that twenty years had really passed to lead them to this moment. Twenty years of change and aging since she'd stood on the outskirts of the Authority City and left her daughter behind.

Another round of tears threatened to descend, and she took a deep breath to chase them away. She needed to clear her mind if she was going to survive today. She shouldn't have reached for those letters. She ran her hands along the sides of her jacket and questioned her clothing choice. It was a ceremony after all; maybe she should have worn a dress?

Carrington could feel the tremble starting again in her hands and she took another deep breath, moving away from the mirror. Her head swam with emotion and she tried to shake it free. She glanced at the clock on the wall and knew Remko would be expecting her any moment. She didn't have time to change into anything else, so she supposed what she was wearing was going to have to do. Moving through the motions of her typical routine, she turned off the lights, rechecked the closed window, locked the door, and descended the front staircase onto the street.

All around her were faces of people she knew. They smiled and waved, pure joy dancing across their expressions; Carrington waved back, masking the panic and worry building behind her own.

Each step toward Trylin's city center, where the ceremony was being held, was familiar. Carrington's legs had traversed this route hundreds of times. But they felt heavy, as if they knew this time the walk was different.

She was about to step off the main paved road into an alley to collect herself when a strong arm wrapped itself around her. Carrington turned to see Lucy Carson smiling at her. Carrington eased a bit and returned a genuine smile.

Lucy looked so much like her mother, Selena; the girl was now in her thirties, with bold, dark features and stunning black hair. Her eyes, however, mirrored those of her late older sister, Arianna, to whom Carrington owed so much.

Like Arianna, Lucy had an incredible gift of intuition,

something she'd learned to tap into as she'd grown in the truth of the Father and spent time learning at Aaron's feet. She was filled with peace and beauty beyond her years, and staring at her now, Carrington couldn't deny her envy.

"How are you?" Lucy asked.

Carrington fought off the urge to divulge all her hidden worry to the woman and merely smiled.

Lucy nodded and pulled Carrington closer as the two women slowly walked the road toward the main gathering. "That's what I thought."

"You shouldn't be here. Lesley will be in a panic," Carrington said.

Lucy gave a soft chuckle and shrugged. "I'm on my way. I just thought I'd check on you first. I know that while this day marks something phenomenal for most of us, it's clouded with fear for you."

"I'm fine, Lucy," Carrington lied. She could feel the girl's eyes on her and suddenly wished to be invisible. She knew even as Lucy opened her mouth to speak that she was going to have to work very hard to keep her walls up around her storming emotions.

"It happens in a flash, like a sneaky fox—suddenly the truth of your identity is replaced by the illusions of your mistakes," Lucy said softly. She paused and nodded to herself before a small smile caught her mouth. "Arianna used to say that to me, and I never understood what she meant."

Carrington could see pain working its way into Lucy's expression.

"She said so much to me in those last few months that sounded like madness," Lucy went on. "I remember desperately wanting to understand. I knew she was upsetting my parents. They would fight over how to handle her rebellion, as they called it, and I knew that if she didn't stop she was headed for trouble."

Lucy paused for a moment, her eyes staring down at her feet as they continued slowly toward their destination. "I went to her once. It was late; I was supposed to be in bed, but I couldn't sleep. I was too worried. I begged her to change, to obey the rules, to listen to our father, to be the girl she once was. I cried and asked her to do it for me, to think about me, because I couldn't lose her. Even then, I knew they would take her from me if she continued.

"She cried too. The bedroom was dark, but I could clearly see her face glistening with tears and broken from pain but with such resolve in her eyes. I remember because it was hard to make eye contact with her. I'd never seen her so sure of anything. Then she walked over to me, knelt so that our faces were close, softly brushed her thumb across my cheek, and said, 'My sweet Lucy, I *am* doing this for you.'"

Carrington's chest ached and she wished she could think of something to say that might offer some consolation, but she came up empty.

"After Arianna's execution, I felt completely responsible. She'd done this all for me—she'd even told me so. We were sisters, and I was supposed to protect her. The shame I carried around beat down on me internally until I bled."

"Lucy, that was not your fault," Carrington said.

"Just as Elise being taken was not yours," Lucy said.

Carrington stopped in her tracks, all images of Lucy and Arianna clearing from her mind. "That is totally different."

"Is it?" Lucy asked. "And now, with Kennedy leaving with the chosen Seven, do you carry blame for that also?"

Carrington swallowed hard against the tight ball forming in her throat. Images of both her daughters filled the space behind her eyes. "I am their mother."

Lucy gave Carrington's arm a squeeze and Carrington fought back the tears threatening to escape. "No, Carrington, their mother is a role you play, but it is not who you are. Like a sneaky little fox, suddenly the truth of your identity is replaced by the illusion of your mistakes."

Carrington wanted to pull away from Lucy's touch and hide in a dark place, but the younger woman's grip was solid and the truth of her words kept Carrington's feet in place.

"Let go of the grievances you hold against yourself, and know all that has happened and will happen is held under the power of the Father. The light that has been our strength will never fail us."

The tears Carrington had been holding back slid down her cheeks and the tremble in her hands resurfaced. Thoughts of her daughters collided inside her head. The one she'd watched grow into a beautiful, independent, secure woman, and the other she'd only dreamed of. One she'd held too closely because she'd let the other be taken.

One who now wanted to leave in hopes of rescuing the other, but all Carrington could think about was losing them both.

Lucy slid her hand up to Carrington's shoulder. "Remember who you are. Who Elise is and who Kennedy is, and who calls them His own."

Carrington knew Lucy was right, but acknowledging that truth would mean giving up her right to be angry and afraid, and she wasn't ready to do that. She wanted to tell Lucy so, wanted to claim Lucy wasn't a mother so she couldn't possibly understand what she was asking Carrington to do, but a loud pounding rhythm filled the air and drowned out her unspoken words.

The ceremony drums had started. The two of them were very late.

2 Remko could feel the vibration of each drumbeat through his heels from where he stood onstage. The wooden platform that backed up to the monstrous Trylin Mountain faced the gathering of every soul that called this simple city home. Everyone but Carrington, who was still nowhere to be seen, though the ceremony was about to start.

Remko knew his wife's soul was on its own journey. Ever since Kennedy had been called to join the Seven. Their daughter's calling hadn't come as much of a shock to him; he'd long ago accepted that his children were not his own and that the truest form of love was in letting go. As he'd once done with Elise, he'd also learned to do with Kennedy. He often forgot, but as Aaron had so often drilled into their heads, the importance was in the remembering.

Now, as he stood before the city he commanded, before the people who had lived for this day when the prophecy of the Seven would be fulfilled, before a city that represented the freedom that came when you let go of your fears and trusted the Father, Remko remembered to hold no grievance against the woman he loved. For she also had to find the power in remembering.

Six drummers, three men and three women, worked the crowd with enthusiasm. They danced to the beats they played as they moved through the gathered people and toward the platform. Children squealed with delight and mothers and fathers beamed with joy. The coordinated pulse of the instruments shook them all with a vibration that signaled the start of a new era.

Remko caught sight of Carrington and Lucy approaching the stage from the left just as the final rhythmic string of joyful sounds was coming to a close. Lucy gave him a silly wink, as if to say it wasn't a real party until she was fashionably late, and Carrington tried an apologetic smile as both women ascended the small wooden staircase and took their places onstage. Carrington beside Remko, and Lucy with the other chosen ones, making them complete. Seven in all.

The drums came to a thunderous conclusion and the city exploded into thrilled applause. The energy swept up and across the stage, and Remko let himself be taken with the spirit of what this moment represented. He reached out and grabbed Carrington's hand to let her know all was well and drove both of his arms into the air, sweeping hers up with his, their fingers intertwined. The crowd's applause grew and the entire mountain felt as though it were trembling with them.

Remko kept his hands high as the city rejoiced. He stole a glance at the woman beside him and she smiled— a genuine, full-faced smile that lit his heart and drove his excitement forward. Suddenly a great wind descended on the gathering, sweeping through hair and clothes, filling the city with hope and crushing the fears that lingered.

Remko closed his eyes and let the wind surround him fully, welcoming the renewal it brought. He lowered his arms as the wind lessened to a breeze and the people began to still. Stairs to the right of the platform creaked and Remko turned to see Aaron step onto the stage. They shared a knowing smile before Remko turned back to face his people.

"Trylin City," Remko shouted, and the crowd once again rang out in applause. "We are gathered here today in remembrance. A single body, united by the Father, embracing the identity He calls us to."

Cheers sprang up from the faces below as Remko continued. "We are here because we were called, as all people are, to discover the truth that lives within us, to acknowledge the heritage we possess, to lay claim to the identity that was given to us, and to grow in the truth of the light that is greater than all darkness. And now we send out those chosen to take that truth to the world."

The crowd ignited with joy, their voices echoing off the stone faces of the mountain's cliffs. Aaron grabbed Remko's shoulder and shook it with excitement. His laugh joined the others and Remko himself let out a cheer.

Aaron stepped forward to address the crowd, and the people fell silent. "For many years you have heard me talk of this day. Many of you remember the moment when each individual on this stage heard the call from the Father to go. Go into the world and make believers of all His children. We must never forget that those inside the Authority City walls are members of our family, of our body, who have simply forgotten who they are. They are blinded to their own salvation, as all of you were once blind. But we will help them see!"

The crowd cheered again, the vibration setting the ground astir.

Aaron continued once the crowd had settled. "It is also important to remember the darkness that floods the streets now. The darkness these chosen Seven will surely face. Led by a tyrant, a man who believes his mind and power are greater than the light. His talons are submerged deep within the city, but do not let this stir fear within you. For the light that lives inside us is stronger than the darkness that lives inside him. He has tricked many into believing lies about themselves, because he comes to steal, kill, and destroy, but he will not be victorious."

Aaron raised his fist into the air, and quickly all the people followed suit. Every person in the city, as one, lifting a single fist to the sky as an intentional calm fell over the gathering.

Aaron spoke. "To the earth and the Father who molded it."

The crowd echoed back their response. "To the earth."

"To the wind and the Father who guides it."

"To the wind."

"To the light and the Father who summons it."

"To the light."

"To His children and the Father who calls them His own."

"To His children."

"We acknowledge!"

"We acknowledge!"

"We accept!"

"We accept!"

Aaron paused, then shouted, "We believe!"

"We believe!"

As the last syllable fell from the crowd's lips, a powerful energy grew from their combined cries and once again rattled the ground. Deep emotion echoed up through Remko's chest and he pulled Carrington under his arm and to his side. He kissed the top of her head as Aaron crossed the stage to where the chosen Seven stood. Their faces glowed with honor and humility, all of them visibly itching to start out on the journey they had been called to.

Aaron waited as the crowd regained their quiet composure and then continued. "Each of you in the crowd represents a pillar of strength and support for those standing here who have been called to go. Join with them in spirit as we send them out with great confidence."

Aaron made his way to the farthest end of the line and took the hand of Lucy Carson. Remko looked and saw Lucy's younger sister, Rayna, beaming in the front row, tears of joy streaming down her cheeks.

"Do you accept the call set before you to follow the

wind, honor the light, and know the Father who created them both?" Aaron asked.

Lucy smiled. "With pleasure," she answered in her quirky way, and several chuckles rose from the crowd. Aaron reached into his pocket and pulled out a small silver medallion fastened to a leather necklace. Lucy tipped her head forward as Aaron placed the piece around her neck. Remko knew the medallion would serve as a reminder of where Lucy's true identity lay, as the road ahead was sure to test them all.

Aaron then moved on down the line. Kane Brant, Remko's nephew. His parents, Ramses and Lesley, watched with joy. Sage Avery, the middle daughter to an original Trylin City family, had been just a baby when the Seers had arrived here. Timmons Gilford, husband to Eleanor Lane, the daughter of Authority member Enderson Lane. Willis Lane, Eleanor's younger brother. Eleanor would be saying goodbye to both of the men in her life. Davis Tollen, the only child of Wire and Kate. The boy had taken strengths from both parents. And finally, Kennedy, Remko and Carrington's younger daughter.

Remko felt Carrington's body tense as Kennedy accepted her call and received her medallion. Remko recognized his own reservations rising, but he knew the path set before his daughter was clear. The truest form of love was letting go.

With each member, Aaron had asked the same question and presented them with the same token as he gave his blessing and accepted their response. He then turned back to the crowd.

"You have taken part in the beginning of the new life that is to come. Let our faith continue to grow and our hearts be steadfast as this new chapter commences. Now, as these Seven have committed to you, so you too should commit to them. Let us celebrate these warriors, as in doing so we celebrate Him."

Aaron again raised his fist high and shouted, "We believe!"

As one unit the gathering did the same, and as their words died off, the drummers began to play again. Applause and cheers rang out; parents and families of the chosen Seven rushed the platform and embraced their loved ones. Remko caught Kennedy's eye, and she smiled as she moved through the gathered mass now on stage and into Remko's arms. He held her tightly for a long moment before pulling back to see the light shining behind her eyes.

Kennedy turned to Carrington, her mother's eyes already brimming with tears, and threw her arms around her neck. Carrington pulled her close, and Remko could hear Kennedy whispering. "It's going to be okay, Mom. I'm going to find her."

Remko's heart faltered and he sensed the all-too-familiar fear creeping into his chest. The endless stream of questions that always led him to one ultimate question: *What if she isn't still alive?*

He felt a pair of eyes on him and glanced up to meet

Aaron's stare. They held each other's gazes for only a second, and then Aaron shrugged as if to say, *Even now you can choose salvation over fear. The choice is always yours.*

Remko grinned and shook his head slightly as Aaron let out a hearty laugh. He was right; even now the choice was his. So he would choose faith over fear and belief over doubt.

3 A deep chill sank into Roth Reynard's bones and he glanced up from his office desk. The room around him was dark; only a small spot on his desk was illuminated by a lamp on the work surface. The air seemed to have dropped in temperature and an uneasy feeling pulsed at the nape of his neck. He scanned the room carefully, searching every crevice for whatever was tugging at his senses. He was certain he wasn't alone.

Movement caught the corner of his eye and the Scientist stood. "Who's there?"

A man stepped out from the shadows and Roth's jaw clenched painfully. He knew this man, though they had never met. Not outside of Roth's dreams. *Aaron.* His chest filled with rage and hate, the power resting inside his dark soul screeching out against the man before him. "You were foolish to have come here," the Scientist said.

"I told you the time was coming, and now here it is," Aaron said.

Roth fought back the shiver starting under his skin. Aaron's words cut like razors in his mind. *I told you the time was coming.* He had told him. For weeks now. In his dreams, in the depths of his sleep. And here the maniac stood, in his office. Or was this just another device of the mind, playing cruel tricks on him? Was his brain plotting against him, colluding with the enemy?

"How did you get in here?" the Scientist asked.

"I walked," Aaron said.

Past the guards scattered through every hallway? Doubtful, Roth thought. "I won't let you walk out."

Aaron's eyes glued themselves to Roth's, and the Scientist could feel their heat, like a pulse of fire. "I think your lack of power over me would be surprising," Aaron said.

Anger boiled in Roth's blood and a rumble turned in his chest. Who was this crazed man—if he could be called a man at all? The familiar lure of power expanded through the Scientist's bones. The dark energy that he held closely reared its evil head as Aaron took another step. "You have come to my kingdom and believe that I would let you leave alive?" Roth asked.

"This kingdom belongs to the light. The people were His first. You are the invader, and their time of returning is near," Aaron said.

Roth spit out a laugh through his clenched teeth. "I own these people. My science saved them. You cannot threaten me here."

"Yet you tremble where you stand. Good—you should tremble. No kingdom created by man shall endure," Aaron said.

The rebel's clear lack of respect for the Scientist enraged

him further. "I will not let you and your people destroy what I have built. I have brought forth the next level of evolution; you can't turn back the hands of time. There is nothing powerful enough to undo what I have done," the Scientist said.

A thunderous gust of wind swept across the room, rocking the floor under Roth's desk and shaking his core. He fell into his chair as the wind whirled around and swallowed everything in its tracks. Papers and dust swirled off the floor like tiny whirlpools all around him. Books crashed to the floor; his desk wobbled violently against the hardwood. Roth raised his hand to his face to block the onslaught of debris.

He saw Aaron through the small slits in his fingers. The man stood, face skyward, a smile plastered to his lips, a palpable sense of ease surrounding him as if the wind were comforting him, not trying to rip him into pieces.

Aaron dropped his face and looked through the tempest toward Roth, an expression of absolute certainty behind his eyes as he spoke. "It is coming. It is inevitable, and it cannot be threatened." A bright light pierced through the wild wind and spread out to every corner of the room. The darkness residing in Roth's chest rose up to protect him from the light, acting as a shield, blocking out his vision. It hissed and twisted as it came face-to-face with the light emanating from Aaron. Roth couldn't see anything, but he heard Aaron's words through the howling of the wind.

"It is certain and eternal. It is freedom for all. And it has already started."

A heavy pounding echoed somewhere through the chaos, but the Scientist couldn't focus past just trying to remain in his seat. He felt his chair give way under the pressure of the wind, and he crashed to the floor, his body surrounded in darkness, the light that felt like flames starting to pierce through, the chill of the suffocating wind inching its way closer. Like fire and ice, the forces crashed around him on all sides. And through it all Aaron's voice rang loud and clear.

"This city will soon be reclaimed by light. The people will once again know their true names. They will be found in the light once again. And the girl Elise will call them all home. She will lead the Returning!"

"Enough—enough!" Roth cried. A tremendous crack echoed through the swirl of insanity and the entire room stilled. The furniture stopped shaking against the floor, the dust settled, and Roth raised his head to see a handful of CityWatch guards stumbling in through his now-splintered office door. They looked around the room in confused sweeps, armed and ready to take on whatever villain was attacking their leader.

"Arrest him!" Roth shouted.

"Arrest who?" one guard asked.

Roth spun his head toward where Aaron had been standing and cursed violently when he saw no one. The dark power welling under his skin buzzed with anger and whispered instructions the Scientist was already formulating himself. Aaron had crossed a line coming here. Enough was enough.

"Sir, are you all right?" a guard asked.

"I'm fine," the Scientist snapped. He wheezed through a deep breath and closed his eyes. Even with his heart rate slowing, his entire body still felt wrecked. He was too old to deal with this kind of emotional stress. "I need to speak with Jesse immediately."

"But it's the middle of the night," one guard started.

"Yes, clearly it's the middle of the night; does that somehow make you incapable of taking orders?"

All the guards stiffened, and the one who had spoken nodded in compliance. "Very well, sir."

"I'll see him in the Council Room." Roth tried to push himself up off the floor. His knees popped as he stood and his brain pounded in response to the movement. He wavered as he stood, and one of the guards rushed over to help him.

Roth pushed the guard away and cursed his aging body. "Just do as I asked."

The guard stood back and nodded, motioning for the others to leave the office.

When they were gone Roth reached out and grasped the edge of his desk for balance as his knees continued to shake. Partly from the lasting impression of Aaron's power and partly from the rage coursing beneath his skin.

The darkness whispered again, its voice coarse and hateful.

"Don't worry," Roth said out loud. "I will crush them all."

/ / /

Roth had regained his composure and walked calmly to the Council Room only moments after sending the guards for President Cropper. The Scientist had waited only a couple of minutes before Jesse walked in, hazy-eyed and still clearing sleep from his mind. Those few moments had allowed the Scientist to refocus and set his mind to the task at hand.

Roth's inner voice had begun speaking to him many years earlier, as the dawning of a new generation had begun in the Authority City. Its words now advised him that the path must be certain and followed without a single misstep.

Roth considered himself a man of science, but he had grown in power and ambition as he allowed the dark energy to invade his life. Now it was part of him; Roth no longer knew the difference between his own skin and the darkness that gave him life. He needed it more than air and food; the energy was necessary for him to continue to thrive into a greater state of power. It gave him clear vision and complemented his greatest strength—his mind. The melding of science and power had influenced all the evolutionary advances Roth had seen fulfilled throughout the city. Yet now the kingdom he had built was being threatened. The darkness hissed violently at the mere thought. It was time to put an end to the madness.

Jesse ran his hand through the side of his hair, pushing the locks away from his ear, and sat at the head of the council table. He didn't look pleased to have been woken in the early-morning hours, but Roth had little concern for how Jesse felt. Even in the dim chandelier light, the Scientist could see the silvery gray streaks growing through the top of Jesse's hair. There was more gray than most men had at his age, but then Jesse was ruling a city, so he faced more stress than most. Roth still saw him as the young archer whom he'd rescued from himself, but now that he was a middle-aged man, it was time he stepped up and did what was best for the community. The Scientist knew the conversation to come was not going to be an easy one for Jesse, yet Roth found himself again caring very little about that.

"We have a problem," Roth said.

"Well, I would hope you haven't had me dragged out of bed for anything less than the storming of the front gates," Jesse said.

"They are storming more than our gates."

"Who?"

Roth didn't need to answer; he could see the twitch in Jesse's face as he was already fully aware of whom the Scientist was talking about. Who else was there?

"Have they been spotted inside the city?" Jesse asked, serious now.

"No, but they are coming."

Jesse leaned back in the chair he was occupying and crossed his arms over his chest. "How can you be certain?"

Roth paused. It wouldn't be honest to say he completely

trusted Jesse. True, the man had served him and the city well, but his affection for the Seers and the girl Elise, now a grown woman whom he had cared for all these years, gave the Scientist pause.

"Aaron came to me," Roth said.

"What?" Jesse asked.

"He warns that they will soon take the city back for the light—a threat I must not discount."

"How did he get into the Capitol Building?"

"That is not important. His message is what concerns me. Greatly."

"He's making idle threats, and you are letting him rattle you?"

"Not idle. I have sensed for some time that something was coming. He is only confirming my fears."

"And why would he do that? Why alert you to them trying to take the city?"

"Because he wants us to be afraid. Because he is falsely confident in a power that will fail him. Because he is a fool."

"Then pay him no mind. We know the Seers in Trylin City couldn't actually pose a physical threat to us. We outnumber them one hundred to one. We have nothing to fear from them."

Roth nodded. Jesse was right, but the darkness coiled inside had been warning him not to take this lightly. Aaron had been perceived as nonthreatening before, and his influence had nearly brought this city to its knees in the past.

Science had proven that the past often repeated itself. Roth would not risk such a thing happening.

"I won't take any chances. I'm making plans to have Trylin handled. I've called you here to discuss the issue of Elise," Roth said.

Jesse straightened. "What does she have to do with this?"

"She has everything to do with this. Her presence has been a continuous threat we should have rid ourselves of when she was still a child."

"She is just a girl, Roth," Jesse tried.

"No, she is one of them."

Jesse stood from his seat. "We had a deal."

"Yes, I know, but deals change."

"I have committed my life to doing everything you asked, being your only ally on the Council while the rest would love to see you thrown into the street. I've served as president while letting you make all the decisions. I follow your orders, and you leave Elise alive. That was the deal!"

Roth noticed the passion filling Jesse's expression. Different than it had been before. Something had changed. "You have fallen in love with her, then?"

Jesse swallowed and pressed his lips tightly together. He glanced at his feet for a moment as if finally letting himself believe what he had long denied, then raised his eyes back up to Roth's. "Is that so wrong?"

"She will never love you back," Roth said.

"How I feel about her is beside the point. You can't break our agreement."

"Aaron named her as a part of this *Returning*, as he called it. She cannot live."

Jesse's face darkened as he took a step toward the Scientist. "You still need me. You can't run this city without me; no one would follow your command. The Council trusts me alone. If you touch her, our deal is off, and I'll leave."

The energy in Roth's chest roared through his mind. His eyes narrowed to slits as he closed the small distance between him and Jesse, striding close enough to the man that he could feel the heat of the anger rising from his skin.

"You think I need you?" Roth began. "The only reason you are still alive is because of me. I pitied you, took you in when the rest of the world abandoned you, when Damien Gold failed you. After your grandfather died, after your father beat you, I saved you. Do not for a moment think that I can't snuff out your life as quickly as I gave it to you."

Jesse clenched his teeth, his jaw trembling as he tried to breathe steadily.

"You can't leave," Roth said. "I own you. You are nothing without me. How dare you spit in my face after I have given you a kingdom? And then threaten to abandon it for a woman? A woman that threatens the very kingdom I gave you to rule? Have you lost your mind?"

"So you would kill an innocent girl over the ranting of a madman?" Jesse asked.

"You would be surprised whom I would kill to protect what I have built." Roth let the edge in his voice linger for a moment before he continued. "Elise has never been innocent. Their blood runs through her veins. She is one of them. She has never been yours."

Roth could see the desperation Jesse was fighting to mask, but it didn't matter. He would see in the end that this was best. Roth would make sure of it or cut him off if necessary.

"I will deal with Elise myself," Roth continued. "I will make it quick and painless for your sake. But if you try anything, I will have her skinned alive, slowly. Is that clear?"

Jesse kept his jaw shut and Roth registered the fear building in his eyes.

"Good." Roth turned and strode away from Jesse. "It will be over and only a memory soon, and then we can continue to walk into greatness." Roth's voice echoed through the large room as he moved across the marble floor and out into the hallway.

Once outside the room, the heavy wooden doors sealing Jesse inside alone, Roth turned to the CityWatch guards and instructed they apprehend Elise immediately and escort her to the bottom level prison cells. She was to be watched around the clock until her execution could be carried out.

Roth wanted to believe he could trust Jesse to do the smart thing, but love was dangerous and vile, and he wasn't going to take any chances.

4 Elise's legs burned as she raced through the trees. Branches scraped at her bare calves, and rocks cut the bottoms of her shoeless feet. Why was she running through the forest without shoes on? She didn't have time for questions as the monster on her heels was gaining. Elise recognized the panic its presence caused, sensed its hatred. She didn't risk glancing over her shoulder; she knew it was still there, breathing down her neck.

"Don't slow down, or I'll catch you," the monster mocked, its voice buzzing in her ears and grating at the insides of her skull.

She pushed herself to move faster, ignoring the abrasive pain thundering in her knees and thighs. She'd sacrifice both legs before she let the beast catch her. Intense wind whipped through the trees to her left and she followed her instincts, moving toward it.

"Run. Run faster, little girl," the monster sneered.

The wind swirled ahead of her and she continued to follow it as if it were leading her to safety, which she knew was crazy because it was only wind. Elise tried to move past the fear in her mind that was threatening to slow her and fought off the panic as the beast's sneering laugh echoed through the air around her.

The path ahead looked as if it cleared, the ground becoming smooth and the trees thinning away. Beyond the clearing, she saw a beach that stretched out toward the sea. She couldn't tell how, but she suddenly sensed that if she could simply make it to the white sands, she'd be safe.

"Don't you step onto the beach, Elise," said the monster, its voice angry and closer than it had been before.

With every ounce of power Elise had, she gave one final push, her lungs feeling as if they might explode, her legs turning to jelly, but her mind crying for the salvation the sand offered.

Her toes sank into the warmth of the white beach and she fell forward, her hands catching her as her palms plummeted deep into the sand. She wanted to stop, to lie down against the warm ground beneath her, but her fear forced her to keep moving forward. Crawling now, she frantically kicked up sand as she scrambled farther out onto the beach.

An angry cry echoed behind her and she dared a glance to see the beast standing at the forest's edge. It was huge—a body like black smoke, fingers extending into razor-sharp talons jutting out of wisps of ebony curls that flowed to the ground and then back up to the place that held some semblance of a face. Its teeth were sharp edges, its eyes hauntingly crimson. It just stood there, rage pouring from its body as its chest rose and fell with each spiteful breath. Terrifying, but seemingly trapped at the tree line.

Elise struggled to steady her thundering lungs. She pushed herself up onto her feet and nearly stumbled backward into the sand again. Her body was still trembling as she watched the beast eye her from its cage. That's what the forest was—its own personal cage. As long as she stayed on the beach, she'd be safe.

"Are you all right?" The voice came from behind her.

Elise screeched in horror and lost the small amount of balance she'd regained. A strong arm reached out and a firm hand steadied her before she toppled over, helping her back to a standing position.

Elise struggled against the stranger's grasp, and without hesitation the hand released her. She spun around, prepared to fight off another monster, but was surprised to find none. It was just a boy, a man rather, maybe a little older than herself, his hands up in a position of surrender, his eyes soft and kind.

"Sorry," he said. "I didn't mean to startle you."

Elise felt her knees tingle and her pulse quicken, but not because she was afraid. In fact, she was overwhelmingly *not* afraid of the stranger before her, which made him feel less like a stranger and more like a friend.

He smiled and her heart seized in response. He was tall, slender but not skinny, pale but not sickly, with captivating blue eyes and light-yellow hair that fell in a long swoop across one side of his face. When he smiled his whole face made the motion, his lips full and his jaw strong.

"I'm okay," Elise said, finally finding her words.

The man let out a sigh of relief. "Good—you looked like you'd seen a ghost."

"I was running from the beast," Elise said, pointing toward the trees.

The stranger followed her finger and shook his head in confusion. "What beast?"

Elise turned and saw that the place where the monster had been standing was now empty. "It must have gone into the woods."

"I see. Well, don't worry; if it comes out, I'll protect you."

Elise looked back at the man and smiled. She believed him. Which seemed odd since they'd only just met, but there was something about his eyes that she trusted.

"I'm Elise," she said.

The expression on his face changed. Surprise took over his features and then turned into joy. "Elise," he said, his voice filled with awe.

"Do you know me?"

He shook his head. "No, just of you."

"Of me? No one knows of me." She said it with a laugh behind her words, as if he must be teasing.

"Many people know of you. You're famous among the Seers."

Elise cocked her head to the side curiously. "What's a Seer?"

"So you don't know, then?" The smile on his face faded, as if he realized something very important. "Are you safe?"

She looked over her shoulder, toward the woods, and thought of the monster that waited for her there. "No," she answered. "I'm afraid." She turned back to face her new friend, but he was gone. And in his place was the beast. Elise cried out in terror as the monster stood only a few feet from her. Its eyes glowed red, teeth and claws poised to kill.

It growled deep in its throat and leaped toward Elise. It was too fast for her, and talons sharp as glass shards dug into the side of her arm and ripped through her flesh. She screamed in agony and shot up in bed.

Her mind was unsure of its position. Half of it still saw the sandy beach, while another part started to register that she was now somewhere else. There was still pressure on her arm where the beast's talons had been, and she tried to rip herself from its clutches. She swatted at the hold, crying out for help.

"Calm her," a voice came, and it sent a notion of reality crashing into Elise's mind. It wasn't the voice of the beast or the boy she'd met on the beach. It was someone else. Someone familiar.

The room around her was dim, but the glow from soft light nearby illuminated her vision. She was in bed, covers pulled up over her legs, her arms restrained by hands. Human hands, attached to human arms. She followed the arms to shoulders and then faces, also human, and not in a towering forest or on a beach.

She had been dreaming again.

"Get her up," the familiar voice said. She moved her eyes to where the words were coming from and saw a CityWatch guard she recognized. Sam, she'd heard some call him. The two other guards holding her on either side did as they were told. They dragged her from bed, more forcefully than she thought necessary. Her mind ran in dizzy circles, trying to catch up.

"What's happening?" Elise asked, her voice cracking from drowsiness.

"Hold her steady," Sam ordered. "Follow me."

They started to move across the room as more reality quickly dropped into her head. They were in her room; the light she saw came from a small lamp she must have left on when she'd fallen asleep a couple of hours ago. Darkness covered the windows; it was still night. Why was she being yanked out of bed in the middle of the night?

"Stop," she said, pulling against the two guards leading her out. "What is going on?"

"You need to come with us. Orders from President Cropper." Sam didn't even glance back as he stepped through Elise's doorframe and out into the marble hallway that led into the grand Capitol Building walkway.

Jesse. "Why?" Elise asked.

"Enough," Sam said.

Elise knew better than to push. It would do her no good. That was the way things worked around here. The way they always had. She didn't have the right to know. Maybe if she had been born in this city, if she'd had parents who wanted her, if the Genesis Serum worked in her bloodstream, then things would be different. But none of those cards had been dealt to her. She was the worthless child of parents who had abandoned her because she was different.

The guards dragged her for several long minutes, making their way down to the lowest level of the Capitol Building, to a place Elise had never been, which was disconcerting since she'd spent nearly every moment of her life within these walls. Fear rattled inside her chest as her eyes scanned the unfamiliar surroundings. It was cold, the floor concrete, the walls gray stone. The lights were scarce and dim, and the sounds of the guards' footsteps echoed as they moved.

Her mind ran with worry. Where were they taking her? Would Jesse be there? Surely he would explain to her what was happening. She trusted him, didn't she? Couldn't she? Yet her instincts told her that something was very wrong.

They finally rounded a corner into a large rectangular room that held barred cells along both the left and right sides. Her fear exploded and her body yanked away from her captors. This was prison.

The arms held her tightly and pulled her toward one of the cells.

"No—stop!" Elise said.

"Inside," Sam said.

"I don't—" Elise tried, but she was no match for the guards' strength. With ease they walked her toward one of the cages and tossed her inside. She nearly fell forward on the concrete floor but managed to keep her balance. She whipped around to free herself, but she was too late. The cell door slammed with a metallic screech that sent a shiver through her bones.

"Wait, please! I haven't done anything," Elise cried. She rushed to the bars and gripped them with both hands. "Please."

The guards barely looked at her before turning to leave. Her mind scrambled with confusion. Her breath was short and heavy, her skin rippling with panic. This couldn't be happening. If she could just get them to listen.

"Stop, please—I don't understand. I didn't do anything!"

"Guards will come for you when it is time," Sam said.

"When it is time for what?" Elise asked as hot tears started to collect in her eyes.

He turned toward her, his face made emotionless by the Genesis Serum pumping through his veins and making him the ever-obedient soldier. "When it's time for your execution."

Her world went cold. Her mind numb. The word *execution* landed on her like a boulder, smothering her ability to think, breathe, act. She watched in frozen shock as the three guards rounded the corner and disappeared, leaving her completely alone with nothing but fear.

5 Elise rested her cheek against the cold concrete floor. Her mind was mush, her eyes dazed, her body numb. It could have been days since the CityWatch guards left her in this cell, or it could have been only hours. It was impossible to connect with time when her mind was captured solely by her impending death.

She shouldn't be so surprised. She shouldn't be curled up on the floor as if this hadn't always been a realistic outcome. She should have seen this coming. Her whole life had been one moment of uncertainty strung together with another, her mind hounded by questions she never got answers to, knowing nearly nothing about her past and being completely unsure about her future. Fear was as close to her as her skin, and dreams were her only escape.

Remember who you are. The words were familiar, as was the voice at the back of her brain.

I am Elise. I grew up in the Authority City. I am twenty. I am alone. My parents didn't want me because I am broken. I am a danger to the community and myself because the

Genesis Serum does not affect me. I am lucky to have survived this long.

A strong gust of wind rustled across the cold floor and pulled at the ends of Elise's hair, silencing her. Tears stung at the back of her lids. She had felt this wind before. Like the voice, it comforted her in the darkness of her dreams and gave her strength to continue through her uncertainty.

No, remember who you are beyond what they say about you.

Elise curled up deeper into herself and tried to push the comforting force away. She was headed to death's door, for who knew what reason, and she wanted to lie undisturbed in her suffering and fear.

Never run from fear.
Walk through the fear.
Only in facing fear can you let it go.
Remember who you are.

"Leave me alone," Elise said aloud. She closed her eyes tightly to stop the tears from escaping. If this was to be her end, then let her go out the way she had always truly been. Powerless.

An image filled her mind. A face she had come to know well. A teacher, a friend, a device her mind had created to keep her alive. Aaron, he called himself when she dreamed of him. A kind man with warm brown eyes and curly hair. The one she'd seen since she was little, who at times felt so real she questioned her own sanity.

She tried to shake him loose, but her mind clasped on to him tightly.

"Do you really want me to leave?" His voice echoed through the air around her head.

Elise opened her eyes. She saw him standing inside her cell, leaning against the bars in the far left corner. His smile was bright even in the dark. She stared at him, bewildered. Was she dreaming? She got to her hands and knees.

She didn't answer his question and so he stayed. The sight of him in this prison made her chest ache. She wouldn't dream anymore after she was executed. The thought struck her as both funny and sad. She would miss Aaron.

"You need not fear death, my dear. Death isn't final," Aaron said. "Besides, you still have so much left to do."

"Why would they let me live this long, only to kill me now? Has it all been some cruel game that I was always just a pawn in?" Elise asked, still bewildered at having a conversation with a figment of her imagination.

Aaron's eyes filled with empathy. "They really are getting to you, aren't they?"

"Getting to me? They have gotten me. Look where I am!"

"Try to remember our times together."

"The times I created you into existence with my mind?" Elise chuckled and swallowed a cry of anguish at the same time. Tears rolled down her cheeks. "What good will that do?"

"It is in remembering that you will be set free."

"How? Are you going to save me?"

He shook his head. "I have never been able to save you. All the power has already been given to you."

Elise dropped her eyes to the floor near her hands. Her mind was trying to protect her, as it always had. Reasoning away the never-ending questions. Why was she the way she was? Why had her parents hated her so? Why didn't the Genesis Serum work on her? Why wasn't she normal? Why did they keep her locked away? Why keep her at all? She shook her head as a new wave of emotion crashed inside her gut.

"At least the questions will end," Elise said. "Do you think there will be peace when it's all over?"

Aaron smiled and shook his head slightly. "It isn't even close to being over. In fact, it is just beginning." He walked to Elise and dropped to his knees beside her. His hand found her shoulder and his touch warmed her cold bones. This dream felt so real! She wanted to cry again, but there was nothing left.

"The forces of darkness will try very hard to make you forget, because the darkness does not want the world to see the light. But try as they might, they will not be able to erase you. The truth runs too deep. It's a strong pulse, full and electric, and when it touches others, they will see the light too."

"Why does my mind talk to me in riddles?" Elise asked the air more than the man beside her.

He chuckled and gave her shoulder a squeeze. "You were called to this. The time has come for this city to be awakened."

"You aren't making any sense."

"You're chosen. Just as your mother and father were chosen before you."

Elise inhaled and held it, searching Aaron's eyes. He'd never mentioned her parents before. Why would he be mentioning them? She searched for words but didn't find them. Her mind was spinning in circles, her weakened pulse suddenly storming the gates.

Aaron continued before she could utter a sentence. "They are coming. You have never been alone, and you have never been powerless. The remembering is important; don't forget. Believe in who you are, and trust in the light. It will save you."

"Who is coming?" Elise asked, but Aaron was already standing. She grabbed for his leg, but her hand moved right through it. Like he was simply an image projected on the air. She looked at her hand in awe, and then somewhere in her mind she remembered that he was merely a figment. Of course he wasn't solid.

Elise glanced up to ask Aaron why he was tormenting her, but he was gone. Once again she was alone.

Elise,

Today was a good day. My head is beginning to feel clear. As if I can finally see through the dark forest of sorrow to the clearing on the other side. I'll admit, I start to feel guilty the moment any sense of peace fills my heart, but that guilt is just another dark forest path to walk.

Today I find myself resting in the truth that you are safe, held in a love greater than the love I have for you, which can only mean it is unconditional. With love that powerful and secure watching over you, what should I fear?

That's the lesson I have been practicing anyway. To trust the overwhelming love I've experienced so many times. Someday I hope I can tell you all about the times I was lost and then found by that love.

Yet even now, the memory of where I came from sneaks up on me at times, and I have to remind myself not to believe the lies that were fed to me. I fear those same are now being fed to you. Lies that your worth is measured and limited. Lies that you are weak and alone, when the truth calls you as powerful as the wind itself. When I feel these fears creep in I try to remember the field where love always finds me in my dreams. The tall golden grass, soft as silk, swaying in obedience to the rhythm of the wind. Love is tangible there. You can feel it in the air and taste it on your tongue. It's all you need; it satisfies all longings.

I wonder if you ever dream of the field? Aaron continues to tell me that you are special. That you have been chosen for a task greater than any of us could understand, and that the power and ability you hold will change everything you touch. Do you have that power now? Do you even know who you are?

I pray they haven't stolen the fire you were born with, the strength that surely comes from your father and the grace I'm hoping you got from me. When I close my eyes, I see you. I wonder how you have changed. Is your hair still dark and full of curls? Are your eyes still warm brown? Do you dream of me? Do you remember me at all?

And just like that, I feel the truth slipping. Life, my sweet daughter, is a cycle of remembering and forgetting. But don't fret: the more often you practice remembering, the less often you forget.

Your mother

6 Jesse moved quickly down the large hallway toward Elise's room. He had been pacing madly for the last hour, ever since Roth had told him he planned to execute Elise. His heart struggled to keep up as his mind grappled violently for any solution. But Jesse knew the Scientist well enough to know that the man always got his way and never made mistakes. Even as his feet pounded across the marble flooring he knew her room would be heavily guarded. Or empty, with her secured in a location far from Jesse's frantic reach.

So this was it—she was actually going to die. For the last twenty years, Jesse had worked to keep Elise alive, to teach her, befriend her, somehow make her feel wanted. It had started as guilt, if Jesse were honest with himself. He'd taken the girl away from her family, stolen her life, only to find the Genesis Serum didn't work on her. He'd struck a deal with Roth then to save her life at least, since he'd destroyed everything else.

He knew caring for her made him weak. He'd even tried to keep her at arm's length, but she pulled him in. He'd felt in awe of her early on, amazed by the rate at which she learned and dealt with her unusual life, as if she knew something the rest of the world didn't. He'd watched her grow, fascinated by the peace and grace with which she carried herself. Eventually, he admitted to himself, his affection and respect had turned to romance. He hadn't even realized how deep those roots went until Roth had said it out loud. He loved her. He hadn't always, but he knew in this moment he did. And now all he wanted was to save her from the fate he'd cursed her with.

He rounded the final corner and saw that the door to her room stood ajar, the lights inside off, not a soul in sight. He stopped. She wasn't here, but then he'd known she probably wouldn't be.

Shame, guilt, anger, and desperation pummeled him. He was the reason this was happening to her, and he didn't know how to save her. Without her, he'd be completely alone in this world. He wanted to save her. He loved her, yes, but he also wanted to save her because he didn't want to be alone.

She will never love you back. Roth's words echoed through Jesse's distraught mind, and he tried to shake them off. He was already alone, but without Elise, he wouldn't even be able to pretend he wasn't.

/ / /

The Scientist sat at his desk. A single lamp was lit in the corner of the room, and even that felt like too much. His head was under attack from an onslaught of pounding, and any trace of light only made it worse.

It was still dark outside. After speaking with Jesse, he'd known there was no way he'd be able to go back to sleep. Then again, he didn't sleep much these days. Or eat, or do anything that might take away from the continued need to gather and protect his power. The enemy was crouched around every corner. Those around him didn't seem to see that the devil was breathing down their necks. But then, most people were blind idiots.

There was a knock at his door and the Scientist called a command to enter. The door opened and a young, handsome man stepped through the frame. He was eighteen years old, his black hair slicked back across his skull, his olive face housing dark-brown eyes and a wide mouth, his torso slim and long like the rest of his frame. He walked with confidence, seemingly friendly and welcoming to those who didn't know him, but to those who saw beneath the charming facade, he was anything but. He had been trained well, and for that Roth was glad. He was starting to believe that this boy might prove to be his only ally. "Nicolas," the Scientist said.

"You asked to see me," Nicolas replied. He moved to stand just in front of the Scientist's desk, his arms loose at his sides, the light from the window catching the angles of his face, reminding Roth how dangerous this boy could be. It was harder to believe something you found attractive would eventually slit your throat when your back was turned.

"We need to move forward with what we have been discussing," Roth said.

"Has something changed since we spoke yesterday?" Nicolas asked.

"I've ordered the execution of Elise. I believe there may be a move coming from Trylin Mountain."

Nicolas raised an eyebrow, trying to hide a smirk that Roth caught a glimpse of. He knew how much Nicolas despised Elise. The boy would gladly kill her himself if ever given the chance. The Scientist gathered that his disdain came from the affection Jesse had for the girl. Nicolas saw it as weakness, which it had become, and Nicolas hated weakness.

"Trylin City has been quiet. I've been watching them as you requested," Nicolas said.

"Yes, but things are changing."

Nicolas didn't look completely convinced. "Changing?"

"There is a rising happening in the earth; I can sense it, and it threatens to cause us harm."

"You want me to march on Trylin, then?"

"Immediately. We shouldn't have waited this long."

Roth watched as Nicolas processed the information. Nicolas was as smart as he was cunning. For those qualities, among others, he'd been chosen for his role here in the Authority City. After disassembling the Authority Council early on, the Scientist and Jesse had quickly reestablished the boundaries under which the Authority would function. Instead of eight members, there were now only four, Jesse included. They had all been hand-selected based on their intellect rather than their bloodline. None of them had been given the Genesis Serum, as they were called to a high level of mental service, and they worked tirelessly as a single-minded unit to pull the Authority City from the dark ages.

It had taken nearly eighteen months to make sure all people inside the city had received the Genesis Serum, and another five months of monitoring to ensure that what Roth had always dreamed of was now a reality. The new Council had then imposed more dramatic changes. They disbanded religion, as there was no longer any need for such nonsense. The Choosing Ceremony had been done away with. The Lints had been brought back into the city to live among everyone else. The CityWatch had been cut in half, as violence had been largely eradicated. Education had been changed to make math, science, and health required subjects for all children, regardless of gender. Gender, in fact, was basically a thing of the past. Besides the physiological differences, the Genesis Serum made them all equal.

In the midst of all this beautiful change, continuing leadership had been addressed. Who would serve in place of the current Authority members upon their departure from office? A mandatory test had been issued to all children under the age of seven, and the four highest scores had been selected. Nicolas Horner was one of them. He and the other three had moved into the Capitol Building during their tenth year and had begun their mentorship.

Nicolas had excelled from the start, securing the highest testing score and showing more promise for the presidential role than the others. The only problem was that in order for them to truly serve on the Council, they could not be given the Genesis Serum, and they were still young. Dealing with their oftentimes erratic emotions was the greatest test of all. Could Nicolas really be trusted as the Scientist hoped? With Jesse's heart reflecting his feelings for the girl, Roth needed someone with a strong backbone to replace him in case their president failed. He saw potential in Nicolas, but was potential enough?

Silence filled the Scientist's office as the old man waited to see how Nicolas would respond.

Finally the boy nodded. "And what does Jesse have to say about this?"

Roth shook his head. "He is clouded currently, but he will return; don't worry." He caught the flash of disapproval on Nicolas's face and ignored his own flare of anger. "You do not need to worry about Jesse. He will do as he is told, as always. Now I need you to act in kind. You need to understand the threat here!"

"If I am honest, the threat is hard to see. Even if the citizens of Trylin were gathering to descend on us, they are barely a thousand strong. They couldn't make it past the wall without being handled."

"The size of the threat is not always the danger; in this circumstance, it is what the threat represents—that is what we should fear," the Scientist said.

"And what is that?"

"The past. The way life was before Genesis renewed it. Imagine all that has been accomplished being undone."

"That would be impossible."

The Scientist nodded. "Yes, I would love to believe that were true, but all great evolution must face the risk of being undone. That is what we are fighting against."

"If Trylin City is such a threat, then why does it even still stand?"

Silence filled the room again, as even the thought of admitting he'd made a mistake filled the Scientist's mouth with bitterness. He knew all greatness came from trial and error, but his failure to recognize the threat of the Seers and Aaron was tormenting him more than he'd ever admit. "The blame for that is mine, unfortunately. I underestimated their power," the Scientist said.

"And what power is that?"

"Belief."

Nicolas gave the Scientist a questionable look.

"Do you know what makes a martyr so dangerous? His belief that what he is called to outweighs basic survival. Believing in anything with enough force to die for it makes you erratic. Now imagine an entire group of people with that same delusion. A cult, committed to dying before letting that belief go. Crazed emotions based on irrational belief that can't be proven with science. I don't trust anything that can't be proven."

"So why now?" Nicolas asked.

An image of Aaron's face danced behind the Scientist's eyes. The man's words drifted through his mind. *It is freedom for all. . . . Elise will call them all home. . . . And it has already started.*

"As I said, there is a rising." The Scientist studied the boy's face as silence again filled the room. He knew something deeper connected them; Roth had always been drawn to him, to the essence he carried. "I know you sense the change," Roth said. "I can see it in your eyes. You've felt the stirring."

Nicolas said nothing, but his face was clear. He felt it.

"Your instincts are strong; listen to them now. The evidence may seem harmless, but you must know there is more below the surface."

Nicolas studied Roth's face for a brief moment, and the Scientist saw resolve cross the boy's gaze before he spoke. "Then we move forward."

"Are you prepared?"

"Everything is in place; we can be mobile by morning. We can send enough CityWatch soldiers to surround the city. Say the word, and we can eliminate them all."

"No, I want them broken, not killed. If they die with their belief, then they win," the Scientist said, standing from his seat. He could feel the familiar trembling in his fingers. "They must be brought into the new era with the rest of us. And their leader . . . I want to personally expose him for the fraud that he is."

Nicolas nodded. "And what of Jesse?"

The Scientist inhaled and clenched his hands tightly together to diminish the shaking. "I will deal with Jesse. After Elise is executed, he will be brought back into the fold."

Nicolas dropped his eyes to slits at the mention of her name and the Scientist felt the corner of his mouth twitch. They shared a common distaste for that girl, and it helped unify them now.

"What I am trusting you with is significant," the Scientist said. "Do not fail."

"I won't," Nicolas said. "And once I have settled this for you, for this city, I want to discuss where I fit into the leadership of the future, because I am ready."

Roth had expected as much from the boy. "Do as you are told, and we will see."

The pain and sympathy in Jesse's eyes when Roth had told him his plans for Elise's execution flashed across the Scientist's mind, and he hoped for the sake of this city Nicolas was indeed ready.

"We are done here," the Scientist said.

/ / /

Nicolas left Dr. Reynard's office before the sun had risen above the city wall. The hallways were quiet, as most of the Capitol Building was still trapped in slumber. His boots clicked loudly in the stillness of the early morning as he walked across the marble floor. His mind was churning in circles, collecting and dissecting all the information swirling in his consciousness.

The warm vibration of power stirred in his gut and he grinned in spite of himself. The Scientist was right; he had felt the shift in the air. The awakening of something strong and animalistic. A power with which he could crush all the empires of the word if he saw fit. He lay awake some nights dreaming of marching into the Council Room and destroying them all, of taking the head seat and ruling this city with purpose.

If it wasn't for the strong grip the Scientist had on President Cropper, Nicolas might have followed through on such inclinations. Jesse may have been strong once, but his affection for Elise had corrupted him, made him soft. But it seemed as though the tide was turning.

Nicolas felt a shadow pulse under his skin, and the familiar twitch started in his cheek. It pulled the corner of his mouth slightly upward and tugged the corner of his eye down. He sucked a deep breath in through his teeth and licked his lips. This was no time to lose control of himself.

He rounded the corner and descended a long staircase to an outer hallway with open arches for windows and stone blocks for flooring. Cold, dark air whisked past him softly and made him shiver. He was ready. Ready for more power, more respect, more responsibility. He had been raised inside these walls, torn away from a family he had long ago learned to stop missing, and sculpted to be a leader. Something he did not take lightly.

He would be a liar to deny the last year had been taxing. Feeling ready to step into a place of power but being held at the sidelines while a less-equipped man steered. President Cropper had the Council's respect, yes; he had their ears, and the people in the Authority City favored him. The CityWatch trusted him. But he lacked grit. He'd swapped it for love, and now they were running scared from a group of religious nuts hidden in a far-off mountain.

Nicolas's cheek twitched again and he shook it off. He bit the inside of his cheek to transfer his emotions from anger to pain and drew blood. An ache pinched his brain from the fresh injury on the inside of his mouth, and he welcomed it.

Ahead of him stood several patrol guards, behind them a large oak door that led to the Capitol Building's main tactical room. The guards ceased their trivial conversation as Nicolas approached. They nodded in respect and waited for instructions.

"Gather the officers and have them meet me here immediately," Nicolas ordered.

Two of the guards nodded and departed, leaving the others to step aside so Nicolas could enter the large room. The door shut behind him, leaving him alone inside the cold space. Another twitch in the side of his face poked at the pain stinging at his cheek. He ran his tongue along the fleshy inner wall of his face to taste the salty-sweet flavor of his own blood.

Again he reminded himself that this wasn't a time for mistakes. He was too smart to let this opportunity slip through his fingers. He would do as the Scientist had asked, collect the tiny Seer threat, and return a hero. Then he would ascend, whether by fortune or force.

7 Willis Lane watched as the beach stretched out and disappeared into the sea. The sand was white and clean, soft and cool between his toes. Behind him, at least two hundred yards back, there was a dense forest. He turned to gaze at the trees that covered the ground in thick shadows and made seeing between them nearly impossible.

He knew he was dreaming. He always knew. It was his gift, to see things beyond normality. It was the translating that was a bit trickier. Often the dreams needed some thought and interpretation. Aaron had taught him to see his dreams clearly, to stretch out his mind to grasp their meaning, much like the sand reached out into the water.

Though he knew he was dreaming, the question he had learned to ask himself was, *Why?* The thought had barely formed in his mind when the girl came stumbling out of the woods. He hadn't even seen the trees rustle, and then suddenly she was there. Tripping over herself and falling into the sand.

Willis started in her direction and watched as she turned toward the woods, backing away in fear, as if the trees themselves were demons. He glanced up, but all he saw were trees. He wondered what she saw.

The girl had pushed herself to her feet by the time he reached her. Unsure of how else to announce himself, he simply spoke. "Are you all right?"

The girl screeched in fright and started to stumble. Willis, aware that this was his fault, stepped forward and grabbed the girl's arm before she face-planted in the sand. Straightening, the girl lashed out violently, ripping her arm from his grip and swirling away with fear and anger on her face.

Willis took a step backward, a bit afraid that she might lunge at him, and raised his hands to signal he meant no harm. The moment their eyes met, he saw the fear drain and found himself thrown off guard. She was like no one he had ever seen before, yet strangely familiar. Black curls that spiraled perfectly down the sides of her face, pink cheeks flushed from running, dark-brown eyes that sparkled in the sun, red lips framed by olive skin. He realized he was staring. But then, she was staring back.

"Sorry," Willis said. "I didn't mean to startle you." He smiled and watched her relax. Man, she was pretty. He waited for her to speak, but she seemed lost for words, her eyes working over his face. He didn't know whether to be flattered or worried.

Finally she spoke. "I'm okay." Her voice was soft and small but sounded kind.

Willis released the tension he'd gathered in his shoulders and exhaled. "Good—you looked like you'd seen a ghost." The second the words came out of his mouth he wished he could take them back. *Of course she saw something terrifying, you idiot; she's been running for her life.*

She didn't seem to catch his complete lack of observation and pointed toward the forest. "I was running from the beast."

There was nothing where she pointed, but then Willis had never seen anything to begin with. He shook his head. "What beast?"

She glanced toward the trees and he saw her face scrunch in confusion. "It must have gone into the woods."

Willis felt a twinge of guilt. He'd asked the question out of pure curiosity, but now he feared he'd made her feel stupid because there was nothing there. "I see," he said. "Well, don't worry; if it comes out, I'll protect you." *Boy do you sound stupid.* It was as if he'd lost all control of his words.

But she smiled in a way that made his chest pulse and he forgot his embarrassment completely. He didn't know why he was dreaming of her, but the way the sun broke through the curls in her hair and the way her eyes danced with fire made him hope he would dream of her often.

"I'm Elise," she said.

Willis couldn't hide the shock on his face. It couldn't be. But then, looking at her again, he could see Remko in her eyes. "Elise," Willis spoke her name out loud more to himself than anything.

Her eyes burned with interest. "Do you know me?"

He shook his head. "No, just of you."

She glanced sideways, nearly rolling her eyes. "Of me?"

Her nose scrunched up as she giggled, and Willis couldn't take his eyes off of her. "No one knows of me."

How could she think that? "Many people know of you; you're famous among the Seers."

She looked at him with a confused expression, and he worried he'd said the wrong thing. "What's a Seer?" she asked.

He tried to hide his own confusion. "So you don't know, then." He suddenly wanted to divulge everything he knew about her, like who she was and where she came from, but a thought stopped him cold. This was still a dream and she'd been sent to him for a reason. "Are you safe?" He should have started with that.

Something in her eyes shifted and she turned away from him. He wished he could take the question back, but before he could make another move, dark clouds rolled in overhead, the sky opened up, and a furious rain spilled down over the beach. Wind whipped harshly across Willis's frame and he staggered to stay upright. He closed his eyes against the vicious change of weather and called out to the girl.

"Elise!" Nothing.

He reached forward and searched for her with his arms but only grabbed at air. The rain fell harder and forced Willis to his knees, wet sand crunching beneath his palms. The need to hold on through the rain was strong; the urge to wait it out and find Elise was powerful, but he knew where this was headed. He bit back his frustration and let go.

Willis awoke, soaked in sweat, the first signs of daylight creating beautiful colors in the sky. He took a deep breath and sat up from his sleeping mat, a mix of emotions playing Ping-Pong inside his chest. Frustration to peace, anger to joy, confusion to clarity, but one resounding emotion trumped all the rest: desperation. He needed to find Elise.

He yanked himself free of his sleeping bag and stood. A faint breeze came with the rising sun, and it felt good across his sticky skin. The rest of the camp was still in deep slumber, his traveling companions laid out around the heap of ash that had been a fire the night before. Seven of them in total. Eight if you counted Aaron, but he rarely stayed in camp through the night.

Willis moved carefully so as not to wake the others. He played the scene from his dream over and over in his mind as he grabbed an apple from the food supplies they'd brought for their journey to the Authority City and headed out to try to walk off his emotions.

Willis remembered having vivid dreams for his entire life. Early on he'd been told that all children dream, but he'd been afraid when his dreams sometimes felt more realistic than the world he faced when he was awake. His older sister, Eleanor, had always encouraged him to dream. Especially when their lives had been turned upside down and their father had abandoned them. Willis hardly remembered the time before living with the Seers, but he knew their father had sent him and Eleanor to be used as Genesis Serum test subjects. They'd escaped, but Willis still wondered what had driven his father to treat his own children in such a way. Since he'd been so young then, it had been easier for him to forgive. Eleanor was older, though, and remembered more. That made her road to acceptance very different from his own.

Remko, Carrington, Wire, Kate, and the other Seers had taken them in and let them freely walk the individual paths set before them. His earthly father may have been blind to the truth, a blindness that let him believe that sacrificing his children was his only option, but Willis had since learned to call another by the name Father.

It was within that relationship that he'd learned to trust his dreams. Sometimes they were simply fantasies, but more often than not they were messages or reminders. A unique form of communication between Willis and the light that guided him. Which was why he couldn't shake the need to find Elise. She was more than just a pretty girl he was seeing in his sleep. He felt connected to her, which sounded crazy but felt undeniable.

He'd asked Remko about her once. Several years ago. Everyone in the city knew of Elise, of course. They knew the story of how Remko and the other Seers had come to the city of Trylin, where the original Trylin One Hundred already lived. Willis had been with Remko then, though he hardly remembered. So he, like most residing in their city, relied on the stories that were told. A child stolen in the night, a call to go west and leave her behind, a plan that was bigger than them all.

Willis had been curious about the whole thing. Had Remko and Carrington really left their oldest daughter in the Authority City, and had they really never tried to go after her? He'd worked up the courage to ask, half expecting Remko to shut him down. But Remko had surprised him.

"I did try to go after her a couple of times, on my own, always while the rest of the city slept," Remko had said. "I just couldn't live with the pain anymore. You won't understand this fully until you have children of your own, but the responsibility to keep them safe eats away at you like acid, especially when you know you can't. All the practicing of faith, all the meditating on trust . . ."

He'd dropped his eyes away from Willis, and Willis had nearly stopped him from having to continue. The pain was evident on the man's face, but Remko had spoken again.

"I just lost my faith sometimes. But I never made it very far before Aaron found me and did what Aaron does best. Helped me remember and walked me home. That never made the pain go away, though. I thought early on that having faith meant I should never suffer. But the pain still comes, every time I think about Elise, which is more often than not, and I was convinced that when I felt pain it meant I'd once again lost my faith.

"It took me a long time to learn that faith's purpose is not to release you from life's trials. Faith gives you the strength to see the trial fully and know that this too shall pass. To hold nothing against the world or the trial before you. To practice true forgiveness.

"As strange as it may sound, I have a feeling that my daughter Elise understands true forgiveness better than anyone, and I hope she gets the chance to teach the whole world."

Willis still didn't really understand what Remko had meant, but the man's words had stuck with him. He took a bite of the apple in his hand. His dream of Elise had him pulsing with new electricity. It was more than admiration and more than curiosity. When each of the Seven had been called, they understood the path—go to the Authority City, and there you will find the hope needed to change everything from the inside out. Willis couldn't shake the feeling that Elise was somehow tied to that hope and to their path. As Remko had believed she would be.

"Hey!" a voice shouted from behind him. Willis turned to see Davis Tollen standing a couple of yards away, the rest of the camp coming to life with the morning. Not as tall as his father, Wire, but just as gangly, Davis had a mind that worked like a machine and an aim that could nail a target dead center every time, and he was the truest friend Willis had.

"You gonna make the rest of us do all the work?" Davis teased.

"Yeah, that's usually the plan," Willis called.

"Seriously," a female voice interjected just to the left of Davis, "no one thinks you're funny, so get over here and help." With that, Kennedy Brant turned back to camp.

Kennedy was the youngest of the group but had more

attitude than all of them combined, something she'd picked up from spending too much time with Davis's mom, Kate, and her own mom, Carrington. It was a wise policy never to cross any of those women.

Willis started toward camp.

"*I* think you're funny," Davis said and winked at Kennedy when she threw him a look that could kill.

What is it with Tollen men? Willis wondered. Both Wire and Davis seemed to be gluttons for punishment.

Sage Avery softly chuckled on the other side of Davis as she rolled up her sleeping mat. Sage was a kind girl, shy and of very few words, but when she spoke, everyone listened, and Willis wasn't sure he could remember a single moment when she wasn't smiling. She carried the light well.

"Sage," Kennedy warned, "don't encourage them."

"Don't listen to her, Sage," Kane Brant said. "If it riles Kennedy up, then it's definitely worth it." Kane was Kennedy's older cousin, but the two might as well have been siblings the way they bickered. Kane was a trickster through and through. If there was trouble brewing somewhere, he was certain to be at the center of it. Many people had been surprised when he'd been called to join the Seven. He was one of the best warriors in Trylin but a doubter of the way of their people. It seemed unlikely that he would be one of them, but no one would dare argue with the calling.

Kennedy glared at her cousin and tossed a rolled-up sack at his head.

Timmons Gilford stepped up next to Kennedy, wrapped his left arm around her petite shoulders, and shook her playfully. "Oh, come on, Kennedy, it's too early for such seriousness." Timmons had married Willis's sister, Eleanor, ten years ago. He claimed to have fallen for her the moment he saw her walk into Trylin City with the Seers. They'd both been only young teenagers then, so he'd waited and pursued until he'd convinced her that she had fallen for him too.

Kennedy shrugged Timmons off, but she couldn't hide the tiny grin forming on her lips. Timmons did that to people—made them feel comfortable and free. He was the guy who was instantly friends with everyone in the room.

"Enough, all of you," Lucy Carson said through a laugh. "We've got to get this camp packed up." Lucy was Momma Bear, and everyone did as they were told. Willis tossed the thin core of the apple he'd been eating into the brush and moved to roll up his own sleeping mat.

"Today's a big day," Timmons said, voicing out loud what everyone else was thinking.

He was right. Today they would reach the Authority City. Everything started today. It didn't take the group long to have everything rounded up and ready to move. They had just finished when they saw Aaron approaching.

Willis threw his pack into the rear of the single van the group was traveling in, feeling the nervous and excited energy from the rest of the group. Davis stepped up beside him and tossed his bag in as well.

"It's go time," Davis said.

Willis chuckled and shook his head. "Where do you come up with this stuff?"

"My dad."

"He's cooler than you, so he gets away with it," Kennedy said, stepping past Davis. "You, not so much."

The rest of the group snickered in amusement as Kennedy moved to jump in the front passenger seat, the others climbing into the vehicle as well.

Aaron reached them quickly, sharing a knowing smile with Willis before the teacher climbed in the back with the others and Willis into the driver's seat.

They rode in silence for a while, all lost to their own thoughts. None of them really knew what was ahead. Trusting the faith they'd honed and the instincts they'd trained was much easier to do when the way was clear.

Willis saw the massive walls of the Authority City as they approached a thick covering of trees. This looked like a good place to leave their vehicle.

The Authority City was larger than Willis had imagined. It was an odd sensation to know he'd been here before but to remember nothing about it. Not the large walls that surrounded it or the sky-piercing buildings that seemed to touch the clouds.

According to the tales of old, the city had once been difficult to penetrate. The strong, barred gates were at one time constantly monitored by the CityWatch Guard with soldiers at every entry point, around-the-clock surveillance of the walls, and patrols that stretched miles outside of the city itself. But since the injection of Genesis, the need for protective measures had lessened.

Most of the CityWatch's resources were spent guarding the Genesis Compound that sat northwest of the Authority City. Since it housed all of their scientific advancements, it had become their most precious resource. In fact, the city gates themselves now stood wide open. Willis could see inside clearly from where the group hid among the trees. And not a guard in sight.

Willis pulled the van to a slow stop under the thick shade of branches and turned the engine off. Everyone climbed out, grabbed what they'd brought, and walked as a unit to the far tree line.

"So, what's the plan here?" Davis asked.

"We'll take an old yet familiar route in through the underground tunnels," Aaron said.

The entire group smiled in unison. They'd heard many stories about the missions of old, many of which had taken place in the tunnels.

"The ones that run under the city? The old water lines?" Timmons asked. "Are they still accessible?"

"They should be," Davis said. He yanked a portable device from his back pocket and Willis just chuckled. Kennedy rolled her eyes before the boy even started talking. "I've made some adjustments to this device, but my dad said it should be able to track geological changes in the parameters along the city's edge, which should give us a pretty clear picture—"

"Are you going to ramble on like that the entire time?" Kane asked. "Because if so, I volunteer to just walk through the front gate."

The others chuckled and Davis shook his head. "Wow, I sounded just like my dad right then, didn't I?"

Willis gave Davis an affectionate pat on the back of the boy's shoulder.

"Totally," Sage said.

"But as we covered already, not as cool," Kennedy said.

Willis turned his attention back to Aaron. The teacher appeared calm, thoughtful, his eyes watching the city, moving over the walls. Willis often wondered what Aaron thought about. He was their guide and teacher, a strong voice when the path seemed bleak, and they all knew he was no ordinary man.

"And once we're inside," Willis asked, directing his question toward Aaron, "then what?"

Aaron smiled slightly. "You'll know." He paused and everyone waited as his expression softened and became almost sympathetic. "Remember, regardless of what's to come, you were all handpicked for this. Chosen by the Father to return to the city and remind the people where they came from."

His voice was somber, his words almost a riddle, as was common with Aaron, but they contained weighty truth that was both welcoming and terrifying. The group digested each word, each of them understanding that the journey ahead would not be easy.

Willis's mind drifted again to thoughts of Elise. The fear and panic he'd seen in her eyes. He looked once more to the towering walls that surrounded the sleeping city. He didn't know what he and his friends would face, but he imagined they would be tested in the days to come. And he hoped for the sake of the city that they wouldn't lose their faith.

8 The screeching of moving metal bars roused Elise from her sleep. She opened her eyes to see a blur of dark movement and felt the strong grip of hands on her arms as she was hoisted into a standing position. Like a punch to her gut, Elise realized what was happening. They had come to take her to her execution.

As it had the night before, her body's instinctual resistance kicked in and she struggled against the guards' holds. But just like every time she resisted, it did no good. She was only inflicting pain into her muscles with no possible outcome other than what was already laid out before her. Death.

She couldn't fight the tears, didn't really see any point in trying. Her arms were yanked behind her and her wrists secured together tightly before she was dragged from her cell. She was then pushed back up the way she'd been brought down, up a narrow stairway and across a hall she didn't recognize, but this time she was taken out through a door and loaded into a black CityWatch transport.

Her mind registered that she was most likely being transported to the Genesis Compound. Everything significant happened there. Outside the city, but always affecting the city. Not that her death would affect much of anything;

most people didn't even know she existed and wouldn't care much if she was alive or dead even if they did know. The Genesis Serum made sure that only what mattered to the city mattered to the people.

An envelope of pain opened up in Elise's chest. She wondered if Jesse would be there. She had expected him to come see her, save her somehow or at least explain what had warranted her sudden execution. But she'd heard nothing from him. Her only ally in this world had abandoned her, making her question whether they had ever actually been allies at all.

She had been kept in the Capitol Building her whole life because she was unusable, uninjectable. Yet moments of happiness had existed, and they were all connected to Jesse. He'd taught her about the Histories of this city, mentored her in archery, given her attention and a relationship that she lacked with everyone else. He was the closest thing to family she'd ever experienced, yet even he had now abandoned her. Just as her parents once had, and just as the world was about to do now.

The drive to the Genesis Compound zipped by. They were pulling up nearly as soon as they'd left. Or at least that's how it seemed. Elise's mind wrapped itself in agony over the ending of all things. She was surprised to be mourning never seeing her room again, or reading her books, or sitting in the Capitol gardens. Those seemed like such trivial things to miss, but then they were really the only things she'd ever had other than her relationship with

Jesse, their conversations and shared moments. Moments that had convinced her someone cared about her but clearly had just been more lies her mind told to help her cope with being utterly alone.

The vehicle pulled to a jerking stop, and Elise was quickly escorted out of the transport and into the Genesis Compound. The building was surrounded by CityWatch guards, vehicles scattered all about. Lines of children who had reached the appropriate age to be given the Genesis Serum filed out of the vans. She watched their playful faces, saw the light and curiosity in their eyes. They'd be different when they came out. Like-minded and cold. Changed for the betterment of the community.

Elise couldn't help but wish yet again that she had been able to be changed. She wouldn't be going to the slaughter now if she had been normal. Her parents wouldn't have left her. She'd understand what her purpose was in life. Instead she found herself here, being led inside to die.

Remember who you are.

Elise felt the voice call to her heart, but she shut it out. Her mind had led her into false traps of hope before. She wouldn't let it do that to her here. The voice continued to whisper to her, to beckon her to a place that almost felt warm, but she ignored it. The guards led her into a small elevator and up to the second floor, then down a stark white hallway to the last door on the left.

Inside the room was a single chair, clean and sterile. Two men in white lab coats stood, one on either side, waiting for her. A tall, thin machine stood to the right of the chair, a sliver against the whiteness of the room. Long wires hung from the bottom, and a screen softly beeped in its center. This was the device that was going to end her life.

Her skin went cold as her heart raged inside her chest. The inevitability of it all made her eerily still. As if moving would somehow make this real instead of just a nightmare. The guards pulled her forward, causing reality to crash through any protective barrier she'd momentarily created, and her heart slowed as her body went numb.

She didn't feel the chair under her as she was pushed onto it, didn't feel the thick straps as they were yanked across her arms, didn't feel the needles attached to the ends of the wires as they were slid beneath her skin, didn't feel the touch of the doctors as they worked, probing and prodding, preparing her for the end. Her mind had gone vacant, her ears filled with cotton so the sounds in the room were muffled, her eyes clouded so that everywhere she looked she saw only through haze. Everything seemed to be moving in slow motion. Yet somewhere deep within the most hidden place of her soul, a voice still echoed:

Remember who you are.

You are chosen for this.

The light is within you.

"We are nearly ready," said a voice through the muffle.

Nearly ready. Suddenly Elise's heart resumed pumping like a speeding locomotive and her entire body trembled. She didn't want to die. She didn't want this to be her end.

Moments ago the room had seemed hidden beneath a sense of thick numbness, but it now felt like it was blazing with intensity. Every sound was louder than it should be, every object crisp and clear, her skin on fire, her blood pounding violently, her mind twisting in circles. Tears rushed down her cheeks and she gasped for air. She couldn't die; she wasn't ready.

"We need to get her calm before we can start," one of the doctors said.

The single guard inside the room started his approach toward her, and it only roused more hysteria within her. And through it all the voice never left.

Remember who you are.

The light is within you.

The voice inside her grew in volume and it ignited a spark of light inside her chest. Small at first, it began to spread out into all parts of her. The fire in her skin turned into a buzzing electricity and she began to cry out as the light covered her completely.

"Get control of her!"

Hands connected with her skin and suddenly the room changed. A different kind of haze covered the room, and everything froze. Cries of anguish echoed somewhere in the distance, but the images exploding across Elise's mind captured her attention. The room melted away to a forest, and Elise saw the guard she recognized as Sam walking with a group—a young man with curly black hair, another younger, leaner one with a goofy grin elbowing a short girl who could have been the guard's twin except for her small size, looking unimpressed by them all as they traveled.

Another image shot across her vision. They were underground now, in a large tunnel of sorts. Tents were set up all over, fires burning, women laughing, and children running. The large guard was there again, as were those who had been with him before. Eating around a table, joking, teasing.

More changes. Now a boy she didn't recognize, holding the hand of a beautiful woman, their eyes filled with love. A proposal. An acceptance.

Change: a young girl standing beside a gravestone, tears streaming down her face.

Change: a couple yelling, a glass being thrown against the wall.

Change.

Image after image flooded Elise's mind. Places she'd never been, people she'd never seen. Memories—but other people's memories.

Her mind ached as each new image flashed like lightning across her brain. The light inside her chest was flowing down into her arms and legs, warming through to her bones, the familiar voice echoing as each picture in her mind changed.

The light is within you.

Help them see.

The anguished cries that had been distant suddenly broke through the haze and assaulted her. "Stop, stop, STOP!" someone screamed.

Elise inhaled and felt the energy that had been flowing through her diminish, the room falling back into normalcy. A severe pounding made her brain feel like mush. All her strength had faded, yet her heart was still trying to pulse out of her chest, her skin buzzing, her lungs aching for air. She was still strapped to the chair. On the ground around her were both doctors and the guard, Sam. All three were moaning in pain, clutching their skulls, rambling about nothing and crying in agony.

The door at the end of the room opened slowly, and several more guards entered with weapons raised. Behind them another man entered, one Elise knew, and a shiver ran the length of her spine at the sight of him. Dr. Reynard. He looked at the three figures wriggling in pain on the ground, then glanced back up at her, and she saw a dangerous look flash across his eyes. She gulped in air, her body trembling as the effects of what had just happened started to take root.

What *had* happened? The Scientist's eyes never left hers as the group of CityWatch guards slowly crossed the room and saw to their own.

Remember who you are.

Something ticked inside her heart, and although Elise wasn't sure what would happen next, she suddenly became very aware that nothing was ever going to be the same. Her head swam, her eyes became heavy, and then her vision turned as black as if someone had pumped straight exhaustion into her veins, and her world went dark.

9 Remko sat at the worn and unfinished wooden table. Old familiar faces greeted him: Ramses and Wire to his right, Kate, Smith, and Eleanor to his left. New faces that had become familiar were also present. Dalen and Cece Avery, Sage's parents; Alisha Cost; her son Keen; and Peter Holts. All five represented original Trylin families. Together the eleven of them acted as a council of sorts. They only met occasionally to address any serious issues that may have developed in the city or to enhance the city's way of life, but for the most part, the city ran smoothly without the need for a governing presence.

Today was simply a routine gathering. It had been several days since Aaron and the chosen Seven had gone, and everyone had agreed that it would be good to meet and see where people's heads and, most importantly, their hearts were. The waiting was supposed to be easy, free from stress until word of a change in the Authority City finally came. That had always been the dream, at least. Remko knew better. There was usually a storm before there was a calm.

Dalen Avery usually ran the meetings, going through a list of routine topics: resources, education, health, etc. Remko tried to listen but found himself distracted by his own thoughts. The weight of the future was heavy, and Remko had felt its constant pressure for days now. He could see anxiety in Carrington as well. Truth be told, neither of them were sleeping well. They were both caught up in nagging thoughts of trouble, whether from the past or about what was to come. They knew that worrying over where they had been or where they were going did them no good, but remembering truth in the fog was hardly ever easy.

Dalen finished the normal list and opened the floor for additional topics of discussion. Remko realigned his focus, trying to be present. Before anyone else could speak, Brock Avery, Dalen's teenage boy, opened the door and strode into the meeting room. His face was worried. He panted as if he'd been running and took a moment to catch his breath.

"Brock," Cece said in surprise. "What is it?"

"We just got reports from some of our scouts that there is unusual movement coming from the Authority City," Brock reported.

"What kind of movement?" Kate asked.

"An army, seemingly headed this way," Brock said.

The entire group erupted, talking all at once.

"What?" Kate said.

Eleanor: "No!"

"Are you sure?" Peter asked.

Brock nodded. "We sent another scout to confirm; we are sure."

"How many?" Wire asked.

"What do we do?" Alisha asked.

"The Father help us," Cece whispered.

Remko sat back against his chair, letting Brock's report settle as the rest of the group continued to chatter. He could feel the familiar rise of fear and panic in his chest. Trylin hadn't seen serious trouble for over twenty years; they were small, hidden in the side of the mountain that both protected them and kept them thriving. They'd never faced an enemy with as much power as the Authority City.

For years after Aaron had led the Seers to Trylin, they'd been on constant alert. They'd been running for their lives for so long, and those instincts and habits were hard to change. The original Trylin One Hundred, already living in the city by the mountain, had eventually helped Remko and the rest of the Seers let go of the daunting sense of threat that they all carried with such vigor. It was time to practice peace and trust, to stop running. To switch their focus to battles of the mind and heart rather than of the body.

That transition had changed them all, and now, looking at the faces of those he'd fought with so many years ago, Remko could see the fear. None of them wished to return to that way of life. At times, those old memories seemed a lifetime away, but some of the pain could still be found freshly stored right under the surface.

"How will we fight them?" Kate asked.

"We need to start gathering our supplies," Smith said. "Place people in sectors with allocated weaponry and a squad leader to keep everyone organized."

"We should start daily sweeps of the outer walls," Peter said.

"I can rig something up quickly to assist with the electrical wiring that runs through the buildings," Wire said.

"Yes, that would be helpful," Alisha added.

Remko's mind couldn't help but be transported back to a time when conversations like this happened daily around fires and in tents as they tried to make the right moves to get them through the next day safely. He'd brought a child into that kind of life. And it was there, in the midst of hatred and chaos, that his child had been taken, the woman he loved had been broken, and he himself had been destroyed. All of which had been necessary. Because in order for his new life to begin, the old one had to be ruined. In order for the woman he loved to be healed, she had to be shattered, and he had finally understood that Elise had always been called to leave so that she could lead them all home.

None of them were the same as they had been, and they couldn't go back to where they'd come from. This time they were called to more.

"I don't think any of that is necessary," Remko said. His voice broke the chaos of voices and all turned to face him.

"What?" Kate said.

"What do you suggest, then?" Dalen asked.

Remko took a moment as the familiar tune played through his mind. A song he heard often, a voice that came with joy and pain as it filled his soul with warmth and cut open his heart all at once.

When peace like a river attendeth my way,
When sorrows like sea billows roll,
Whatever my lot, Thou hast taught me to say,
It is well; it is well with my soul.

"I know the natural reaction is to be fearful, to want to fight back and protect ourselves, but that is what we would have done before, and we are not those people now," Remko said. "Think of all we have learned since then. Think of the ways our minds and hearts have been changed. I don't think we should prepare to fight—"

"We should be prepared not to," Kate said, finishing Remko's sentence.

Silence filled the room as the idea of going against the natural instinct to defend themselves sank in. Even Remko could feel the panic blossom as the thought of letting go truly seeped into the meat of his mind. Not to fight was an unnatural reaction for the body, but then it was just a body and had no ownership over his soul. It was from his soul that he was learning to react, and his soul sang, *It is well.*

"So we just let them come kill us all?" Dalen asked.

"We let them come, and then we practice faith and forgiveness," Remko said. "We show no resistance and hold no judgment, and then we just see what happens."

"Or we could leave," Eleanor said. "Take everyone and travel farther into Trylin Mountain."

Several heads nodded in agreement, but Remko shook his. "As the Seven, many of them our children, were called to be brave and go, I believe we are called to be brave and stay. Running is just another form of resistance. If we run, we might as well fight."

More silence wrapped them in its clutches, each mind turning over what the future might hold, working through the emotions of what that might mean, and deciding what to do next.

"I suppose the time to practice all we have learned has come." Wire's voice was small and filled with concern, but it was resolute. He reached over and took Kate's hand. She gave him a soft smile and a nod before Wire turned his attention back to Remko. "Let them come."

Remko smiled at his dear friend.

Dalen was also nodding. "Let them come."

Eventually all sitting around the table were of one heart and one mind. They would not run, and they would not fight. They would live by their faith, and when the fear came, they would walk through it.

Or at least they would try.

March 21, 2273

Sweet Elise,

I'm not sleeping again. Your sister was called to join the chosen Seven. She's the last one to be called, but I think I knew it was coming long before she told us. Your father is thrilled, as is your sister, Kennedy, but my heart is broken. It seems I am the only one who senses the danger she will now face, or maybe I'm the only one who cares.

She's only eleven. I know it could be years before the time for them to leave comes, and I know that those she would travel with have been training since they were children. I know this is the path chosen for her—I fear I've always known—but to think of her actually leaving . . .

And so I can't sleep. The wheels in my head won't stop turning. The voices that call from the dark corners of my bedroom and haunt me while I'm awake won't leave me alone long enough for me to forget. Then, once I start down the road of fear and worry, it always leads me to one place.

Back to you.

I've been writing you these letters for nearly fourteen years, hoping one day I'll hand them all to you and you'll see that I never stopped thinking of you. I still turn my head toward the cry of a baby only to remember that you wouldn't even be a child anymore.

If you're alive at all. My hand trembles even as I write the words on the page, but no one can confirm that you are, and I am starting to wonder if holding on to an image of you living and thriving is wreaking havoc on my mind. They tell me to have hope and faith, but faith for them is easy because none of them are your mother. None of them carried you for nine months or slept while you were snatched from their side. None of them know this pain. So faith seems impossible.

I'm trying not to give up, because I'm your mother. And after all the ways I've failed you, to give up on you as well would be terribly cruel. So I'm trying to have hope and faith, but what if I can't?

Your mother

10

Elise woke with a start. She inhaled and lifted her head and shoulders toward the sky but was stopped in her tracks. She tried to use her arms to push herself up, but she couldn't move them. She glanced down to see she was strapped to a chair, the same kind she had been strapped to for her execution.

The thought gave her pause, and her mind searched for data. The last few hours of memories swirled back into place all at once. They had tried to kill her and something had happened to her. No, *from* her. Light, piercing and hot, filling her with power and rattling the minds of those around her. The images she had somehow seen from each of their pasts crashed into her skull again, and a pulsing ache started in the front of her brain. What was that? How had she done that?

The rush of questions was nearly as painful as the rush of memories. She recalled Dr. Reynard entering the room. What had happened afterward? Where was she now? Why was she alive? Shouldn't she be dead? She remembered the look in Reynard's eyes and shivered. He'd seen her do whatever it was that she had done. Again the question of what she *had* done flitted through her brain.

She yanked at her restraints and knew within seconds there was no way she could get herself free. The leather straps were thick and tight enough that they were leaving marks against the bare parts of her skin. She moved her eyes around the room, noticing that although the space was very similar it wasn't exactly the same as the one she'd been in earlier.

The walls were light but not quite as white as the other room's. The chair she sat in was not as modern. This floor was dingy from time and use. There was a single door— steel, not white. The ceiling was made of large, square metal plates. And she was alone—no guards or doctors in sight.

Her mind returned to the events of earlier. She glanced down at her skin, half expecting to see singe marks from the way it had felt like it was on fire. She searched inside for the spark that had lit her inner flames and found nothing. She listened for the voice that had been present. Nothing.

The door in front of her creaked to life and she tensed. It opened slowly, two guards stepping inside first, followed by the Scientist. Elise trembled as he walked into the room, followed closely by a smaller man in a lab coat. None of them looked familiar except for Dr. Reynard, and for the first time she wondered what had happened to Sam and the two doctors she'd affected.

She'd affected? The thought seemed preposterous. It *was* preposterous, but she struggled to find any other description. Whatever had happened to her—through her—had done something to those people.

"Elise," the Scientist said.

His voice sounded as evil as his presence felt. Every encounter she'd ever experienced with him had left her with a sour taste in her mouth. She was repulsed by the way his skin barely hung on to the bones in his face, by his ashen complexion and dried lips. She feared the way his eyes seemed to drill holes into her soul, as if he were looking to extract whatever he found.

"Well, well, aren't you a surprise," the Scientist said.

"Where am I?" Elise asked.

"The Capitol Building."

Elise looked around, confused.

"A part you've never been to. There are many unused sections of this grand building, as you are quickly discovering," the Scientist said.

"Why?"

"I needed to have you close enough to monitor constantly without causing suspicion. And there is no closer place than under my own roof. See, Elise, I was surprised by your . . . reaction earlier today. Do you know what I'm referring to?"

Elise swallowed and kept her mouth shut. The darkness playing over his facial features wasn't encouraging her to speak.

"How did you do it?" the Scientist asked.

"How did I do what?" Elise said.

Dr. Reynard inhaled, studying Elise with intensity. "I always told Jesse you were a stupid girl; don't prove me right."

Elise didn't know how to respond. Equal parts fear and anger rolled around in her chest. "I don't know what you're talking about."

The Scientist considered her words for a second. "You broke their minds."

"I broke . . . ?"

"Yes. You brought back memories they shouldn't have. More troubling, you reversed critical components of the Genesis Serum in all three of them. A serum I know extremely well with effects I was confident couldn't be erased."

Elise saw a flash of rage wash over Dr. Reynard, and she felt more fear. He was surely going to kill her right here. "I didn't—" she fought.

"I watched you. I saw you connect to something and attack my men!"

"I don't even know—"

"I watched you strike them all down without lifting a finger. How, Elise? How did you do it?"

"I don't know! . . . I just . . . You were trying to kill me!" Elise swallowed, trying to control her trembling emotions.

Again he paused and considered her. "I'm still going to kill you." There wasn't a bead of emotion in his voice, as if taking her life would be nothing at all. "But not yet."

He nodded toward the guards, who left the room only

to return carrying a steel crate. Elise's instincts raged under her skin at what could possibly be inside. The man in the white lab coat removed the top of the crate and took a small package from within. Then he started for the right side of Elise's chair. He set the package on the ground and pulled a small controller from his pocket. With the press of a button, the chair beneath her started to decline.

Her heart roared to life inside her rib cage. She struggled against the straps securing her, but to no avail. The chair lurched to a stop and the back of her head smacked the hard headrest. Lab Coat opened the package, yanking out small, flexible patches connected to long wires. He started placing the patches all over Elise's bare skin, under her shirt, along her arms, on either side of her neck, and on both ankles. The patches were cold and menacing. She couldn't move; she could hardly breathe.

"Science is simple, Elise. For every action there is a reaction. Some neurons lie dormant until the correct input comes along and activates them. They need just the right amount of push to fire properly," Dr. Reynard said.

Lab Coat pulled a metal box out of the crate and connected the ends of the wires running from her skin into the box's top along with different-colored switches. He flipped one, causing the box to buzz to life and sending Elise's body into a panic.

"Please—I don't know anything about what I did!" Elise cried.

The Scientist cocked his head and gazed over her.

"I believe you. So let's find out, shall we? Let's see just how hard we have to push." He nodded to Lab Coat and the man flipped another switch.

Electricity fired through each wire and into the pressure points where the flexible patches met Elise's skin. Her entire body tensed, razors of pain exploding across every inch of her flesh and digging into her bones and muscles. Her jaw locked in agony, her head rattling like the tail of a snake. Her eyes rolled back into her head so she could only see darkness; her lungs felt as if they might burst. Lab Coat flicked the switch off and the lightning shooting through her joints eased, but the pain stayed, silent tears escaping the corners of her eyes.

"We just need to find the right stressor," the Scientist said. "Again."

/ / /

Willis felt like his blood had been replaced with ice. The air around him was dark and freezing. He didn't know where he was, but his heart knew enough to pound maddeningly inside his ribs. An uneasy tension stirred his bones, and he tried to recall where he'd been.

Searching through his memories, he remembered entering the Authority City earlier that day, following Aaron to a safe location where they would be staying, and settling in for the night. He probably had gone to sleep soon after that, though he couldn't remember doing it. If he had, then this darkness was all in his mind.

He must be dreaming. Though this dream felt odd and unfamiliar. He held his hands up to try to make out something in the darkness, but he found nothing. He'd never experienced such blackness. Through the dark he heard a whimper and froze. He wasn't alone.

He waited for it to come again. It did—soft but painful. The noise was too small and faint to ascertain who was making it. Female, male, child, adult, he couldn't tell. All he knew was that it was filled with suffering.

Willis felt a rush of anxiousness. If he could just see something, maybe he could find his way toward the person and help. A shiver passed through him as the chill in the air sank deeper into his skin, and the whimpering came again. This time Willis determined it was coming from straight ahead of him.

The darkness continued to disorient him and kept him from getting his bearings. He needed a plan. He couldn't just start walking blindly in the direction of the whimpering and hope there was ground to meet his feet and not a huge black hole. He edged forward slightly, slowly, one toe at a time, his hands outstretched. He'd hardly started moving when his hands brushed up against something ahead of him in the dark. The sudden presence of something solid caused him to jump, and he was relieved no one was there to see him.

Willis used both hands to explore what was before him. It was smooth but filled with tiny bumps and imperfections. Plaster, perhaps. He slowly worked his hands down toward the bottom and found that it met the floor where he stood. Moving his hands upward, he found it stretched farther than he could reach. It was a wall. Good—where there was a wall, there was a floor. Usually.

He followed the wall for a while, and then the darkness started to lessen and fade to gray. There had to be light somewhere to make such a thing happen; with this realization, Willis quickened his pace. The whimpering grew stronger, and he knew he was getting closer. The mysterious light shining in the dark was strong enough now that he could make out his fingers against the wall, and he could see that just ahead of where he stood, the wall ended in a corner.

A long cry rang out, close enough to him that he was now certain it was female. A thought crashed into his skull out of nowhere. *Elise.* He rushed forward and around the corner to see a single spotlight, twenty yards ahead, hanging from the ceiling above a long white medical chair. The rest of the room was empty, all a black void except for the light, the chair, and the girl strapped to it.

The girl. The one who had filled his mind and his dreams for days. She was strapped down tightly by thick black bands, wires and tubes coming at her from all directions, their ends buried under her skin. She was frozen in pain, her eyes closed, her face twisted in agony. She shivered from the cold, silent tears running down the sides of her face, and Willis found his entire being shaking with anger.

Before he could react, someone else entered the space.

A huge creature, more beast than man, with long, dark talons for fingers, dark-red eyes, and sharp, metallic teeth. The beast stared at Elise with a deep hunger and licked its lips with a long, rotting tongue. Her eyes shot open as the monster approached, and at the sight of him, another shrill scream escaped her throat.

Willis's body took over then, his feet racing forward, legs pumping like pistons, not thinking of what he'd do once he reached the beast. The only thought he had was *Save the girl. Save Elise.*

When he was still several yards from her, the ground began to collapse and fall away. Like decaying stone, it crumbled into dust and disappeared, forming a widening circle around the chair and separating Willis from Elise. He pulled back barely in time, his feet sliding forward and nearly taking him over the edge of the newly hollowed crevice. He looked down into the black void that seemed eternal and then back up to where Elise was. The gap was too wide to jump.

He darted to his right, running after the decaying floor as it continued to fall away. Willis pushed himself to move faster, to outrun the destructing stone. He only needed to get ahead of it long enough to make the jump across, but as he increased his speed, so did the crumbling. As if whatever acid was eating away at the floor had a mind of its own.

Winded, his chest begging for air, Willis slid to a stop. Elise was now completely surrounded by the black abyss. An island in the center of darkness, alone with the beast that had been slowly inching toward her.

Desperation clawed at Willis's insides. *Save the girl!* screamed through his skull.

But he couldn't. There was no way to cross the ravine. Her screams echoed against the blackness that surrounded them, and each note sliced through his heart like a blade. *Save the girl.* It burned like fire under his skin.

Willis's heart rose up into his throat as the beast stopped just beside Elise's chair. Her eyes met its glowing stare, and she started thrashing at the straps that bound her.

"Elise!" Willis yelled, his voice breaking from the emotion collecting in his chest. "Elise!" He couldn't get to her, but she should know he was here. She wasn't alone.

"ELISE!"

The beast raised its eyes from the girl to Willis, its mouth turning up in a snarl. Even from where he stood, Willis could feel the monster's hateful energy. It washed over him with heat and his soul shivered. It felt like he was looking at the devil himself.

But he wouldn't stop, not even in the face of evil incarnate. Willis swallowed his raging fear. "Elise! Elise, look at me!"

She must have heard him then, because she started to turn her chin his way, and the beast reacted in kind. It roared at the sky and lifted its clawed hand over her chest.

No.

The monster plunged its talons down into Elise's chest and her mouth opened in a silent cry.

"No," Willis cried. "NO!"

A cloudy white haze filled Elise's eyes, and horror rocked Willis to his knees as she gasped for air. "Elise," he whispered, his mind reeling from shock.

A deep, cruel laugh bounded up from the beast's chest and shook the ground where Willis knelt.

Save the girl.

The laugh echoed in Willis's ears, rattling his bones as he clenched his eyes shut. *Wake up, wake up.*

"I will kill her, Willis," a voice said, sweet and teasing. "You can't stop me." It was the beast. Then the laughter returned, working its way down Willis's back and into his stomach.

Willis pounded his fists into the ground and focused.

Wake up, wake up.

Save the girl.

Wake up, Willis. Wake up!

Willis sat up in bed, taking a desperate, deep breath, his lungs starving for air. The room around him was thick with moisture, hot and sticky. He couldn't breathe, and he needed to get out of here. He scrambled from his sleeping mat, nearly knocking over the small table in the center of the room where the rest of the Seven were sleeping. His head spun and ached. A thunderous pounding steadily pumped between his eyes, making him squint as he stumbled from the room. Down a small hallway and out through the side door, into the cold night air.

The stars above were bright, and the light caused another wave of pain to crash against his head. Willis struggled for breath, falling against the brick wall of the building. He tried to calm his lungs through the panic that was still exploding in his chest.

It was just a dream.

Deep breaths.

Fear not.

But it wasn't just a dream. It was a nightmare—her nightmare. She was in trouble; he knew that as surely as he knew that the blood was pumping in his veins.

Save the girl. An echo that slipped through the cracks of his fear and sounded in his brain. *Save the girl.*

Willis took a deep, long breath in through his nose and let it out through his mouth.

Save the girl.

Message received loud and clear.

11

Roth Reynard stood with an arm behind his back, reading through the doctor's findings. He had been testing Elise the past two days, putting her body through rigorous circumstances to try to detect the cause of her perplexing ability. Find the center of her power. A power he couldn't help but covet. The darkness inside him cooed lustfully at the thought of it.

Power like that was a waste in the hands of a stupid child such as Elise. And dangerous. Yet he didn't want to destroy the power inside her; harnessing it for himself would prove much more valuable. Unfortunately, getting her to react the way she had back at the Genesis Compound was proving extremely difficult.

"Nothing," Roth said. He could feel his frustration building. He slammed the report down on the desk beside him and it snapped against the silence.

"We are trying, sir," the doctor said.

"Not hard enough."

"We are pushing her as close to death as we can without causing long-term effects—" the doctor tried.

"Push her harder! Do you think I care about long-term effects? We need her to activate that energy again so we can understand it. Extract it if possible. So do whatever is necessary!"

"Yes, sir," the doctor said, bowing slightly and leaving Roth alone.

The Scientist moved to the window and looked down into the streets of the Authority City. How had she done it? The lingering question that haunted him day and night. The way she had reached into their minds and changed the effects his drug had on their synapses. As if she had rewritten their mental code. It had been thrilling to watch, and unnerving. The three who had been affected were still recovering at the Genesis Compound. Their minds slowly being re-erased, brought back to a place of total control from Genesis.

The scientific questions this girl raised were enough to get Roth's blood pumping, but the prospect of what she could offer him roused something more sinister. The door behind him opened, and Roth cursed under his breath. He hated to be disturbed.

"You sent Nicolas and the CityWatch Army without consulting me?" Jesse asked, his voice heated and raised.

"Watch your tone in my office," Roth fired back. He turned to see Jesse ablaze, standing just inside the doorframe. "I told you I was going to handle the Seers."

"Yes, but to go behind my back . . . The Council is asking a lot of questions about the move, Roth. You should have consulted me so I could cover you," Jesse said.

"I didn't think it necessary. And I was trying to be respectful of your . . ." Roth trailed off. He wasn't sure what to call the pretend grieving that Jesse was experiencing. After Elise's outbreak, Roth thought it best to keep the knowledge about her to as few people as possible. Jesse hadn't made the short list. As far as the Authority president was concerned, the woman he loved was dead.

Jesse dropped his eyes away from Roth, his fists balling at his sides. Roth found himself becoming irrationally irritated at the weakness Elise caused in his protégé.

"The Council requests your presence at the next gathering," Jesse said, his tone calmer.

"I don't care what the Council wants; that's why I placed you in charge of them," Roth said.

"They'll insist."

"I trust you know how to deal with them."

"Do you? Trust me?"

Roth stared at Jesse for a long moment. "Can I?"

Jesse paused but kept his eyes locked on Roth's. He was angry, mourning, miserable even, but Roth knew Jesse had nowhere else to go. He was a smart man. He acted as if being in his position was torture, but that position afforded him power he'd never had before. And with Elise out of the picture, he wouldn't compromise it. Roth was sure of it.

"Of course you can," Jesse said.

Roth nodded. "That's what I thought."

/ / /

Elise had never known darkness like this. It invaded her mind and erased time and reality. This kind of darkness made you question whether you were still human, made you wonder whether life still existed. But then, she knew she was living, because she still had nightmares before being pulled out of sleep to face more torture. She wished the darkness would envelop her and stop rousing her back to life only to suck her underneath again.

The beast was always there in her nightmares. Stalking her chair, ripping into her flesh. Acting as another form of torture while the man in the lab coat left her to recover from near death.

Elise gasped for air as her eyes sprang open. Her throat burned and she coughed painfully as she tried to inhale enough air to fill her lungs. She remembered water, lots of water. Drowning, she thought. They had tried to drown her.

Her eyes blurred at the pain in her shoulders and neck. She was strapped to the chair that had become her only constant, her arms numb, her chest bruised. She looked around at the familiar room. She was alone again, but they would be back. With new ways to push her over the edge, each time expecting some great power to come out of her. But there was no great power in her. It had been a fluke, nothing more. She was nothing more.

You are stronger than you know.
Remember who you are.

Elise shook her head. The voice always came when she was alone. It let her suffer in silence and then showed up when she needed it least. Even in the thickest darkness it came. Part of her wanted it to stay; part of her wanted it to leave. All of her wanted it to save her from this misery.

"I already told you; I can't save you," someone said in front of her.

She glanced up to see him there. Aaron, standing a couple feet away, an image projected from her mind. "Then why come if you can't save me?" Elise asked.

"To help you remember you don't need to be saved. You already are; you have just forgotten."

"Look at me! Look where I am!"

"I am looking at you, but what I see and what you see are very different."

Elise huffed and dropped her eyes to the ground. "What could you possibly see?"

"I see the precious, chosen daughter of the Father, filled with light and power unlike anything this city has ever seen."

Elise shook her head. "Your words mean nothing to me."

"I know you have felt Him calling to you. The still, quiet voice in the darkness, the one that has always been with you, telling you truth, reminding you who you are."

"That isn't real," Elise said, closing her eyes tightly. "Just like you aren't real. None of this is real." Tears silently slid the length of her cheeks.

"Elise, let go of your fear. Listen to what He calls you," Aaron said.

The room filled with the familiar presence of wind. It floated over her and dried the tears rolling down her face. It wasn't cold, like the wind she sometimes felt out in the Capitol gardens, but rather warm and comforting.

"Let go and remember who you are," Aaron said. His voice sounded distant, an echo bouncing back to her ears. She didn't open her eyes to see if he had gone; she didn't want to risk that the wind would leave with him.

I am always with you.

I am the light inside you.

Hear what I call you, daughter of the Father.

Daughter, Elise thought. A foreign concept that she'd only ever heard from the wind. How could such a thing be? She was broken, unwanted by all. Hadn't she only created this wind to feel some sense of belonging? Was this not all just a trick of her mind?

The wind whipped more urgently now, moving into every inch of the room. Heating the cold chair beneath her, buzzing with comfort and love. Another round of tears dried in its wake as it circled around Elise's frame and seemed to tug at her.

Remember who you are.

Remember what I call you.

Daughter of the Father.

Elise desperately wanted to believe that she was more than just an unwanted child, that she mattered, but fear held her back. To let herself believe and be wrong . . . Elise couldn't risk that. She opened her eyes and *saw* the wind swirling around the room. Light and warmth floated with it as it swept over every corner. The walls and floor vibrated with it, everything caught up in its path.

"I can't be what you say," Elise cried out against the rustle. "The Scientist is wrong about me, and so are you. I am not what you all believe." Hot emotion filled her face, and tears rolled from the corners of her eyes. The wind filled more than the room. It filled her entire being, moving around her body, igniting her spirit, and battling against her overwhelming fear. It seemed almost to be lifting her from the chair where she was strapped, carrying her up into the air, covering her completely.

You are stronger than you know.

Daughter of the Father.

Remember who you are.

Something slammed against the closed door in front of her, and immediately the wind dissipated, leaving her with just the coldness of reality. Another sound rocked against the steel door, followed by a softer thud, the sound of moaning after that, and Elise strained against her straps. Her doorknob jiggled, and fear erupted in her chest. They were coming back for her.

The doorknob went still and Elise waited, her imagination conjuring up images of more torture. Her body braced for what was to come as the knob shook again. This time the center twisted as whoever was on the opposite side unlocked the door and pushed it open.

His face came into focus and Elise went numb. It

couldn't be. The boy from the beach stood just inside
the doorframe, his hand still holding the knob, chest rising and falling with vigor, eyes filled with determination.
She watched his face flash with anger and sympathy as he
looked across the room at her. His eyes widened with shock
as his hands balled into fists at his sides.

Neither of them said anything for a long beat, and then
the handsome boy seemed to shake off whatever was rolling
around inside his head, softened his expression, and took a
step toward her.

Elise tensed. She didn't know anything about this boy.
He was just another figment of her imagination, yet here
he was standing in the flesh. Or was she imagining this,
too, just as she'd imagined Aaron? She was having a hard
time telling the difference. She was probably asleep again
and dreaming this entire situation. This couldn't actually
be happening; the boy from her dream couldn't actually
be standing across the room. That would be insane.

"Hi," the boy said.

"Hi," Elise replied.

The room felt like it was filled with a new intensity that
overwhelmed all her senses. Elise told herself to stop staring at his face, but he was staring back at her, just like in
her dream, and she couldn't get her eyes to move from his.
There was something familiar in his gaze, as if something
was understood between them, even though they'd met
only once before. A voice inside her mind reminded her
that he was imaginary, that she must be sleeping.

Still, something in him called to something in her. Something deep and grounded and eternal. Elise just knew, without knowing how, and that scared her.

"We don't have much time," the boy said.

"What do you mean?"

"Before they come back for you. I need to get you out of here." He moved toward her slowly, so as to not startle her, and reached her with a couple of long strides.

"You can free me?"

"I can try."

"And go where?"

"Somewhere you'll be safe. Anywhere would be better than this." His eyes scanned the room again. "What have they done to you?"

Elise didn't want to talk about it, but a tremble of pain cascaded down her back at the thought of being nearly drowned or electrocuted again, and she was suddenly desperate to leave. "Get me out of here." She didn't know him, but that didn't matter if he could save her from this nightmare.

He nodded and started working at releasing her straps. He did it quickly and then carefully helped her sit up. Her feet shakily met the concrete floor and intense pain ran the entire length of her body.

"Can you walk?" he asked.

She noticed his hand still holding hers, his other firmly on the middle of her back, and she found herself distracted from her own pain. He was touching her; he had undone her restraints. He was more than a dream. Her wind whirled and she felt like she might throw up at his feet.

She looked up and held his gaze. She didn't want to die here in this room. "Yes," she said and used all her strength to push herself standing.

"I'm going to help you, but you have to trust me," the boy said.

Elise wasn't sure why, but she did. It wouldn't matter what she might encounter in the next couple of seconds. She wasn't willing to take her other option.

"Okay," she said. "Let's go."

12 Elise followed the boy down the long hallways that led from the room where she had been held. The guards stationed outside the door had been knocked unconscious and were slumped against the walls, their heads cocked to the side, their eyes closed. She glanced up at the boy again and paused for a second, but it was barely a heartbeat before she remembered what going back meant.

She would die if she stayed here, locked away in this prison until the Scientist got what he wanted from her. Though if they were caught trying to escape, they might both be killed. Then this boy's blood would be on her hands. She suddenly realized she didn't even know his name. He might be killed because he was foolishly trying to save her, and she didn't even know his name.

Elise didn't actually know anything about him at all. Why did her heart trust him when she did not even know his name? How had he found her? Where had he come from? Why did he even care? The questions hit her brain like small pebbles flung with annoyingly accurate aim.

They reached the end of the hall, and the young man held up his hand for Elise to stop. She did, and he reached into the inside pocket of the jacket he was wearing and pulled out a handheld device she didn't recognize. It flashed to life when he tapped the screen. She tried to peer closely enough to see what the images on the screen were, but the boy read the display too quickly and then tucked it away.

"We have a couple of minutes before the patrolling unit makes their way back toward this section. So we have to move quickly, but quietly," the boy said.

"What's your name?" Elise blurted out. She hadn't meant for it to slip past her teeth, but sometimes her words had a mind of their own.

The boy smiled, the one that made Elise's heart quicken, and shook his head. "I guess I should have told you that already. My name is Willis."

"I'm Elise."

Again he flashed her that brilliant smile. "I know. You ready?"

She had more questions, but clearly this wasn't the right time. She didn't know him, but he was rescuing her, so she would hold to that and ignore the rest. She nodded and Willis's smile turned to a determined grin. He then returned his focus to the mission at hand and slipped around the corner, Elise on his heels. They stayed pressed against the wall, crouching low as they quickly moved toward their destination.

The hallway they passed through was thin and dark. It ended in stairs that they climbed quickly. Every inch of her body ached, but she ignored the pain and tried to keep up with Willis. The top of the stairs landed them in another hallway, much larger and more familiar to Elise. She had probably walked this one before. It had marble floors and decorated ceilings.

They moved down the side of this hallway smoothly, encountering nothing but air. Willis slowed suddenly and placed a finger to his lips as Elise nearly slammed into him. Worry streaked across his face and he began searching the area around them. Elise heard it then—the echoing of boots, headed right toward them. She thought he'd said they had several minutes. Who was coming?

She also searched the hallway, but all she saw was the wall, floor, and ceiling. Suddenly Willis was pulling her back the way they'd come and across the wide hallway. Elise glanced over his shoulder to see a door a couple of feet away. They reached it and the boy twisted the knob. It didn't budge. The footsteps got louder, and Elise's heart rammed into her throat. They were going to get caught.

Willis yanked Elise along as they continued to move back in the direction they had come from, trying each door they came to. All were locked. They could hear voices now as the patrol of guards got closer.

Finally a knob twisted free, and Willis pushed open the

door, stepped through, and pulled Elise inside. He closed the door softly as she turned to survey the room. She hadn't been inside this room before. It looked like an office of some kind but appeared never to have been touched. It was set up perfectly, all necessary office supplies in their proper place, but it had no life of any kind. It was a placeholder, as so many of the rooms in the Capitol Building seemed to be.

Willis touched Elise's arm to grab her attention and opened his mouth to instruct her, but before he could, another door that led into the room on the far left wall began to open. Elise froze, and Willis couldn't move fast enough before a guard stepped around the opening door and into the unused office. His eyes met the two standing in the room, and a moment of confusion passed over his face before recognition set in. He knew Elise; all the guards knew her.

He started toward them, his mouth flying open to speak, but Elise only heard his command over her shoulder as Willis pushed her back out through the door and into the grand hall.

"Stop!" the guard yelled.

Elise slid out across the marble floor, and Willis kept his hand clenched tightly around her arm to steady her. Now more echoing footsteps bounced through the large hall. Elise suspected the patrolling unit had heard the shout and was headed toward them. As soon as the thought entered her mind, two more guards appeared in front of them, the third one exiting the unused office behind them.

Willis pulled Elise down the hall in the opposite direction of the imminent threat. They ran, their feet pounding against the floor, as they tried to put distance between them and the guards. All three were rushing after them. Elise could hear their shouts and the crackle of a radio as one called for backup. Dread filled her heels and made it hard to push through. There was no way they were going to get out of this.

"Here," Willis said, and she followed him as he made a quick turn down a smaller side hallway. It was much darker than the grand hallway and only held a couple of doors on either side before ending in yet another staircase. Willis jiggled every handle as he sailed by each door. He moved like a machine, Elise noticed, her lungs straining for relief. Keeping up with him felt impossible. All the doors were locked, so Willis headed for the stairs. The guards had rounded the corner into the small hallway now, only a handful of seconds behind them.

"Stop, in the name of the Authority," one of them called.

"Willis," Elise said, her mind filling with terror. Maybe they should just stop? They were going to be caught anyway; maybe if they surrendered, the Authority wouldn't kill him. Her fate was already sealed; she'd been a fool to think she could change it.

"Come on," he said, reaching for her hand without pausing.

The moment their hands met, she was filled with an unusual sense of peace. He had come for her. She held his hand tightly and pushed past the throbbing ache in her thighs and the blinding worry trying to overtake her mind. *Just keep moving.*

The stairs twisted up onto a landing, and another long hallway stretched before them. This hallway was carpeted, with two doors framed against the wall to their left. Willis pushed on the first door and it opened, leading into a small sitting room. Elise rushed in and slammed the door behind her. Her eyes scanned the room and found that the far wall held two windows. Beyond them lay the gardens that stretched over a dozen yards toward the stone wall at the perimeter of the Capitol's property. They must be on the east side of the building, Elise thought. If they could get out onto the lawn, then she knew the gardens better than anyone, and she might be able to shake these guards.

The idea filled her with a new measure of hope, and she moved toward the windows. They were only two stories up, but she knew this side of the building had balconies. If they could drop to one . . .

Quickly she moved from one window to the next. Both were shut tight.

"Elise," Willis said.

"If I can just get one of these open . . . ," Elise said.

She yanked again on the window's hardware, trying to shake it loose. She knew these opened. They had to. Something screeched against the floor behind her and she glanced back to see Willis pushing a chest in front of the door. She turned back to the window and continued to pull, splinters from the wood digging into her fingers.

Willis stepped up next to her and squatted, placing his shoulder under the window's middle ledge. He pressed up through his legs as Elise pushed with her palms, both of their faces red with effort, and the window squeaked open just a hair.

They looked at one another and she saw excitement flash behind his eyes.

The closed door behind them began to shake with force, and the chest blocking it shuddered. It wouldn't hold for long.

"Again," Willis said.

Elise nodded, and again they focused all their combined energy on the window. It slid up a couple more inches as something heavy began to pound against the center of the blocked door. The sound of wood cracking echoed through the sitting room, and fear buzzed through Elise's mind.

"Again," Willis said.

They pushed once more, Elise digging for strength she wasn't sure she had, and the window finally slid open. The bottom half slammed against the top, and Willis and Elise peered down. Just as she'd remembered, there was a small balcony just below. She exhaled a heavy sigh of relief.

"I'll lower you down first and then come after you," Willis said.

Another crack of wood bounced around the room and Elise nodded.

She turned and climbed out the window backward, as if she were headed down a ladder, bracing herself with Willis's arms. He began lowering her, moving so that his torso was lying across the window's ledge. A loud snap came through the window, and Willis turned his head over his shoulder. Shouts followed the snap, and Elise knew the guards had broken through the barricade.

Everything happened quickly after that. Willis was yanked away from the window, and he released his hold, dropping Elise several feet to the stone balcony's floor. She hit hard, the vibration spreading up through her feet. Her knees buckled and she fell onto her hands, the blow piercing through her already-bruised shoulders.

She could hear the struggle that was taking place above her—a loud crash and an angry wail—as she struggled to push herself up against the spinning pain in her head. Through the haze, she heard the noise upstairs stop. Elise stood shakily and looked up, hoping to see Willis's head poke through the window. But nothing came.

Willis!

Panic took her then. What was she supposed to do? She looked through the glass doors that led from the balcony back into the Capitol Building. Something moved inside, and before she could react, a guard opened the door with his weapon raised and his face stern. Elise kept still as he moved out onto the ledge. Another guard appeared behind him and marched toward her. It was over. She had been foolish to believe it was ever anything other than over.

13

Willis's eyes fluttered open as images blurred in and out of focus. He felt like he had cotton in his brain; everything was foggy and stuffy. Something overhead was turning, blades cutting through the air, which he thought was odd. The ceiling was white, and as he looked slowly around the room, he saw four beige walls that stretched down to hardwood floors. His eyes moved back skyward and he realized that the spinning object was a ceiling fan, turning slowly, circulating the smell of chemicals.

The back of his head pulsed with pain, and when he tried to move his hands toward the ache, they didn't budge. He glanced down and saw that his arms were strapped at his sides. He felt the cold of steel as he registered that his entire body was being restricted against something solid. A chair, he thought. Two wide white belts were across his chest, two more across his legs.

The cotton in his head was clearing now, and voices drifted through the air to his right. He turned his head to see two men dressed all in black, one talking with an old man in a white lab coat, the other holding back a beautiful girl. *Elise.*

All the memories of the past several hours crashed against his mind at once. He'd been told to save her, and the light had led him. To the Capitol Building, down into underground tunnels, up to a lower level where she was being held. Each step was foreign, but he trusted the whisper, the light, the instinct that was more than he understood. They'd almost made it out.

His body reacted before his mind had finished digesting the situation, and it yanked violently at the straps around him. He had one pulsing thought that cut through the jumble in his brain: *Save the girl.*

"Oh good, you're awake," the old man with the two guards said. "And faster than I would have thought. You must be well trained."

"Let her go," Willis said.

"You're going to lead with that? How disappointingly predictable, and really rather a waste, since you were trying to steal her from me."

"Where am I?"

"That seems irrelevant."

"Who are you?"

Darkness flashed across the old man's face. "The fact that you don't know confirms my suspicions about you," he said, "which means the time is indeed upon us."

As the old man talked, Willis slowly began working at one of the straps. By bending his wrist as far as he could, he could just reach the lower buckle on his right, away from the prying eyes of the guards. The strap was tight and thick, but with enough time, he thought it might not be impossible to get free from.

"What suspicions? What 'time'?" Willis asked, the fog in his head now completely clear and his mind working properly. *Just keep him talking.*

"Don't play the fool now, boy; you've already proven you're smarter than that. How many are there of you? Is he with you?"

"Is who with me? I don't know what you're—"

The man chuckled hatefully. "Very well, then. So the Seers have managed to infiltrate the city? There can't be that many of you, so what's your purpose?"

"Let him go, Dr. Reynard," Elise said.

The old man snapped his head back to glare over his shoulder at Elise, and Willis caught her eye. She looked desperate, defeated. She was swaying a bit too, as if she weren't completely in control of her body.

"What did you do to her?" Willis asked.

"Gave her something to settle her nerves," the man said.

"You have me back; please don't kill him," Elise said, her words slower than they had been a moment ago.

"Oh, I don't intend to kill him. No, death is a waste when one can instead transform," Dr. Reynard said. He walked back across the room to a long, thin table against the wall. On it was a silver tray holding a large syringe filled with yellow liquid. He lifted it up and surveyed it with pride.

Dread inched its way into Willis's mind.

"I don't plan to kill any of you. I'm just trying to save you from yourselves," the doctor said, turning back toward Willis. "You're young and were probably taught by that mad leader that choice is necessary for happiness. The truth is he may be right, but evolution isn't much concerned with happiness. Humanity's primary goal is longevity. To survive as long as possible. We have found that choice has a rather negative effect on survival."

"So that's how things are done around here?" Willis said, still working on his restraints. "You just take away every person's choice until they are numb robots that merely survive?"

"I don't expect a mind as flooded with nonsense as yours to grasp the big picture; besides, it doesn't matter. In a couple of minutes, you'll be in transition, and all your worries will be gone."

The doctor took several steps toward Willis, the liquid in his syringe sliding about. "After I take care of you, I will finish what I started with Elise, hunt down the others you came with, and extinguish the false power you believe choice gives you."

"I won't let you," Willis said.

"Why do people always say that? As if you are in any position to be making such a claim. You can't stop evolution. Regardless of the trash Aaron has filled your head with, this has always been the path of humanity. It's time that you all joined us in the future."

Dr. Reynard looked to one of the guards over his

shoulder. "Prepare him," he said, and the guard nodded and moved to the front left side of the chair. He did something that Willis couldn't see, and the metal chair began to lower backward until he was stretched out as if lying down to sleep. The movement forced Willis to stop messing with the strap at his side for fear of getting caught, and as the doctor approached, it was impossible to ignore the panic racing in his heart. He needed more time.

The chair came to a stop and jolted Willis's bruised head against the hard steel, sending a ripple of pain down his back. The old man grabbed Willis's forehead and turned it toward the right so that his neck was elongated and vulnerable. The doctor's touch was like ice, his hold firmer than Willis would have guessed. Doubt and fear dropped into his body like stones. This couldn't be happening. He'd followed the call.

"Your pulse is racing," Dr. Reynard said. "Don't be afraid; it will all be over soon." He moved the syringe's needle toward Willis's neck, and Willis tried to pull against the old man's hold. His desperation for survival intensified.

"Don't fight what's good for you, boy," the doctor said. "You should feel lucky. You're the first of many Seers that I plan to bring into the new era. You'll be an example of the power of science and forward thinking. Once the tiny hope of the Seers is destroyed, all that will remain is the future—my future." A small chuckle fell from the old man's mouth, and Willis nearly erupted with fear. He could feel the presence of the needle even before it touched his skin.

"Welcome to the new world, boy."

/   /   /

Elise's mind swirled with agony and fog. She tensed as Dr. Reynard lifted the syringe from the long table beside her. She knew what it was, but her body was heavy with drugs, so she could do nothing but watch as the Scientist headed for Willis.

After being detained on the balcony, Elise had heard a voice on the guards' radios ordering them to bring her back to the basement. Elise had thought about throwing herself off the balcony; she knew all too well what waited for her in the basement. But they had Willis, so she hadn't.

The moment she'd entered the subterranean level, her old friend Lab Coat had greeted her with a syringe made just for her. She'd barely had a moment to register what was happening before the needle was deep in her arm. Then she'd been led to her familiar room and seen Willis strapped in her familiar spot. Terror had filled her bones. *She* had done this to him. A boy she knew nothing about had risked his life to save her, and she was now going to get him killed.

Willis came to a couple of moments later and the sick mental game that the Scientist was playing began. Elise tried to get Dr. Reynard to let Willis go, but even as the words left her mouth, she knew all resistance was useless. And then her head had started to swim. Her body felt like jelly, wobbly and uncentered. What had they given her? She tried to wade through the muck collecting in her brain, but it was thickening with each moment.

Elise watched Dr. Reynard continue toward Willis, the boy completely unable to do anything to stop the man from taking his freedom. A freedom he deserved, a freedom that made him who he was. He'd gambled everything to save her, and now he would lose it all. Elise couldn't let this happen. Her heart raced and her mind turned as she searched for something, anything.

Out of the darkness of her mind, a single voice came.

You have great power in you.

Remember who you are.

Elise struggled through her desperation. For days she had been trying to harness the mysterious power that Dr. Reynard so coveted, trying to make the torture stop, with no luck. Her head felt heavy, and she slumped against the guards holding her. She was powerless.

Let it go, Elise.

Fear not, and remember who you are.

Find the light.

With no options left, she let go of her searching, let go of her pain and panic, let go of her need to find her power, and just acted. As the Scientist leaned toward Willis with his syringe, Elise felt the buzz of energy gather in her chest, and she let her instincts take over.

Blinding light pierced through Elise's head, as well as blinding pain. She heard the cry from the guard next to her as he dropped to his knees, and then the room around them vanished and the scene changed. Just like before, the scenery around her took on images of places she didn't recognize. A childhood home with broken wooden fences. A small shared bedroom, bunks stacked three high. Rain dripping through a leaking ceiling into tin buckets placed on the floor to catch the water. Screaming between a man and woman. Trembling children.

Then it changed. A young teenage boy in training sessions at the CityWatch barracks. Wandering eyes that followed a specific girl through town. Flowers presented and rejected. More barracks training.

With each new moment, Elise felt the strong emotions connected to the scenes. Someone else's emotions, invading her chest. Fear and pain. Loss and need. Loneliness. Anger. Self-pity. It felt as if they all might overwhelm her. She couldn't even begin to hold on to the images as they cascaded past like moving pictures.

Suddenly another wave of memories crashed against the first. Completely different, the emotional pull uniquely its own. Somewhere in the distance more cries of agony echoed, but she was too far down the rabbit hole of someone else's mind to pinpoint specifics. The new memories were all of a small child: his first steps, his happy home, his loving parents. The feelings were warm and comforting, on the opposite side of the spectrum from the first set of emotions.

The two strains melded together in a hurricane of emotional weather. The energy shot through her like lightning, electrifying her senses. She felt afraid that she'd gone too far, that she wouldn't be able to climb back out of these people's minds. The more fear she felt, the more hesitation filled her gut, and the deeper she seemed to fall.

Let it go.

Fear not.

Elise shut out the anxiousness that made her hands tremble and let the voice wash over her.

Remember you are called.

With a deep breath, she opened her eyes and saw that it wasn't just her mind that was filled with light; the room itself seemed to be vibrating with color. She was kneeling, the guards on the floor beside her, both clutching their heads as light danced through the air around them.

The light soaked its way into her skin and filled her with weightlessness, as if she could float right off the ground. Joy tingled through her blood, and a new sensation overwhelmed her. Confidence. Suddenly anything felt possible. As if she were commanding the waves that had so often threatened to drown her. As if the air around her were waiting for her next order.

Remember who you are.

Elise still wasn't sure who she was—the question had traveled with her all of her days. But she knew she was more than she had previously believed, and that filled her with power. She was much more.

/ / /

A scream of pain bounded through the room just as the tip of the needle touched Willis's neck. Dr. Reynard snapped back, drawing the syringe away. His hand released Willis's forehead, and Willis turned his head toward the sound. Elise had somehow dropped a guard to his knees. The man was gripping the sides of his skull and grunting in pain. Elise was also on her knees, her eyes closed and dancing violently back and forth behind her eyelids.

Willis stared as a glow lifted off her shoulders. Powerful energy filled the room, an energy Willis was familiar with, and all fear vanished from his mind. Seconds later, a breeze, soft but sure, floated through the room, touching the hairs on his arms and calling forth his strength.

"Get him up!" the doctor yelled at the other guard. "Get her away from him!" The second soldier moved, reaching Elise and his fallen friend in several long strides. He went to rip Elise away from the other guard, but he was too late. His eyes rolled back into his head and agony escaped his throat.

Brilliant light radiated out of Elise, overtaking the room and heating the chill that had been there before. The second soldier fell to his knees, crying out as something worked its way through his mind.

The old doctor stumbled backward, the light nearly forcing him to the ground. "No, no!" he screamed.

Willis could see the trembling in the man's body and the

power-crazed look in his eyes. The old man focused in on Elise, her eyes still closed and light still pulsating from her body. Hatred like black oil dripped from the doctor's eyes as quick, labored breaths slithered through his teeth. "That power belongs to me!"

Willis yanked and struggled with all his might against the straps. He twisted his shoulders and ankles, trying to get enough space to slip free. The straps cut into his skin and scraped at his muscles. He ignored the pain and pulled harder.

Elise's eyes snapped open, staring forward and right through everything in the room. She was caught up in another place entirely, but Dr. Reynard was focused completely on her. Out of the corner of his eye, Willis saw him moving, holding something that reflected off the light vibrating from Elise. The cruel look on the old man's face was certain, and all the trained sense in Willis's body surged.

Save the girl.

With a fierce cry, Willis yanked one final time at the straps, and the ones around his torso finally loosened just enough for him to snap his arms free. In one swift move, he was sitting up, ripping the second set of restraints from his legs, and bounding out of the metal chair. He crossed the room toward the old man and wrapped his hands around his brittle chest from behind.

The doctor thrust his head backward and it connected with Willis's chin, causing him to stumble and lose his grasp on the old man. The doctor whirled and moved toward Willis, the object in his hand clear now. It was a knife. He slashed it in the air at Willis, and Willis stepped back to avoid it just in time. The man charged at him and Willis slid behind the chair that he'd been strapped to, shielding himself from the blade. The crazed look on the doctor's face intensified. Rage pumped through the veins in his neck and he screamed out in bitterness, thrusting toward Willis again.

Willis rounded the chair and saw that the syringe was lying on a desk in front of him. He dashed for it, the doctor on his heels, then turned, swinging his arm, syringe poised, and implanted the needle in the meaty part of the old man's arm. The doctor cried out in pain as Willis injected the yellow substance out of the syringe and then ripped the needle from the man's flesh.

A fog passed over Dr. Reynard's eyes, and his lips faded from violent red to ash. Then his knees buckled forward, and he collapsed to the floor.

Willis stood for a moment, panting and tensely waiting for the man to strike again, but he just lay there as still as stone, and Willis wondered if he had killed him. He ignored the prick of guilt, reached for the knife that had fallen on the floor to his left, and turned his focus to Elise.

He slowly crossed the room to her, knelt beside her, and hesitantly touched her shoulder. Like a vacuum, the light sucked itself back inside Elise, and she gasped for air. Fear filled her eyes and she automatically pulled away from Willis's touch.

"It's me," he said softly. "I'm just going to cut these restraints, okay?"

She gulped for breath, as if the wind had been knocked out of her, and Willis sliced through the plastic bands that bound her. She pulled her hands free and nursed her raw wrists, her eyes wandering around the room.

"We have to go now," Willis said.

He didn't wait for her to respond but swept her up in his arms and left the room behind, both guards still writhing on the floor and the liquid from the syringe eating away at the mad scientist's mind.

My beloved Elise,

I'm up before the sun today. The days are cold and the nights are freezing, but the mountain helps protect us from the bitter wind. I should probably be trying to get more rest, for I know what is ahead of me over the next few days. The time has come for the chosen Seven to leave, and my head is a mess with conflicting emotions.

I can't decide if I'm happy, worried, angry, afraid, or maybe simply all of them at once. The entire city is alive with an electric energy and excitement like I have never seen. Many have been dreaming of this time for decades. It signifies hope and freedom, the chance to return to the home we all left behind, to be reunited with the people still trapped there, to complete the journey we were all called to.

But beneath the surface there is a strong sense of fear too. It's hidden well under the excitement, but I can feel it like a steady pulse. What if it doesn't work? What if we have waited all this time only to realize that nobody wants to be saved? What if all of this was for nothing?

We're supposed to have faith, to recognize that doubt is only possible when we lose sight of who we are, and we aren't supposed to judge ourselves for losing sight, which is the hardest part, my love. If I'm being honest, which I feel like I can be here with you in this safe place that we share, I am living in a constant state of judgment.

I judge myself for losing sight of my true nature. I judge myself for needing to remember. I judge myself for aging, for feeling weak and tired. I judge myself for the blame I carry. And I judge myself that I can't let it go. I know I shouldn't, and then I judge myself because I do anyway.

Maybe that's all this life is, really. Waking up each morning and forgiving yourself. Forgiving the world around you. Seeing things with clear eyes and letting go of the grievances we hold on to for dear life. Maybe that is the only way to really find peace.

It's hard to do when the darkness creeps in. When thoughts of you flood my mind or when I'm overcome with worry for your sister. But I am trying to see myself as I hope that you see yourself: blameless, whole, lacking nothing, perfect. For the love given to us calls this forth.

The darkness is real and dense and ever present. But I will try.

For you.

For Kennedy.

For myself.

Your mother

14

Elise swam in and out of consciousness as she was carried from the Capitol Building. Fuzzy images of the grand hallway filtered through her mind, followed by a back door, the vibration of stairs, a damp tunnel, a dark night sky, and finally the smell of grass and pine. Her body shifted as Willis moved along his exit route, but Elise's mind was too fried to wonder where they were headed.

She was aware that her brain should be trembling with questions, but instead she felt completely at ease. The light and energy that had radiated from her was still swimming around inside her head. It alleviated her worry and silenced her doubt. So the questions stayed at bay for a while, and she just rested in the knowledge that for the first time in her life she felt connected to herself.

Not the body that she lived in or the mind that she carried but the soul that was deeper. The part that housed her power. It was almost as if she'd known it was there, maybe even unknowingly interacted with it from time to time, but suddenly, in a moment of clarity, she'd released it upon the

world. And now that it was awakened, Elise couldn't put it
back to sleep.

Not that she wanted to. In fact, all she really wanted
to do was drown in it, escape with it, block out the rest
of reality and dwell in it. The power, the confidence, the
peace. To think she'd had it within her this entire time.

But as the minutes passed, the world around her
started to chip away at the protective layer that the
light had created. Then the questions started to sneak
through. What had happened? How had she done that?
What had she done? How had they escaped? Where were
they going?

She felt her mind and body stirring as Willis paused and
set her down. He took heavy, shallow breaths, and Elise
saw sweat glistening across his forehead in the starlight.
She took in her surroundings. This was not a place she'd
been before; it was outside the Capitol Building's walls.
Collections of shops and houses stood all around them,
their foundations planted along the pavement of a thin side
road. There were hardly any lights on, leaving the buildings
dark and still. If Elise had to guess, she would say they were
in the outskirts of the city.

She could feel Willis's eyes on her and she wondered
what he was thinking. He had, after all, been with her, seen
what she'd done. Was he judging her? Afraid of her? He
already seemed to know more about her than she did herself, so maybe he wasn't surprised at all.

As if reading her thoughts, Willis huffed out a breath.

"I was expecting some crazy things from you, but that was . . ." His words faded to silence.

She felt a familiar pinch of sadness bubble inside. Another chunk of the light disappeared from her mind as she remembered that there was still so much she didn't understand.

What she did know was that she was just a girl.

Chink. Another piece gone.

That she wasn't in command of her life.

One more, vanished.

That they may have escaped for now, but death was still coming for her.

Pop.

That she wasn't actually that powerful at all.

The peace that had only moments ago felt as close to her as skin was now gone, and in its place was the reality of what she had done and what it would mean.

"Are you all right?" Willis asked.

His words yanked Elise from her own mind, and she tried for a fake smile but couldn't manage one. She was suddenly filled with overwhelming fear and doubt. What had she done? Without thinking about it, she glanced down at her hands in wonder. She had caused such pain and misery with them. She was a weapon. The idea made her tremble.

Willis reached out and laid his hand on top of hers, but she jerked away. She didn't want to hurt him too. His eyes held a somber empathy that made Elise uncomfortable, and she shivered against the cold night.

"We need to keep moving," Willis said and took a step forward, but Elise didn't move. Her feet were glued to their place on the street, her body and mind questioning all of her choices. Her mind reeled. It was all too much for her.

"How did you know how to escape?" she asked the stranger before her. Because Willis was still that—a stranger. But before he could answer, the dam holding back Elise's queries broke. "How did you even find me to begin with? And where are we going? What are we supposed to do now? We can't outrun them; we can't hide from them. This is insanity!"

"Elise—"

"I was just trapped in a room being tortured so someone else could use this," she said, thrusting out her hands.

"Elise, please—"

"What am I? You saw me; you saw . . . What is happening to me?"

"I don't know."

Elise felt her anger rise. "You know more than you're telling me, though. I want to know what you know."

"Elise, we are in danger just standing out here."

"I've been in danger my whole life! I won't move until you tell me what you know about me."

Willis sighed. "Your name is Elise Brant. Remko and Carrington are your parents. They live in a city west of here called Trylin; they are some of the original Seers. You have a younger sister; her name is Kennedy. She is with me in this city along with five others who were called here. We escaped the Capitol Building because I have been training for this my whole life, and I found you because I was called to you. But as far as who you are? The only person who can answer that is you. That's the journey we all go on, the search for ourselves."

Elise felt like a bucket of cold water had been poured over her head. "No." She shook her head. "My parents didn't want me because I'm broken."

Willis's face filled with sympathy. "Is that what they told you?"

Her brain struggled to absorb all the information he was giving her. She had parents and a sister? Her sister was here? He was called to her? The more she reviewed the information, the more questions she had. It couldn't be true, what he said. It couldn't.

She took a step away from him, and he calmly raised his hands as to not spook her.

"I have been living with the light the majority of my life," Willis said. "I was raised in a place that encouraged me, and everyone around me, to interact with it. But I have never seen anyone channel it the way you did back there."

At the mention of the light, Elise's soul yearned for another dose. How quickly it had vanished; how quickly she had forgotten the way it made her feel. It had given her a sense of identity, and she had abandoned that for fear in a single moment.

"Aaron can help. He'll know—"

Elise felt her breath catch in her throat. "Aaron?"

Willis's eyes lit up. "So you know him."

Tears filled Elise's eyes and her lips trembled. "He's real?"

"Very real. And he's here in the city with us." Willis took a step toward Elise, slowly. "The way the light moved through you and became an extension of you, I don't know what that means, but if you come with me and let me keep you safe, then I promise to help you find out."

For the second time that night, Elise searched Willis's face for any reason to run the other way, but she still only saw sincerity when she looked at him. He had spoken about being called; the Seers being called to the city, him being called to find her, and hadn't she herself dreamed of being called? Maybe this was where that calling started. She gave Willis a nod, and he responded in kind.

With a chilly breeze at their backs, the two of them started off toward whatever the future held next.

/ / /

Jesse followed the pack of CityWatch guards as they led him toward the Scientist. Roth had been found in an old, unused medical laboratory room with his mind destroyed and his eyes nearly lifeless. Two guards had been with him, both stumbling about, spouting off impossible memories from the past, but neither of them coherent enough to recall their names, much less what had happened. The entire situation was madly unreasonable. What could have possibly happened to cause such confusion in two of his guards?

He walked through the doorframe of another room. The Scientist's bedroom was very different from his office. It was well kept and clean, thanks to his housemaid, and almost warm. It was coated in browns and golds, had large windows, sturdy furniture, and more space than any one person needed. The old man was lying on his bed, eyes closed, hands placed on top of one another across his chest as if he were readying himself for a coffin. But he was still breathing, his chest rising and falling slowly.

Several men in lab coats stood around the Scientist's bed, reading the measurements beeping through the medical machine that they'd hooked Roth up to. Why they were here, and what they hoped to accomplish, was beyond Jesse. They all knew how Genesis worked; there was no going back from it.

"What else was found with him?" Jesse asked.

One of the guards stepped forward. "Nothing, sir, just the empty syringe. Both of the guards were huddled in the corner. The straps on the medical chair were ripped loose, though, so it appears someone broke free from them. There's no way of knowing if that was before or after Dr. Reynard was injected."

Frustration rippled across Jesse's back. How had this happened? He needed time alone to think.

"I want everyone out," Jesse said.

The others in the room paused and looked at their president with confusion.

"I said out!" Jesse yelled, and the room came back to life. It cleared quickly until only Jesse, his old mentor, and the beeping of machinery were left. Jesse walked toward the bed, his eyes passing over the man's body. He looked so fragile lying there, unconscious and mindless. Jesse had never thought of the Scientist as weak, but seeing him like this made him so.

Jesse pulled the wooden desk chair from its place against the wall and set it next to the bed. He sat, placing his elbows on his knees, and dropped his skull into the palms of his hands. He rubbed his fingers in tiny circles along the top of his forehead, hoping the pressure would abate. The beeping gave a steady pulse to the room, and Jesse lost himself in thought.

A soft knock sounded at the door and Jesse cursed under his breath. The invader didn't wait for a response. The door opened and a small man in a lab coat entered.

"I thought I asked for the room?" Jesse said.

"You did, sir, but I think there is something you need to know," the man said.

"What?" Jesse snapped.

"It's about Elise, sir."

Jesse's skin went cold at her name and he stood from his

chair. "You had better have a good reason for mentioning her."

"She did this to Dr. Reynard," the man said.

Confusion racked across Jesse's brain.

"Well, not this exactly, but she's the reason he's in this state."

Jesse grounded his heels into the floor to keep himself from lurching angrily at the puny man in front of him. "You must be mistaken. Elise is dead." Even the words hurt, and Jesse tried to think of a good reason not to have this lab-coat wearer thrown in prison.

"No, sir. I was working on a project with Dr. Reynard concerning her abilities when this happened."

"Her abilities?"

"I think you should sit down, sir."

/ / /

Elise followed Willis to a dilapidated factory. It was small, with redbrick walls and broken windows. They stood outside as she looked the structure over.

"This is where you guys are staying?" she asked.

"I know it's not exactly the Capitol Building, but it's safe," Willis said.

Elise nodded. That was already more than the Capitol Building had ever been for her.

Motion to their right caused them both to tense, and Willis moved in front of Elise to block her from sight. After only a moment, she watched his shoulders ease, so she glanced around him to see a familiar face approaching.

Aaron.

Elise stepped out from behind Willis and stared at the living, breathing representation of what she had been certain was only her imagination.

"Hello, Elise," Aaron said.

His familiar voice caused her sore bones to relax and her head to spin.

"I know you have questions," he said. "I'll have answers for some; others you'll discover on your own. Most you already know the answers to." He smiled at her, and she felt it hard not to smile back. "I was just about to take a walk to see the sunrise; would you like to join me?"

Elise glanced at Willis and he smiled too, nodding toward Aaron and heading into the old factory. The moment he was gone she wished he would return. He really did make her feel safe, and without him she felt very vulnerable. She looked at Aaron's kind face and then timidly followed him through the still-sleeping city streets, down short alleys, and around a couple of corners, until they came to a large brick building that had a ladder reaching up one of its walls.

Aaron took the ladder swiftly, without much effort, and Elise followed, working to get her tired, bruised limbs to climb each rung. Once at the top, Aaron reached down and assisted her up and over the roof's edging until she was standing securely.

The roof was flat with a large, groaning generator sitting in the center but otherwise free of debris. The city stretched for miles in all directions; thin smoke billowed from dozens of chimneys, cattle roamed out in fields to the west, and streetlights illuminated the lonely roads below. The scene was picturesque, especially seen from a viewpoint that Elise had never experienced or even imagined. There really was so much life in this city that she knew nothing of.

"Beautiful, isn't it?" Aaron asked.

"Yes," she replied.

"This is one of my favorite spots in the city. I've found myself up here many times to reflect on the people below. Watching them remember, and forget, and change." He paused and looked past Elise toward the two giant matching buildings at the farthest end of the city. Elise knew they had once been used to house the women who were not selected during the time of the Choosing Ceremony. Now they just stood empty.

"Things were different on the outside then, but the same blindness existed within the soul," Aaron said, staring at the looming fortresses. "I met your mother then."

The word *mother* still sounded foreign to her, and she wasn't sure she could fully accept it.

"You knew my mother?"

"I know her still," Aaron said. "Very well."

Elise wanted to ask him a million questions, but the words seemed to get stuck behind the feeling of injustice rising in her gut. It seemed as though everyone knew things that had been hidden from her, hidden behind lies she had been told and blindly believed her whole life. Like they were all in on some sick joke that she was the butt of. She had a family that was alive in a faraway place she hadn't even known existed. The man from her dreams was real and leading a group of people called the Seers, yet Elise still felt like she was wading through the dark, trying to figure out where she fit.

"I've seen you from up here," Aaron said.

"Then why didn't you ever come to me?"

"I did."

Elise shook her head. "In my dreams? I didn't even know you were real."

"Of course you knew. We spend so much time struggling with what we think we don't know that we miss the truth underneath that gives us all we need."

"Every time I think I understand what's going on, I feel like the rug gets pulled out from under my feet and I realize I understand nothing." The weariness of the last several hours began to creep under her skin.

"Well then, let's start with what you think you know and understand," Aaron said.

"Well, I know nothing is actually as it appears to be. I know that I don't know anything about this city, or my past, or where I come from. I understand that everyone around me has kept me in the dark, but I don't know why. I understand that for some reason I've been kept basically imprisoned my whole life, but the reason is a mystery to me."

"Those are all things related to the forms of this world. The buildings, the roads, the clothes we wear, the lives we think we own. I want you to look beyond that. Look to the true identity that lies within you. That is what you need to understand; when you do, the rest all falls away."

"I don't know how."

"Remember the truth, the voice that calls to your soul. I know you have heard it. What does it tell you?"

Elise searched her mind but found all her thoughts consumed with the frustration of her present condition. She couldn't reach beyond the clutter crashing around inside her brain. "Nothing. I hear nothing."

"Stop searching for what you think the answer should be, and just feel the first thing that comes."

Elise closed her eyes and stopped trying to push through the madness. She did as Aaron suggested and just waited. The moment felt eternal before the familiar whisper came.

Remember who you are.

She wanted to remember; she wanted the freedom that Aaron so easily carried, but who was she? A girl nobody had wanted, kept locked away because she was different, lied to, used, manipulated. The voices of doubt rose higher the further Elise tried to push into herself. What was she even doing here, on this roof? Why had this power been given to her? She was useless.

Suddenly the world seemed to fill with shadows. All

around her they billowed up from the roof, moving toward her, giving her menacing looks, as if they had faces, as if they wanted to devour her whole. They stirred a deep-seated fear that rattled Elise's bones.

"Elise," Aaron said.

Elise opened her eyes and exhaled. There was nothing on the roof but her and Aaron. She shook her head. "I can't."

"But you already have," Aaron said. "You've seen the light, felt its power. It is already within you. All you have to do is turn toward it."

"I can't! I'm not the one you want. I'm just a girl! This power shouldn't even be mine. You asked me what I know—I know I'm not enough for this."

As the words left her mouth she could feel the shadows again, creeping up her back and wrapping their fingers around her neck. She wanted to run from this roof, hide somewhere where they couldn't find her, shut all of this out. Aaron was wrong about her. Willis was wrong. She couldn't be called to this; she wasn't enough.

Remember what I call you.

Somehow the tiny voice sneaked through the mounting fear, and Elise felt the shadows quake at its softness.

"The shadows cannot hurt you, Elise," Aaron said. "They are only shadows. Let go of the lies they tell you and see who you truly are."

The comforting voice came again, still soft, hardly audible, but powerful, and with it came the light, piercing through the shadows of her mind, calling forth a power that was housed within her. It boiled up into her chest and down through her arms. Faster than it had before, it seemed to flood her entirely.

"What do you know now?" Aaron asked.

Remember what I call you: Daughter. Chosen. Called.

"Who does He say you are?" Aaron asked.

A delicate wind ruffled the ends of Elise's hair, and the light in her mind flowed down through her fingers and toes. "Daughter," she said. "Chosen and called."

As the words left her mouth, the gathering energy multiplied, pressing against the inside of her skin, wanting to break free, as if at any moment the power would consume her entire being and tear her apart. A cooling rush expanded from her shoulder, and she opened her eyes to see Aaron resting his hand there. A smile spread across his face, his eyes filled with dancing fire.

"Again," Aaron said.

Daughter.

"Daughter," Elise answered.

Chosen.

"Chosen."

Called.

"Called."

Aaron nodded. "The truth will set you free. It is the reason you are here now, in this place, for this time." He spun her around so that Elise was facing the rest of the city, and she gasped.

"See the world with new eyes," Aaron said.

Colors of all varieties danced before her. Golds and blues, purples and reds. Waves of color poured over the buildings and streets as if a haze had been lifted and all that remained was the vibrating beauty of what really was. Her heart raced and her mind spun, all doubt crushed by the light. It no longer sat caged in her mind but flowed out through the ends of her fingers and swept across the sky and down into the streets.

As if she were part of the light itself. But then, wasn't she?

Daughter. Chosen and called.

She was the light of the world. She didn't need the voice to tell her; she felt it in every molecule of her body. She felt filled with power by her true identity. As if she'd been standing on the edge of a cliff, her toes dangling freely over, the rest of her so close to knowing and only needing a push; the truth of who she was yanking her free of the edge. And she felt as if she were flying.

Tears dripped off Elise's chin, and she dropped to her knees, the voice of truth speaking warmth over her. The wind wrapped around her as if it were love itself. She trembled in the midst of the One who called her daughter, the One who was the light, the One who gave His power to be her own.

All that you see before you I have given. Your inheritance is power beyond comprehension. What shall you fear, then? Who shall stand against you? Remember what I call you. See the world with new eyes. Walk in my truth, and be the light of the world.

A new sensation washed over her then, an awe-inspiring sense of love and acceptance that brought forth another round of tears. A feeling of worthiness that Elise had never experienced. As if she were perfect in that moment, flawless and unable to fail. Because He called her daughter and gave her His power, filling her with perfect love that made her the light of the world.

Elise opened her eyes and saw that the vibrating colors were gone, the wind had died down, and the fiery light bursting from within had quieted. But she didn't fear, because nothing was as it had been. She knew more now than she ever had before. It was as if all the lies in her mind had been replaced with truth, and the ground under her feet could no longer be shaken.

She took a deep breath and let it out. Even her breathing felt new. She glanced at her hands and saw power instead of weakness. She pushed herself from her knees with purpose instead of doubt. She looked at Aaron and saw the same joy she felt, saw love instead of unfairness.

The sky was now painted with the first colors of morning. Elise and Aaron said nothing for a long moment on that rooftop. They didn't need to. A bond of truth connected them now. Aaron finally broke the stillness with a soft chuckle and walked over to the roof's edge and sat. Elise followed.

"I have waited a very long time for this day," Aaron said.

Elise sat down beside the man. "And what happens now?"

He smiled. "Now you change the world."

Elise moved her eyes away from him and watched as the city below started to awake.

She could feel Aaron's eyes on her. "Are you afraid?" he asked.

She thought for a moment. "I feel like I should be."

"Why?"

Elise could still feel power vibrating over her skin and filling every pore. "Changing the world doesn't sound easy."

"Don't be afraid. This journey was laid out for you long before the beginning of time. The power you have is an incredible gift."

She glanced at her hands again, and visions of the power that had coursed through them returned to her mind. "So when I touched those guards . . ."

"You were calling for their truth, which is the same as yours. They have been numbed by the Genesis Serum and blinded to what is real, but the truth still exists within them. As it is your inheritance, so it is also theirs. The darkness can't rob people of that, only hide it. You have been called to uncover it."

"Will people resist?" Elise asked.

Aaron nodded. "Yes, some will. But that's okay. Even their blindness now is okay. Only because they are blind can they now be awakened."

Elise shook her head. "You talk in a lot of riddles."

Aaron laughed and swung his arm around Elise's shoulder, pulling her close. "I've been told that before."

15

Elise followed Aaron down from the roof and back to the old factory. Her mind still swam with colors and warmth. The sky felt different; the earth felt different; she felt different. Her body felt new, or maybe just finally awake.

Willis was waiting for them as they approached, and Elise couldn't ignore the way her heart bounced at the sight of him. How quickly this boy had maneuvered his way into her head. It seemed insane that twelve hours earlier she'd thought he was just a figment of her dreams. He was much more than that.

Willis nodded to Aaron as they shared a silent line of communication, and then Aaron turned to Elise and once again placed his hand on her shoulder. They held each other's gaze and Elise suddenly got the impression that she was headed forward without him.

"You're leaving?" Elise asked.

Aaron smiled. "I never go far."

Elise felt a twinge of panic pull at her chest. "But I can't do this alone."

"You have never been alone; the light has always been yours. Remember it."

Aaron gave her shoulder a final squeeze, shared a warm smile with Willis, and left. Elise watched him walk down the road and around the corner. The whole time her mind wanted to scream after him to return, but the truth of what she had experienced stopped her. The light was still with her; what should she fear?

"He does that," Willis said, yanking Elise back to the present. "Don't worry; you'll get used to it."

Elise took a deep breath. "I can't imagine getting used to any of this."

"You ready?"

Reality dropped into her head like a stone. There were others like her inside the building before her, others from a home she had never known, a sister she couldn't even imagine. Was she ready? She gave Willis a weak smile, nodded, and followed him inside.

It was smaller than she would have imagined a factory to be. The walls were made of all red brick, the floors of cool cement, the windowpanes clouded with time and dust. The building clearly wasn't in commission anymore, but at one point it had been used to produce flour. Old tan sacks were strewn here and there in the large main room. Dust lifted into the light of the moon that streamed in through the windows as they crossed the floor.

Willis led her down a hallway to the left of the

factory lobby and toward the door at the end. As they approached, muted voices drifted through the air. Elise felt her stomach tighten. Nerves crashed like waves through her chest, and she tried to ignore the urge to turn and run. The people who sat behind that door knew her. Or at least knew where she came from. They represented the life she'd dreamed of and was now suddenly terrified to discover.

More incredible, her sister was behind that door. A girl with blood the same as hers but a history that was completely separate. What if the natural bond that was supposed to hold family together only came with time and interaction? Did the title *sister* really mean anything at all? What if they disliked one another?

By the time she and Willis reached the door, her heart was thundering inside her throat. She thought for a moment that she might be sick as he reached down, turned the knob, and pushed open the door.

"Willis, where have you been?" a female voice said.

A second voice, this one male, started, "Yeah man, you can't just take off—"

The room fell quiet as Elise stepped through the frame and into the space.

It was a pretty large room; the only pieces of furniture were a couple of long wooden tables with benches connected on both sides. They were pushed against the left wall, leaving the center of the room clear. Sleeping mats were laid out neatly around the floor, and a fire burned within a tall metal bin in the center, giving the room an orange glow. Half a dozen mysterious faces stared at her as she entered and stood beside Willis. It was hard to read their expressions in the dark light, but their energy was clear. They were all on edge.

"Guys, this is Elise. Elise, these are the Seers," Willis said.

No one spoke. Several of them glanced at one another in shock, but one girl, standing in the center of the room behind the fiery bin, stared at Elise with such intensity that it made her skin buzz in response. She dared to lock eyes with the girl and knew this girl must be Kennedy. Her sister.

Her little sister.

The girl's face was round, framed with soft black curls much like her own. She was smaller than Elise, but her eyes, blue like a deep ocean, held such fire, such fearlessness, that Elise suddenly felt as if this girl could teach her way more about the world than she could teach in return. The fear and worry Elise had carried with her into the room shifted. It was no longer for herself. In one moment, it transferred to the stranger before her, and without even meaning to, Elise suddenly wanted nothing but good for her. Maybe the bond of family existed regardless of inter- action and was something that connected them at a deeper level.

The entire room stood frozen, no one sure what to say or do. Elise wasn't sure what she'd expected, but she felt like she'd stepped into a place she wasn't wanted and wasn't prepared for. She wasn't prepared for any of this.

Kennedy was the first to move. She slowly stepped around the bin. "How?"

"I've learned to follow my intuition, just like you," Willis said.

"And you're sure?" Kennedy asked.

As Kennedy moved closer, Elise saw the emotion collecting on her face. Her eyes were watery, her lips quivering. The urge to rush toward her trembled through Elise's feet.

Willis nodded. "Yeah, I'm sure."

Kennedy stepped close enough that only a foot separated the sisters. The rest of the room remained still as the younger girl's eyes washed over Elise's face. She bit the inside corner of her mouth and gave a small nod. "You look like him," she said, barely above a whisper.

"Who?" Elise asked.

"Dad."

The word crashed against Elise's heart like a battering ram. Kennedy wasn't just her sister, which was overwhelming enough; she also represented the truth that Elise came from someone. She had a family, a place she belonged.

Tears gathered in her eyes and she fought to keep them from pouring down her face. "Will you tell me about him?"

Kennedy smiled and reached for Elise's hand, which she cradled softly in her own. "I'll tell you everything."

/ / /

Roth's mind was still. He was surrounded by empty, dark space, his eyes open but seeing nothing. He was alive, he thought; he sensed air flowing in and out of his lungs, blood pulsing through his veins, neurons firing in his brain, but he was no longer sure what being alive meant.

His existence was foggy, his memories unclear. And then he was standing in a space that seemed to stretch eternally. The floor beneath his feet was solid but he sensed no other distinguishing factors; the sky above was black, the air to both sides of him the same. He was standing in utter darkness.

He wondered if he should be afraid. But then he felt a familiar power whoosh around him, the materialized form of the darkness itself. It was hot on his skin, violent as it raked across his figure and pushed him to his knees. Roth knew the darkness well, and he welcomed it to fill him as his brain started to piece together what had happened.

His mind had been taken. Erased by that stupid child he'd foolishly let live. She'd cursed him to an eternity of numbness, and now he was powerless to destroy her.

No, the darkness whispered, *you still have my power.*

"I'm hardly even alive without my mind!" he screamed into the void.

I can give you back your mind.

Roth tried to breathe through the harsh movements of

the darkness around him. It pushed into his flesh and past the protective coating around his mind. It slithered into every inch of his body, painfully injecting itself into his deepest crevices. "How?"

How is not important. What matters is your obedience.

"My obedience?"

Yes. I will give you back your mind, but you must give me what I need.

"What do you need?"

Your blood.

"My blood?"

It is the key. I am the key. It is time for me to spread among the people and save this city from destruction.

Roth could feel the comforting pulse of darkness under his skin, in his veins, filling them fully and circulating to all his organs. This was a power he knew he'd tapped into before, but never with such magnitude. The pain intensified as his skin seemed to expand, somehow growing without breaking. Roth cried out, feeling his frail bones rattling and his muscles tearing. The darkness was changing him, altering him from the inside, making him the perfect weapon. Its perfect tool.

It is key. The blood is key.

Abruptly the voice vanished and the darkness faded as Roth's eyes fluttered open. His eyes were dry and he blinked a couple of times to moisten them. He swallowed and it burned. His head was filled with the sound of his unsteady heart and ragged breath.

He was in a room—his room, he thought. As more came into focus, he saw the fan spinning overhead, adding a soft hum to the room. He saw the tubes running from his body to a tall machine on his left. The machine added a tiny beep to the space.

He was in bed, his body ached, and his memory was fuzzy, but one thing was clear. *The blood is the key.* His blood.

The darkness turned inside him, spurring him to move. He sat up slowly, taking deep breaths and readying himself for what must happen next. He yanked the tubes from his arms and chest, the machine beeping loudly in protest, then falling quiet completely.

Roth swung his legs out from under the covers and was hit by a wave of cool air that dried the sweat covering his body. His feet met the ground and the pressure sent painful vibrations up his legs and into his back. He noticed a pitcher of water across the room, sitting atop his dresser, and he suddenly desperately needed it. He moved toward the dresser like a stumbling baby just learning to walk and didn't bother with a glass as he brought the pitcher to his lips. Water spilled down his chin and shirt, but he paid it little mind. The water crashing down his throat made him feel alive.

His memory started to clear. Elise. The Seer boy. The dark vision. The voice speaking with such clarity. *It is time for me to spread. The blood is key.*

Roth's mind and body seemed to have been taken over

by the beast inhabiting his chest, and he moved with purpose now. Toward the cabinet that stood by his bed. To the top drawer. Yanking it open, he found nothing he needed and moved to the second. Tearing through the contents, medical supplies falling to the ground, Roth scanned the drawer for the tool he needed.

Finally his fingers found the large, thick syringes at the back, and he yanked all of them out. Hastily, without following proper protocol, Roth popped the plastic cover off the first syringe's needle and inserted it into a thick vein in his arm.

He drained himself. The dark-red substance filled the vial. Somewhere in the back of his mind, a tiny voice urged him to stop, argued that this was madness, but the beast was driving now, and as the first vial filled, Roth prepared the second. And then a third, until half a dozen thick, dark vials of blood rested in his shaky palm.

His head swam, but he knew he wasn't finished. The darkness wanted something more, and he was powerless to object. His feet moved as if thinking on their own, his legs trembling, the tiny voice certain he would collapse at any moment, but his master drove him forward.

Out of his room and into the hallway, bright with the afternoon sun. The light stung his eyes, the heat made him sweat, but he ignored it all to push forward. He knew where he was headed, could picture what was coming next. What needed to happen in order to eradicate the light from this city.

That's what this had become. A battle between the
light and the darkness. Roth caught his weary reflection
in a mirror that hung in the hallway and paused. Paler
than ever, moisture glistening on his face, lips nearly blue,
but it was the darkness that had devoured his eyes that
made him stop. He was fully captured now, and all he
saw was power. The corner of his mouth pulled up into
a cruel grin and he moved forward with more determination than before.

He saw his destination ahead. Two guards stood outside
the Council Room doors and gave Roth shocked looks as
he approached.

"Dr. Reynard," one of them started to say.

"Open the doors," Roth ordered, but it wasn't his voice.
Not completely. It was being overshadowed by something
else. A hiss he was familiar with. The darkness was talking
for him now.

"Sir, I don't think—"

Roth didn't stop moving and pushed past the guards
and through the closed doors. The room was occupied, as
he'd known it would be, and all heads turned toward him
as he entered.

Jesse and the other three Council members sat around
the large oak table, their faces frozen in horror at seeing the
dead walking around freely.

Jesse stood, his face draining. "Roth?"

Roth was no longer just Roth. He could sense the darkness spreading through the deepest parts of him. He was

being worn like a suit now, but he didn't mind. He was the host and he was being used by complete and utter power. He felt as if this had always been his destiny. The weariness and shaking that had plagued his body was gone, and all that remained was power.

"You're awake," a Council member said.

"How is this possible?" another asked.

"Roth," Jesse said, "what is going on?"

"Enough," Roth spat. The others tensed, noting the change in his voice.

"Roth," Jesse said again, stepping away from his seat.

The darkness ignored him and focused its attention on the other three Council members. "To those of you who have mistrusted me, who have rejected me . . ."

"Dr. Reynard—" one of the Council members interjected.

"Silence!" the darkness commanded, using Roth as a mouthpiece. "I have been calling to you, opening doors toward the future, and all of you have refused me. All except one." Roth looked at Jesse, a dark haze crossing his vision. More darkness was taking over. Roth tilted his head and smiled. "I see who you really are."

The other Council members glanced at Jesse, and Jesse opened his mouth and shook his head.

The darkness snapped Roth's head back straight and nearly hissed as it spoke. "You others could have had power beyond your wildest dreams. Instead you will have nothing."

"You can't come in here and threaten us!" a member said.

Roth's mouth split open in a wide cackle that echoed off the ceiling. "You have no idea how threatened you are."

"That is enough!" the councilman yelled. "Guards!"

"That isn't necessary," Jesse said and turned toward the guards. "Stay where you are."

Roth glanced over his shoulder calmly to see the two guards who had been outside now standing like stunned puppies just inside the room. They looked as if they didn't know which way to turn. Pathetic little pawns all but dead to the world. He had done that—numbed them, started their evolution—but they were meant for so much more. The next stage of transition was upon them all. *The blood is the key.*

Roth glanced at his hands and saw that he was still holding several large vials of blood. Yes, the blood. He stepped toward Jesse, and the entire room backed away. A grin played on Roth's face. They were scared of him. They should be.

"I'm done with this, President Cropper," the councilman said again. "Guards, take this man back to his room."

"Stand down!" Jesse snapped at the man.

"Enough is enough!" he said.

The guards moved hesitantly forward, but the dark creature was already several steps ahead. Turning toward the approaching guards, Roth's body moved as if he had been trained for battle, fluid and with speed he'd never before possessed. A few long strides across the Council Room, and he was at the guards' sides, their reactions far too slow for Roth's superhuman speed.

Before either guard could stop him, Roth had grabbed the weapon tucked at the side of the shorter of the two guards. He raised the weapon and sent a shot flying through the air and into the middle of the talking councilman's head.

The room fell into slow motion then, except for Roth. He was still functioning in a higher state of being. Cries of anguish filled the air as fear crawled along the faces of the other men.

The guards tried to apprehend Roth, but the darkness was too skilled and strong to be taken. He ducked as arms reached for him, then came up and landed a hard blow to the first guard's skull, hard enough to send him to the floor cold. The second guard hesitated as his partner fell, and Roth easily used the butt of the weapon he had just secured to send him to the floor like a sack of bricks.

Without a second thought, and before the rest of the room could respond, Roth raised his weapon. He sent two more shots across the room, one for each Council member who had rejected the lure of the darkness. The bullets landed with incredible accuracy, one through a heart, the other through a brain, both instantly fatal.

The room fell into a deathly silence. Roth lowered the gun and stared at Jesse. The president's face was white, his eyes wide, his lips trembling. Roth crossed the room and ignored the way Jesse flinched as he approached. Jesse knew the darkness more intimately than he was willing to admit. He must have felt this coming; he, too, was chosen for something more.

Roth held out the vials. "Change is once again upon us. You have felt it, you have tasted it, but you have not yet completely given yourself to it. It is time!"

Jesse looked at the vials and shook his head. He took a deep, audible swallow, composed his face, and met Roth's black eyes. They stared at one another for a long moment.

"What happened to you?" Jesse asked.

Roth grabbed Jesse's hand and placed the vials in his grasp. "I ascended, and you can too. Do what you were made for. This will save this city from the light."

Roth's head began to ache again. His legs wobbled, and his stomach turned. He felt as though the power that had been housed inside his gut was being drained from him like water. He stumbled backward, and Jesse caught him before he could fall.

"Roth," Jesse said.

Roth reached up and touched the younger man's face, his eyes losing their dark haze and the rest of the bright world coming into view. He heard boots stomping down the hallway, and he knew more men were coming.

"Take the blood—the blood is the key," Roth said. His

voice was returning to normal, but a tremendous ache was attacking his body. He struggled to breathe as the world faded in and out of focus, and he saw Jesse's lips moving but heard nothing.

Then the world went blank.

16 Nicolas stood beside a thick tree under the cover of heavy pines and stared at the city that stood only a couple of miles ahead. Night was starting to fall, and the army behind him, spread out through the woods, had started their evening tasks. Setting up tents, lighting fires, reporting to their commanding officers.

Nicolas kept his focus pointed toward the target. Trylin City was built into the side of a mountain with a massive stone wall enclosing it. It was protected by its surroundings, closed off from the rest of the world, nearly impenetrable with only a single visible entrance through the front gate. So gathering and securing the residents inside, as he'd been ordered to do, relied on finding a way in.

Or waiting them out. Eventually the people inside the city would need resources that would require them to step out from behind their mother's skirt. But time was of the essence, and Nicolas wasn't interested in lazily wasting days as they waited for the citizens of Trylin to move. He wanted to strike but knew they needed to be smart about it.

They'd been here watching the city for a couple of days now. Every morning Nicolas sent out groups of scouts, trying to determine weaknesses in Trylin's protective fortress. It was only a matter of time before they discovered an entry point, and then the city would be his.

Nicolas pushed himself off the tree and turned back toward camp. He walked past gatherings of CityWatch soldiers moving about in the fading daylight. All nodded their respect as he approached, but Nicolas wasted no time in acknowledging them. He headed for the largest tent, the communications and tactical meeting point, sitting nearly dead center among the rest. As Nicolas approached, one of the two guards standing watch outside pulled back the large flap to allow Nicolas to enter.

He stepped inside and found a small group of officers huddled around the main table. They turned at the sound of Nicolas advancing and their collective whispering fell silent. Nicolas paused momentarily, getting the sense that they weren't thrilled to see him, and then continued toward the table. He didn't care for discussion involving this mission to take place without him present; in fact, he forbade it completely.

One of the officers must have sensed Nicolas's displeasure with the situation, because he quickly began to speak up. "We were just about to bring this to you," the officer said, speaking faster than was necessary and nearly choking on his words.

"And what is that?" Nicolas could feel his quick temper beginning to boil under his skin. His familiar tic flared to life in his cheek.

"We received orders from the Authority City. We have been instructed to return," the officer continued.

Nicolas worked to keep the surprise off of his face. "Really?"

"Yes, the order came through just now."

"On whose authority?"

"President Cropper's."

"We are under the authority of Roth Reynard. We act on his orders alone."

"Dr. Reynard is no longer fit for leadership," one of the officers said.

Nicolas sent the man a puzzled look, and the officer glanced hesitantly at the others before continuing. "He has been given the Genesis Serum."

Nicolas felt his temper threatening to explode through his chest, but he bottled it before it erupted out of his mouth. Nothing was said for a long moment, and then Nicolas broke the tense silence. "That's impossible."

"The report is clear."

"How?"

"We were not given all the details," another officer said.

Nicolas was already done listening to them speak. "Why am I just being told this?"

"We were only informed a moment ago, sir."

Again Nicolas let tense silence fill the tent. His mind turned in angry circles as images of the old man living as a lemon with the rest of society crashed into his imagination. The Scientist would have been the first to say he was nothing without his mind. Who would have done this to him?

"The details are unclear . . ."

The officer continued speaking, but Nicolas's mind was already moving on to what their next action should be. He only partially listened as the officer reported that President Cropper had ordered all CityWatch personnel to report immediately to the Authority City. If Dr. Reynard no longer had his mind, then that meant control of the city was left solely in the hands of Jesse. A man Nicolas knew was too weak to rule. Jesse had been a pawn, easy to control and bend to the will of the Scientist. Not a leader. He'd let a girl bewitch him, for crying out loud.

Thoughts of Elise crossed Nicolas's mind and he interrupted the officer speaking. "Has there been confirmation on the execution of Elise Brant?"

The officer paused and shook his head. "No, sir."

Nicolas's rage banged against his skull like a caged animal as the enormity of the situation became clear. This didn't feel right. Had Jesse done something to Dr. Reynard to save the foul girl he loved? Roth had been Nicolas's greatest ally; he'd been the one to truly see the threat that the Seers and Elise presented. Jesse had always been blind to how toxic she was, and he'd always treated Nicolas with distrust because Jesse knew Nicolas saw his weakness. Jesse knew Nicolas was a better fit to rule and that his time was coming. But now, with the Scientist incapacitated . . .

Nicolas could feel a tremor starting in his hands and

he balled them into fists. The twitch in the side of his face pulsed, and as was his habit, he bit the inside of his cheek to maintain control. His mind rapidly calculated the situation. The Scientist was down. Elise could easily be alive. Jesse and the Council were making choices for the city. And the CityWatch army was being ordered to return. To what? To a leader who would surely sink the civilization Dr. Reynard had worked so hard to build?

No, Nicolas thought, he wouldn't let this stand. "Enough," he said.

The officer stopped talking and Nicolas could feel his confusion, but he ignored it. He continued running scenarios, tumbling through options, tearing away at possibilities, looking for a clear path. There was something in the air; change was coming, and this tragedy with the Scientist only gave more proof to that. The dark essence that had been slowly invading his chest stirred.

The Scientist's demise had not been part of Nicolas's original plan, but he might be able to use this to his advantage. The Council might follow Jesse, but only because a stronger candidate had not yet presented himself. And without the Scientist to steer Jesse correctly, the president's facade would fall and the Council would see him for the weakling he was. Nicolas could use that.

Another guard stumbled into the communications tent, his chest heaving and his face red as if he'd sprinted a mile to get here. He took a stabilizing breath and nodded in respect to both Nicolas and the officers.

"What is it?" one of the officers asked.

"We've taken prisoners, sir—a family of four, leaving the city from the north side of the mountain."

Clarity sprang to life inside Nicolas's skull. Exiting from the north meant they hadn't departed through the front gate. Another way out meant another way in. Perfect.

"Wait outside," Nicolas said to the guard, who nodded before stepping back out of the tent. Nicolas then turned his attention to the officers. "We are not leaving," he said.

"But, sir, our orders are—"

Nicolas hardly heard him; his mind was already looking forward to a new future. What would the Council think if he delivered an entire culture of formerly free-thinking people, now controlled by the Genesis Serum as the rest were? They would see then what he was capable of. Jesse would fail, as weak men do, and when he did, Nicolas would be there to push him aside. Then the real change would begin.

"We will be operating under my command from here on out," Nicolas said, cutting the officer off as he continued to babble about protocol and rules. The men looked at one another and Nicolas stepped forward, drilling them with hateful stares. "Is that going to be a problem?"

"No, of course not," an officer said for the group.

"Good. We take Trylin tomorrow. Spread the word."

The officers nodded and Nicolas stepped out of the tent and addressed the young guard waiting for him. "Take me to the prisoners."

The guard started off and Nicolas followed. He would take this city, rid the world of the Seers once and for all, and then return to the Authority City and deal with the infection there.

/ / /

Elise sat beside Kennedy on a long platform above the empty factory floor. Both of their feet hung off the edge, dangling comfortably in the empty air.

After she had been introduced to the rest of the group, Elise had followed Kennedy here so they could spend some time alone. The first couple of moments had been filled with long, awkward silences and uncomfortable pauses, but these had eventually melted into curiosity and wonder. Elise had so many questions, but for every one she posed, Kennedy had two more.

Questions about the Authority City, the Capitol Building, the Genesis Compound. Elise tried to answer them the best she could, smiling at her younger sister's childlike wonderment. Elise was vividly aware of how different she felt. Her reactions, her feelings, even her voice sounded different to her now. Subjects that once might have brought pain now felt insignificant in comparison to the power she knew was growing inside her. As if the moment on the roof with Aaron had followed her, the room around her buzzed with the energy of something greater. It made her wonder if this presence had always been with her, but even as she asked the question, she knew the answer was yes. It made her smile to herself.

"Sorry," Kennedy said. "I'm probably asking too many questions."

Elise turned her attention back to her sister and shook her head. "No, you aren't. It's perfect, in fact. I like listening to your voice."

Kennedy turned her eyes away from Elise, light-pink circles forming across her cheeks. Elise worried for a moment that she might have embarrassed her and reached for her hand. "I'm sorry."

Kennedy shook her head and smiled. She looked straight ahead, but Elise could still see the emotion sparkling in her eyes. "I'm not really a crier," Kennedy said. "Not that you'd know it from the way I've been acting today." She turned back to Elise. "I've probably thought about you every day of my entire life. Who were you? What were you doing? Were you safe? Would I ever meet you?" A tear slipped past her bottom eyelid. "It just seems unreal that you're actually sitting beside me right now."

Elise paused and thought through her words carefully. "I'm not sure I ever dreamed of family. I was convinced my family didn't want me, so it was easier not to want them."

Sadness filled Kennedy's eyes. "We always wanted you. I can't believe they told you we didn't want you." Her expression changed to anger quickly. "That monster."

"Which one?" Elise teased, but Kennedy's face was hot with rage.

"They called him the archer, but you call him president," Kennedy said. "He's the reason for all of this."

"Jesse?" Elise was taken aback by the vitriol in Kennedy's voice. "He's the only one who's ever been kind to me."

"Kind to you? He stole you from us!"

Elise gave her sister a horrified look. For the first time since realizing her family hadn't abandoned her, a single question pulsed inside her brain: How had she gotten here? She couldn't believe her mind hadn't wandered there already. If her parents hadn't abandoned her, then why was she here while they were somewhere else? Was it possible Kennedy was speaking the truth? "Stole?"

Kennedy nodded, her nose scrunched up in fury, her eyes drilling angry holes into the ground below their feet.

"He manipulated our people, gained their trust, and then, under cover of darkness, because he's a coward, he had you stolen away, right from our mother's side."

"But why?"

"He'd better hope I never get close enough to him to ask him that."

Elise's mind ran in circles. Her only friend and perceived ally had been her captor? But he had always shown such affection for her. He'd gone out of his way to make sure she was taken care of. On the other hand, he had abandoned her first to death by execution and then to the Scientist's torture. And he had kept her locked away from the world and lied to her about her past. Had he been manipulating her into believing he cared for her all along? She suddenly felt violated. She'd trusted him, and he'd played with that trust.

The voice of the Father whispered in her pain.

Remember who I call you.

Elise could feel anger and vengeance filling her chest. They should have to pay for what they'd done to her.

You are the light of the world. What shall you fear?

"Elise?" Kennedy asked, her tone softer now.

Elise looked at her sister and searched for the power she'd felt so strongly on the roof. The power that had made her feel worthwhile, like she was more than an object terrible men had played with. "Sorry," she said. "There's just still so much I don't know."

Know who I am, and therefore know who you are. Daughter of the Father.

Elise took a deep breath and exhaled. Time to practice remembering. Time to let it go. She could feel the anger gripping her heart tightly. This was easier said than done.

"I'm sorry, Elise; I shouldn't have put so much on you all at once."

"No," Elise said, squeezing Kennedy's hand. "Don't be. I'm more than what they made me believe I was. I just have to remember."

Kennedy chuckled. "You get that from Aaron."

Elise smiled and shook her head. "It's still so strange to hear you talking about him."

"Why?"

"I always thought that he was only mine, an invention of my own making."

"Yeah, he makes you feel that way, and he kind of is, in a way. He is something to everyone, but in such a personal fashion that it feels exclusive."

"Where did he come from?"

Kennedy laughed out loud at this. "If you can get Aaron to tell you where he came from, I'll eat that entire cardboard box down there," Kennedy said, pointing to an old, dirty box on the factory floor.

Elise scrunched her nose in disgust. "Gross."

And the two girls laughed together, softly at first, but it quickly spread into something more powerful, until their laughter was echoing off the walls and making the steel ledge they were sitting on vibrate.

"Kennedy," a male voice called, "we need you."

Elise glanced down to see a scrawny boy standing below. Davis, she thought his name was.

"We're kind of in the middle of something," Kennedy said.

"We heard from Trylin," Davis said.

The concern in his voice made Kennedy tense, and Elise knew something must be wrong. Both girls stood and headed back down the thin stairs and toward the room where the Seers were camped.

Panicked voices drifted down the hall as the two girls rounded the corner into the room.

"How can this be happening now?"

"We have to go back!"

"What's going on?" Kennedy asked.

Elise stepped inside behind her sister and tucked herself into the corner of the room. She caught Willis's eye and saw the fear moving through his face. All of them looked afraid, and her heart quickened.

"I was finally able to conduct a radio transmission with Trylin," Davis said. "The city is under siege."

"Under siege? Who? How?" Kennedy asked.

"Apparently the Authority feels the city is a threat. There's an army parked outside the front gate," Timmons said.

Elise watched the color drain from her sister's face.

"Nothing from them for twenty years, and now they've sent an army after us?" Lucy said.

"Do they know how many?" Willis asked.

"They estimate nearly four hundred," Davis answered.

"Too many," Timmons said.

"Don't forget how secure Trylin is. The army is parked outside for a reason," Sage said.

"Yeah, until they find another way inside," Kane spoke up from his spot against the far wall.

Sage shot him a piercing glare.

"Do you honestly think the Authority would send that many soldiers if they didn't plan on taking the city? They'll find a way in," Kane said.

"He's right," Willis admitted. "There's no way Trylin can stand."

"We have to go back," Sage said.

"We can't go back; we were called here," Lucy said.

"Our families are there! What are we supposed to do? Just let the Authority army kill them?" Sage demanded.

"We can't just stay here," Davis said.

"Where's Aaron?" Sage asked.

"Not here, naturally," Kane said.

"Enough, Kane! We need to stay calm," Lucy said.

Kennedy moved then, toward the mat where she had been sleeping, and started packing her bag.

"What are you doing?" Timmons asked.

"What does it look like she's doing?" Davis moved to do the same with his own things. "We need to go help them."

Elise stood still, nearly becoming part of the wall, her mind racing. They wanted to leave the city, to return to where they came from, and she didn't blame them. But the power she'd experienced on the roof, the force she was carrying around under her skin, flared in rejection. She couldn't leave. She was exactly where she was supposed to be.

"Everyone needs to relax so that we can think this through clearly," Willis said, trying to assert some control as Sage moved to start packing her things as well. Elise watched as the group continued to argue, but their voices fell silent to the energy swirling inside her mind. She felt the pull of a familiar fear and anxiety, but she was different now, and she didn't let it overtake her.

Then another voice joined the madness: a voice only she could hear, the only voice that mattered.

Remember what I call you. Daughter.

You are the light of the world.

There was more movement from the group, and it looked as though they were all now preparing to leave. A pocket of sorrow opened up in Elise's gut. She had just met these people, and now they were going. She would be alone. Again.

Chosen and called, beautiful light of the world.

She knew she couldn't leave with them. She watched her sweet sister scoop a few final things off the ground and shove them inside her bag. Saw the panic and worry lining her beautiful face. Elise hadn't even known this girl existed twelve hours ago, and now the thought of being separated from her was almost enough to shake her resolve.

Stand with me and you cannot be shaken.

Elise felt eyes on her and she glanced up to see Willis looking right at her. His face was filled with questions, but once their eyes connected, she watched his eyes change to understanding. He seemed to know what was happening inside her head. She felt the light glowing inside her chest, never far from the surface, and she wanted to assure him that what he'd done for her was not for nothing. He'd broken her out of her prison so that the light could set her free.

They held each other's gaze for a long moment before

Elise noticed that the room had gone still. Everyone was looking at her now, some of them already packed, others, like Lucy, still standing beside their belongings. But all of their eyes were on her.

Kennedy stepped forward hesitantly, her face twisted in concern. "You'll come with us," she said, her voice full of confidence but her eyes unsure.

"Of course she will," Sage said. "I mean, you have to."

A devastating sense of regret toppled over Elise's head, and she didn't want to tell them the truth. But even as the pain of reality hit her, the wind and light from which she drew her strength engulfed her with peace. She breathed it in, and it steadied her pounding heart. And without having to say a word, she could see they all knew she wasn't going.

Anger flashed across Kennedy's face and Willis dropped his gaze.

"You have to come," Kennedy said.

"I can't," Elise answered, her voice as steady as the light pulsing inside her.

"Why?" Kennedy asked.

"Because I am supposed to be here."

The air in the room grew heavy and Kennedy started shaking her head. "No—you were never supposed to be here. You were supposed to be with us. With our family!"

"Kennedy, please—"

"I came here for you! I promised Mom I would bring you home. How can you choose this city over us? Over me?"

Elise opened her mouth to respond but was cut off by new movement to her right.

"Nobody move," a voice said.

A man stepped into the room, arms forward, gun pointed, and the whole room froze.

Elise recognized him immediately: Sam. And he wasn't alone. Another CityWatch guard entered behind him, his gun also raised, his face unfamiliar to her.

"Hands up, all of you," Sam said. The group did as they were told, slowly dropping whatever they were holding and raising their arms. Sam turned to Elise, no fear behind his eyes, no reaction to her at all. He had forgotten their first encounter—or rather had been made to forget. He was blind again.

A twinge of fear twisted in her stomach, but then she remembered who she was and that everything that happened was supposed to happen. This moment was not by chance. She was the light of the world; who could stand against her?

The thought unveiled something new within her. She saw Sam as she herself had once been. He was wandering, lost to his own truth. Had she not been lost herself? The light had come to her; could the light not also come to him?

Call forth his light, Elise.

"Elise Brant, you're under arrest by the authority of President Cropper," Sam said.

Call it forth.

"I'm going to need you to come with me," Sam said.

Elise took a deep breath and felt the charge in her bones. She closed her eyes, letting herself be overcome with the light burning inside her, and with a single push, released it.

17

Willis finally understood why Elise was so important. Before, he'd simply believed because he trusted in his own call, but now, watching her from across the room, he understood. The guard was only inches from her, and Willis had been a single second away from moving to protect her. But before he could process anything further, the room began to shift. The same way it had shifted in the Capitol Building. As if someone had reached down and wrapped the space in plastic, enclosing them and blocking out anything other than the energy radiating from Elise.

A force rushed through the room, its power physically rocking Willis where he stood, and he watched as the guard in front of her began to buckle at the waist. He fell to his knees and gripped his head in agony.

Willis heard gasps from the other Seers and tried to keep himself standing against the strong power pulsing from Elise. It filled his blood and penetrated deep into his bones. It called forth a fire under his skin that cleansed all the fear and doubt that had been swimming around inside his head with the news from Trylin. He could feel heat coming from Lucy, who stood only a foot to his left. He looked that way and saw her face pulled in shock, her eyes wide as she watched Elise.

Willis scanned to the other Seers in the room. All of them were visibly affected by the change in the room's atmosphere.

Light was shimmering from Elise now, filling the space around her in an outline of gold.

Then Kennedy fell to her knees, the second guard only inches from her. She reached out to grab hold of him and he buckled at her touch as if her hand were on fire. He cried out and dropped to the ground. Kennedy clenched her eyes tight and it looked as though the light, now swirling through the air, was digging its way into her chest.

Even as the thought crossed his mind, an explosion ransacked his own chest. It was as if someone had plunged a hand into his middle, bypassing his heart, to the place where his soul hid, yanking forth power he'd only imagined. His knees hit the floor, then his palms.

He tried to breathe through the awakening of power in his body, through the shock of the transformation racking his mind. Suddenly the ground beneath his hands was cool, and he opened his eyes to see golden grass sprouting between his fingers. The burning sensation was gone, as was the room around him.

In its place was a field. Strands of wheat danced as far as the eye could see; large, beautiful trees stretched into the air, a crystal-blue cloudless sky overhead. It was still and quiet. He knew this place. Had heard others speak of it. The Father's field. Many transformational stories had taken place here, because every inch of land was covered in perfect love, which made it more powerful than magic.

Willis pushed himself up off his knees as his heart eased into a peaceful rhythm that matched the swaying of the grass. The wind swirled across the top of the tall wheat strands, pulling at them softly, twisting them about, and bending them playfully. Willis felt mesmerized and couldn't tear his eyes from the way the wind moved. It circled toward him, and as it approached, Willis found himself nervous over the encounter.

What if he wasn't prepared for how strong the wind was? What if it knocked him over, or what if it passed right by him? He couldn't understand why he was so concerned with the wind, but he felt his heart fall out of its steady rhythm as it drew closer.

"How much time we all spend trapped in resistance," a familiar voice said from behind him. Willis didn't turn his gaze from the swirling wind; he wanted to keep his eyes on it. He didn't want to miss his chance to touch it if it came by.

He felt Aaron approach, the man's shoes whispering over the ground.

"I just don't want to miss it," Willis said.

"And what makes you think you'll miss it?" Aaron asked.

"It could pass by me without stopping."

"And would you feel complete if it did stop?"

Willis thought about this for a moment before answering.

"Yes," he said. "I think touching the wind is what I've been missing."

"I see. Well, what if I told you that you couldn't be completed, because you already are?"

Willis turned his head toward Aaron then. "I'm not, though—not like Elise."

"But you are. In fact, you and Elise are exactly the same. The wind will not pass you; that's impossible, because it is already in you."

"But I've seen the power she has."

"Believe you can move the mountain and you will. Believe no man can stand against you and they will not. The same power that lies within her also lies within you. It resides within all those who belong to the light. Stop resisting your true identity. Step into the truth of who you are."

"What if I can't?"

"Of course you can. That's what you were created to do."

Willis turned his attention back toward the field and searched for the wind. It was nowhere to be found. He felt a strong sense of panic and skimmed his eyes violently across the top of the wheat.

Nothing. Just as he'd feared, the wind had passed him by.

Aaron placed his hand on Willis's shoulder, and the touch reignited the fire Willis had felt under his skin while standing in the room with Elise. "Look within you for what you seek," Aaron said.

Willis closed his eyes and searched his heart for the

truth. Beneath the darkness he carried, past the regret, past his insecurities, under the cover of pain, something pulsed. He reached for it, meditated on it, and called it forth. With a burst of movement, light rushed up through his chest and filled his entire being. It streamed out through the pores in his skin and down into the ground at his feet. Willis opened his eyes and saw that the entire field seemed to be glowing with the light beating from under his skin.

Wind, strong and steady, whipped through the field around him, encircling him completely. It danced across his skin and ruffled the ends of his hair. Beside him, Aaron clapped his hands together in triumph. Willis felt his own excitement bubbling inside, and he started to laugh aloud toward the sky. How wonderful it was to be filled with light.

"Yes," Aaron said with a final clap. "Now we can begin."

The clap resounded in Willis's eardrums as the field faded away and was replaced with the factory. He was still on his knees, his eyes facing the concrete floor, the room quiet. He lifted his chin and saw that the others were kneeling around the room as well. Elise was standing in the same corner, while both CityWatch guards looked around as if they didn't know where they were. Willis pushed himself to his feet and locked eyes with Elise. She smiled warmly, and his heart jumped. Her skin still seemed to be glowing slightly, and the fire behind her eyes was intoxicating. He smiled back and managed to pull his eyes away from her.

He stepped over to help Lucy to her feet as the others all worked to stand on their own. They'd each had their own experience with the light, he could see. Sage's eyes brimmed with tears. Timmons's as well. Kennedy's face was flushed; Davis's chest rose and fell quickly. Kane was the last one to stand, his hands shaking, his eyes still glued to the floor.

Whatever had happened to each of them, Willis was certain of one thing: None of them would ever be the same.

/ / /

Elise watched as the light slowly faded from the room, and her mind became clear. The memories of the two CityWatch guards receded, leaving her with her own thoughts again.

Three things had been different this time. First, she hadn't needed to touch Sam as she had before to initiate the recalling of his memories. She didn't know if this was because she had already had contact with him or if she was just starting to understand the power inside her more fully.

Second, Kennedy had affected the second guard, not Elise. Though she'd gotten a glimpse into the soldier's past, he hadn't reacted to the light until Kennedy had touched him.

Finally, the memories hadn't ended with either guard withering in pain as before; in fact, they were now looking at her as if they were completely different people. Their eyes scanned the room for some sort of clarification as to what had just happened to them. She had no idea what this meant, but something in her spirit felt more at ease this time.

It was hard not to feel as if she still had no idea what she was doing here. Why had she been given this power? Why had she been called? But she knew that to judge herself would mean to resist her true identity, and to resist would mean to separate herself from the light.

Elise was suddenly aware that she was believing in truths she'd never learned before. She wasn't sure how, but it felt as if bits of life-changing knowledge were launching themselves at her and sticking to her heart, embedding themselves deep, as if she'd known them all along and was just starting to remember.

Sam stood, his eyes on Elise. He opened his mouth to speak, but emotions choked his words. Her heart melted with his as tears filled his eyes and spilled over his bottom lids.

"I remember," he said. "I remember everything." He took a sharp breath and sniffed back tears. Shaking his head, he ran his fingers through his hair. The second guard had backed against the closest wall and was rocking side to side, lost in his own thoughts. Both of them aware and entirely sane. The light had rid them of the Genesis Serum's effects completely. It was a cure. The light that she carried was a cure.

Lost in her own thoughts, Elise hadn't noticed that

Kennedy and the others were all staring at her until Kennedy reached out and touched her arm. Elise looked up and met the group's eyes, each of their expressions encased in awe and wonder. She smiled and placed her hand on top of Kennedy's.

"You were right," Kennedy said, her voice barely above a whisper. "You're supposed to be here, and I will follow you."

Elise's heart leaped.

"So will I," Lucy said, and Elise looked at the woman as they shared a knowing smile.

Sage was nodding in agreement beside Lucy, tears still sliding down her cheeks.

Davis gave Elise a solid, strong nod, and Timmons chimed in with the same.

Elise caught Willis's eyes, and for a long moment, they just held one another's gaze. He smiled and heat rushed up her face. "There's no way you're getting rid of me," Willis said.

Elise bit the inside of her lip to keep her mouth from splitting into a grin and noticed Kane watching her from the back of the group. She looked at him and waited as he stared back. There was a darkness that played across his face, one filled with fear, and she knew that unlike the others, he wasn't convinced yet.

She nodded to him that it was all right, and he dropped his eyes away. He would follow because everyone else was, but there might come a time when he questioned their path. Elise wasn't worried, though; the light came to them all in its own perfect timing.

"Now what?" Kennedy asked.

/ / /

Carrington shot up in bed, breathing heavily in the cold night air. She let her eyes adjust for a moment before removing herself from bed, careful not to wake Remko. She pulled on a thick gray sweater and headed for the balcony. She clicked the door closed softly behind her and took a deep breath of the chilly air.

The day had been filled with emotion. Wire had finally connected with Davis, and they'd reported that everyone was safe. But the moment of overwhelming joy had come when they'd learned that Elise was with them. Safe and alive.

Remko had held Carrington for a long time as she'd cried into his shoulder. Their baby girl was alive, had been all this time, and she was finally rescued. But somewhere during those long moments, Carrington's utter joy had begun to turn to fear. The emotion had become second nature for Carrington, so she hadn't been surprised when all the happiness had converted itself to anxious worry.

Now she was having nightmares. Night terrors where she never saw either of her daughters again because the Authority City disposed of them both. Where she spent the rest of her days in agony, knowing that she never should have let Kennedy go. Where she woke up with the same gnawing feeling that all of this was her fault.

She'd started all of this. Twenty years ago, when she followed the call of her soul and left the Authority City, she'd started this chain reaction. Now she couldn't escape the fear that if she'd only been content to do as she was told, then maybe so many wouldn't have been lost.

Light flickered in the distance, beyond the front gates, where she knew the Authority army was crouching in wait. How long could the residents of Trylin really wait out the impending threat? Or how long before the army found another way to gain access to the city? They wouldn't survive an attack from an army as large as the one standing at their doorstep. Carrington knew the plan was to not resist. To practice what they had been taught and even try to see their enemies as their brothers. To hold nothing against them.

But what if they found a way to break down the gate and came in with guns blazing? Were the Seers supposed to just roll over and die? Would they all be casualties of Carrington's original choice to go against the grain? Would she get all of these people killed? The door creaked open behind her, and she glanced over her shoulder to see Remko walking out onto the balcony. He'd pulled on his own heavy sweater and grabbed a wool blanket from the closet. He offered her a loving smile, his dark eyes capturing the light even out here in the darkness. Her choice might have brought them here, but it had also given him to her.

He sat on the wooden bench along their home's brick wall, and she moved to join him. She nuzzled down next to him as he draped the wool blanket around them and pulled her close. They sat quietly for a while, watching the stars fade into the early-morning haze. She matched her breathing with the steady beat of his heart and tried to release the tension gathered in her shoulders.

"I'm sorry if I woke you," Carrington said.

"I wasn't really asleep. It doesn't seem to be something that comes to me as easily as it once did."

"They say that happens when you start to get old."

"Is that what we are doing?" Remko asked. "Getting old?"

"I'm afraid so."

Remko shook his head and rubbed the outside of Carrington's arm. "No—I prefer to think of us as beautifully aging."

Carrington shot him a playful grin. "Whatever delusion you need to deal with those graying hairs."

His eyes grew wide. "My hair is not graying," he said, instinctively moving his hand to the tips of his curls. "Is it?"

Carrington bit the inside of her lip to keep from laughing and gave a small nod. "I didn't want to tell you and add any more stress, but in the right light . . ."

His face became almost boyish, as if he'd just discovered his imaginary friend wasn't actually real, and Carrington couldn't hold back her amusement.

"I'm glad you're having a good laugh at my expense," Remko teased, pretending to be very offended.

Swept up in the moment, Carrington leaned forward and kissed the man she loved through her giggles. His lips were warm and welcoming against her own. His strong arm dropped around her waist and pulled her closer. And for a moment, the rest of their problems faded. She forgot to feel shame and anger with their situation, and she let herself get lost in him.

Their love had formed against all odds, and with the threat of each new danger, it had grown instead of diminishing. They could have let their pain and anguish snuff out the flame that burned between them; it would have been easier to let it die. But Remko had always pursued her, and Carrington had always run back to the thrill of his embrace. Sometimes it felt like all the world did was take from them, but it was in these small moments that she remembered it also gave her a greater love than she'd ever thought possible.

She pulled back from her husband and laid her head on his shoulder. He squeezed her close, and they chatted as they watched the sun begin to peek up over the horizon. About the past, about the future, about their fears and worries. Carrington felt her heart sink whenever he mentioned Elise or Kennedy, and she tried to keep it off her face. But he knew her better than she knew herself.

"We'll see them both again," Remko said.

Carrington swallowed against her pain. "You always say that with such confidence, as if you actually know."

"I'm just practicing faith—" he started.

"Please, Remko," Carrington said, pushing herself off his shoulder, and he let the rest of his sentence die silently. Carrington could feel all her concern and panic filling the space between them. Their perfect, lovely moment gone, and their harsh reality present.

"Carrington . . ."

"I can't hear about faith. I'm so tired of having to suffer to find my faith. I just want my girls to be here and safe. I just want this war to be over. I'm so tired of it all!" She knew her voice was stronger than necessary, but she couldn't seem to keep it controlled. She rubbed her fingers across the front of her forehead and sighed. Shaking her head in frustration, she stood from the bench when Remko tried to run his hand down her back for comfort.

She didn't want to be comforted, or convinced, or led to the truth. She wanted to be mad. She wanted to be justified in her pain and loss. She wanted the world to recognize that she deserved to be miserable and angry after everything it had put her through.

"I know," Remko said, "but you won't find any peace unless you let it go."

"Maybe I don't want to find peace," Carrington said. "Maybe I am content to mourn the loss of my daughters."

"We have not lost them."

"But they are not here. They're in that city, where they are constantly at risk." Carrington pointed toward the woods, where hundreds of CityWatch lay sleeping. "And what about us, Remko? How can you possibly believe we will survive what is ahead of us? There is a monster storming the gates, and you want us to just sit and wait. Are you not afraid?"

Remko opened his mouth to answer but was cut off by a loud pounding on the bedroom door. He turned to look and stood. Carrington took several short breaths and tried to collect herself as Remko walked back into their bedroom and toward the door to open it. She moved to stand in the balcony's entrance and saw Wire's face.

Wire looked from Remko to Carrington with panic in his eyes. "They're in the city."

18

Nicolas had gathered a small group of CityWatch soldiers just before sunrise. A couple dozen whom he trusted, their guide a pathetic Seer who had folded like paper the moment Nicolas had started to threaten his family. He'd led them around to the north side of the mountain, where a break in the rock, hardly large enough for an average-size man to squeeze through, had been cut out of the cliff face. Nicolas would have assumed it was merely a shallow dent, but once inside, the Seer made a left turn and led them through a much larger opening. The mountain had deceptive angles. It really was a magnificent fortress.

They maneuvered through the rock tunnel quickly, making good time and moving like a well-trained force. Nicolas could feel his new sense of power rumbling under his skin. Once inside, they would open the front gate for the rest of his troops to enter and seize the city without any problems. They'd all been instructed to hold their fire. Death was not their objective; Nicolas would honor the Scientist in that way. Besides, he knew the Council was soft, so bringing back the lost mountain city people changed for the good rather than murdered in cold blood would only increase his appeal in their eyes. Something about competing for the Council's approval left a sickening taste on his tongue and made the tic in his cheek activate, but he pushed past them both. This was the way it had to be until total control was his. Then things would change.

By the time they reached the opening that led into the back end of the city, the top of the sun was piercing the horizon, filling the sky with light-pink hues. Nicolas ordered their helpful Seer bound and placed in the care of a guard as Nicolas took the lead. He kept the group moving swiftly through a back alley and behind a row of two-story brick buildings. The city was quiet, slumber still holding it in its clutches.

Nicolas turned toward the soldiers, who had already separated into three groups. He sent two squads in opposite directions with instructions to scout out any hidden surprises. Nicolas had heard enough about the Seer leader, Remko, to know that he could be dangerous. Once a CityWatch guard himself, he was clearly familiar with tactical training, so they were to keep their eyes peeled for signs of an ambush.

Nicolas took the third group with him as they headed for the main gate. They scoured rooftops and dark corners as they moved. Their weapons stayed raised and ready, but the city remained eerily still. Nicolas had expected to run into trouble sooner and was almost uneasy about the lack of resistance they were encountering. He knew the Seers' reputation; he'd heard about the days before the Genesis Serum had cleansed the Authority City. Nicolas had been tensed for a fight, but as he and the handful of others moved toward the front gate, it seemed as though they were moving through an abandoned ghost town. Still, he stayed focused, turning his emotions down to a dull hum. But he couldn't ignore an irritating pulse at the back of his mind. Something was not as it seemed.

Nicolas continued to lead the guards forward with confidence until he spotted their destination ahead. The sun was now lighting the empty streets, and he held up his hand to still the moving soldiers behind him. The tall stone wall that enclosed the city had a single wrought-iron gate with thick cylindrical bars crossing both vertically and horizontally in tight formations. There was a power center on the left side that was used to control the gate—an easy enough target, and their path was clear.

It can't be this easy. Nicolas glanced both right and left, searched the rooftops nearest him, and motioned for the guards behind him to carefully scout the surrounding block for any threats. Remko and his people had to be somewhere; they couldn't have simply disappeared. Were they truly letting their enemy storm the streets while they cowered inside the surrounding buildings? Surely they knew it would only be a matter of time before Nicolas found them all, rounded them up?

They had been sent with enough Genesis Serum to dose the city's population twice over. Nicolas hadn't known what to expect, but this was something he hadn't anticipated at all. Several soldiers signaled that all was clear, and Nicolas slowly moved out from the alleyway in which he'd been standing and made his way toward the main gate. The guards remained in their positions around him, watching for attackers, and Nicolas made it to the gate before a guard to his right motioned that he saw something coming.

And so it would begin. Nicolas turned around, his weapon armed and ready, the guards around him moving into a tight unit as a single man approached. He was silhouetted by the rising sun, and Nicolas was taken aback when the man's face finally came into view.

He looked so much like Elise that Nicolas had no doubt this man was the famous Remko Brant. He approached at a steady pace, his arms hanging comfortably at his sides, no clear sign of a weapon. He was walking alone. The sight was odd to Nicolas. Either this man was completely mad to approach a dozen armed men by himself, or he was incredibly brave. More likely, this was just the beginning of some defensive plan, so Nicolas told himself to be mindful of everything that happened in the next few moments.

Remko advanced until he was standing only yards from Nicolas and stopped. Nicolas waited, his focus on Remko. He shifted his gaze from the right to the left of the man ever so slightly, searching for unexpected company, but never took Remko out of his sight. What was he waiting for?

Nicolas kept his weapon poised and took several steps forward. Remko didn't move, so Nicolas took another step, motioning for the guards behind him to stay put. "What game are you playing?" Nicolas asked, his voice echoing through the empty streets.

"There are no games here. I've simply come to welcome you to Trylin," Remko said.

Nicolas paused. "To welcome us?"

"Yes. We have a saying here that we live by. Let all who come, come."

"Seems like a dangerous way to live."

"It's the only way to truly find freedom."

Nicolas studied Remko's face. The man seemed to be genuine in his welcome. Nicolas again searched for a weapon and saw none. Was the man truly unarmed? His mind calculated the situation. This moment was too important for the city of Trylin to simply give in. Surely they knew the Authority army had been camped in the woods for days. Probably they had known the soldiers were coming before they arrived. So what was the citizens' plan?

"You've come unarmed," Nicolas said. "Why?"

"I've seen enough bloodshed in my lifetime. I only want to try and avoid more," Remko answered.

Nicolas was surprised by Remko's nonresistant behavior. He'd expected to meet a great warrior, one who had out-smarted the Authority on numerous occasions, but the man who stood before him seemed to have long ago suppressed his fighting nature. Nicolas wasn't sure whether that would make this easier or more difficult.

Nicolas lowered his gun slowly, keeping it cocked and ready to be fired. "And the rest of your people, the ones watching from inside these buildings—are they sick of bloodshed as well?"

"I can assure you, no one here wants war with you."

"You must be aware that we easily outnumber your fighters? When I signal to open that front gate, your city will be overwhelmed with CityWatch soldiers. So tell me, what will your move be then?"

Remko shook his head. "We have no moves; you are welcome in our city."

The twitch in Nicolas's cheek flared into rhythm. Something more had to be happening. He couldn't imagine these people were just going to lie down and be taken after years of fighting for their freedom. He took another couple steps toward Remko until the men were standing only about a yard apart. "Forgive me for not fully believing your statement of surrender. You wouldn't be willing to tell what you are actually planning, would you?" Nicolas asked.

"I have told you," Remko responded. "Our plan is simple, and that is to practice what we believe."

Tic, tic, the vein in Nicolas's cheek pulsed. "So you just give up your freedom?"

Remko smiled. "No, we secure it."

Tic, tic. Nicolas ground his back teeth together. He could feel rage starting to boil under the surface. His years of practicing containing his emotions were beginning to fail him.

Remko kept his face clear as Nicolas stared into his eyes, searching for indicators, but all he saw was steadiness. This man was filled with something he believed gave him power, and the darkness that crawled under Nicolas's skin wanted to kill that belief.

Nicolas took another step toward Remko, his mind churning with a new motivation. He wanted to destroy this man's confidence. He wanted to break his steady facade; he wanted to own him. A tiny voice at the back of Nicolas's mind told him to stay true to task and not get swept up in his emotional reaction to this man, but Nicolas was struggling to listen. "You actually believe surrender will bring you freedom, when your surrender to me will ensure the exact opposite. Yet still I can see your belief is very strong."

"I believe in a freedom that goes beyond this world, and yes, my belief in that is everything."

"Power is everything. Power can break belief."

"I would argue that there is no stronger power than belief."

Nicolas could feel the dark tentacles of his soul curling around his heart, pumping it for him. "We will see," he said. The Scientist had been right about these people. Their belief was dangerous, but Nicolas wasn't worried. Crushing their belief had just become his new destiny.

"Open the gate!" Nicolas cried over his shoulder, and

the mechanical beast roared to life behind him. Within moments, the entryway was filled with black-clad soldiers, all armed with weapons.

"Search every corner of this city. Gather them all; no one stays behind," Nicolas shouted, and the black mass descended on Trylin. He looked back at Remko's face, the man's eyes still sure and true. *Yes,* he thought, *it will all begin with this man.*

/ / /

Elise studied the faces that stared at her from around the fire. The room was quiet, the others lost in their own thoughts. None of them had really been able to sleep after their experience last night, so they'd stayed together, attempting to make sense of what this meant for them all and trying to decide where they were supposed to go next. They all looked to Elise for answers, but the truth was, she hardly knew what was happening either.

She'd spent the last several hours battling the cycle of remembering and forgetting, each time the remembering becoming less difficult and the forgetting less permanent. Sam and the other guard, Franklin, had stayed with them as well, Franklin hardly saying a word, his fingers still shaking even hours later, and Sam spending much of the night catching up on all he'd missed with his nephew, Davis.

After a while, Willis had retired, Kennedy had fallen asleep sitting beside Elise, and everyone else in the room had retreated to their own minds. The room was still now as the first signs of morning peeked through the windows. Elise was starting to feel a deep fatigue working its way into her bones and thought maybe it was finally time to sleep.

She had almost willed herself to stand up and walk to a sleeping mat when Willis stepped into the room, his eyes wide, his breathing heavy.

Davis, sitting to Elise's right, took Willis's state to mean trouble and stood quickly. "What's wrong?"

Willis shook his head with a tiny smile pulling at the side of his mouth. "Nothing. Nothing's wrong."

Davis let out a disgruntled sigh and sat. "Got me up out of my chair for nothing, man."

"Sorry," Willis said and locked eyes with Elise. She gave him a curious look, but the excitement playing on his face made it hard for her not to smile back.

Kennedy stirred to her left and brushed her hair out of her face. "What'd I miss?" Her voice was gravelly from sleep.

"Nothing—just Willis rushing in here, in a state of panic I assumed, but no, he's just really excited about making flirty eyes with your sister," Davis said.

"Yeah, that about sums it up," Timmons added.

"Sorry," Willis said again. "I had a dream."

"He does that," Lucy said, her words directed toward Elise.

Elise smiled, unable to rip her eyes away from Willis. "I know."

"Is this awkward for anyone else in the room?" Kane asked.

If Willis heard them, he wasn't showing it. "I think I know what we have to do next."

That grabbed the room's attention, and all the playful teasing fell away.

"What do you mean?" Lucy asked.

He moved to the empty spot beside the fire and sat. "I saw a handful of places. Some with small amounts of people, others with larger numbers. We were going to each of them and starting revivals in pockets throughout the city. Each place different, always the same result: awakening." He paused to gauge the group's reaction, but when no one said anything, he continued. "Each place I saw was specific. The first was a newly constructed building, actually still in the works. There were half a dozen men there. I have a strong sense about this place."

"You want us to truck to some random building based on a dream *sense*?" Kane asked.

"I know how it sounds, but I can't shake this feeling," Willis insisted.

"And what are we supposed to do at this place?" Kane asked.

"Practice," Willis said. "Figure out how this works and the roles we each play."

"Great, yeah, that makes perfect sense," Kane said.

"Maybe it was just a dream," Kennedy suggested.

"It wasn't. I can't explain how I know, but after my

experience with the light . . ." He trailed off, his eyes getting lost in the memory for a moment before he refocused on the group. "It wasn't."

"Let's go, then," Elise said.

The rest turned to her, curious expressions on their faces. She pointed to Willis. "He dreams—that's his gift. It makes sense that the light would communicate with him that way, and haven't you all been trained to trust your instincts? What are they saying to you now? Because mine are telling me to trust Willis."

She held his eyes with her own and nodded. A smile broke across his face, bright enough to light the room, and she felt her head spin.

The rest of the group took a moment to process, and Davis was the first one to speak. "Do you even know where this place is?"

"I do," Sam said. "There aren't many new buildings in the Authority City, and only one that is currently under construction. If the building you saw was an active job site, I can take you to it."

"It means crossing the city, though," Franklin said. The group was startled by his participation because he'd barely said a word since the incident last night. He was young, in his late teens, Elise guessed, with red hair buzzed close, hazel eyes filled with questions, and a strong chin. He caught Elise's stare from his place across the room. "I have nothing to go back for. I was born into this world the way it is now. I didn't know there was anything to miss until last night. I didn't even know the light existed, and now . . ." He got choked on his own words and shook his head. "I'm just saying, I'm with you now. I don't want this to be taken away from me."

He glanced at Sam, and Sam gave him a knowing nod before turning back to Elise. "We can get you there. We know all the active patrolling routes, and as long as we keep Elise covered, the other CityWatch guards won't think anything of us traveling with the rest of you. Nobody knows your faces."

"Someone should stay here and try to reconnect with Trylin," Davis said. He held up a small, handheld device that looked like a walkie-talkie. "I know I can get this contraption to work; I just need some time alone with her."

"Her?" Kennedy said.

"My dad calls it Roxy, so yeah, *her*."

"We don't have any weapons to protect ourselves," Kane said, and Timmons nodded in agreement.

"We don't need weapons," Lucy reminded them. "We are here to save these people, not hurt them."

"Anyway, we do have a weapon," Kennedy said. She turned her eyes to Elise. "If anyone tries to harm us, we'll just have Elise make their brains explode."

"That's not what—" Elise started.

Kennedy placed her hand on her sister's arm and chuckled. "Relax; I was kidding. Kind of. You do have a great power, though, and you brought out a power in me, in all of us. Maybe Willis's dream is right, or maybe he's out of his mind. Either way, where you go, I go. We were brought back together for a reason; we do this together." She looked back at the others, her hand still resting on Elise's arm. "All of us. Let's go try and figure out how this works."

Timmons was the first to stand. "Well then, what are we waiting for?"

19

Nicolas watched as the people of Trylin stood gathered together in the main city street. It hadn't taken long to pull them all into one place, partly because there were not very many of them but mostly because they had all come so willingly. It was as if they'd decided as a group that they weren't going to fight back. A few had stepped out of line, and Nicolas had ordered the soldiers to forcefully put them back in their place, but most had been easy. Too easy. As if they were eager to accept their destruction.

All of them seemed to be following the same radical belief that filled Remko. It gnawed at Nicolas's mind. It was fascinating to see an entire flock of sheep walk off a cliff, but the darkness in him despised their complacency. Their belief was no doubt sincere, but how far would it carry them? How far until a human's true nature took over and the peace was shown to be just another mask?

"You don't have to do this," Remko said. "We can show you another way."

"Your way? The path in which giving in to your enemies is the answer?" Nicolas asked.

"Turning the other cheek so that no man controls freedom."

"Yet here I am." Nicolas glanced across the gathering of Trylin people. "Controlling your freedom."

"Greater is the light within me than the darkness that is in the world," Remko said. His words washed over Nicolas like hot water, burning at his skin and causing him to pause. *Tic, tic.*

Nicolas took a deep, steadying breath. "Let's see if that is true." He grabbed Remko's arm and escorted him toward the crowds. The people had been placed in large groups, watched carefully by the CityWatch soldiers that surrounded them. Nicolas could see their fear as he moved Remko through the horde and into the open space that had been created for the next phase. Nearly three dozen armored vans, each large enough to transport at least thirty full-grown men, had been driven inside the city gates and parked across the front of the open space, serving as the perfect backdrop.

Nicolas tugged Remko out into the middle and led him toward the armored vans. The Seers watched the two with apprehension. Nicolas handed Remko off to two very large guards. He moved into the center of the open area. "Bring her out," he ordered, and from behind the large group to his right, two more guards emerged, dragging a beautiful blonde from the crowd.

Gasps and whispers ran through the gathered people. Some began to cry, while anger flashed across some of their faces.

Carrington looked up at Nicolas, and just as before with Remko, he was taken aback by how much of Elise he saw in her. The shape of her face, her beautifully perfect skin. But more than that, it was something similar behind her eyes. Elise got her spirit from her mother's side of the family.

She glanced over her shoulder at Remko, and Nicolas followed her stare. He could see the muscles in Remko's neck tightening, but he stood perfectly still, his eyes on his wife's, his expression filled with love. *Tic, tic.* Nicolas shook off the sudden urge to shoot Remko between the eyes and remembered his purpose here. The bigger goal. Secure their obedience, return them as a gift to the Council, and take the throne. That was all that mattered. But first, he wanted to resolve a bit of the tension growing in his muscles. He wanted to see how deep their faith really ran.

/ / /

Carrington was brought to where the leader of this detachment stood. He was young, she thought, younger than she would have expected. He smiled at her as she approached and he almost looked normal, but she knew how deceptive a smile could be, and it was clear from the reflection in his eyes that he meant her harm. Fear coiled in her gut.

"Carrington," the young man said, "what a pleasure to finally meet you. My name is Nicolas."

She said nothing in return and glanced again at Remko.

Her husband's eyes were filled with strength, but she recognized his concern as well.

"I've heard a lot about you," Nicolas said. "The girl who ran away and started a war. You really have made quite a name for yourself."

Still she said nothing. What was she supposed to say? All she could see was the fear she knew so well clouding her vision. All she could think about was that fear filling her mind.

"Quiet, I see. Elise is like you in that way."

As if he'd stabbed her with a knife, pain exploded in her gut. She tried not to tremble, but it was nearly impossible, and she sensed her emotion welling up in tears that she fought to hold at bay. A hundred questions came with her agony. He knew Elise? Had this monster done something to her? Too many questions to calculate, and all of them shaking her resolve.

She looked again at Remko, and his face was starting to break. They were supposed to be standing in surrender, practicing what they preached; they were supposed to be the pillars for the others watching. If they broke, everyone would follow. But how were they supposed to hold steady in the face of this?

"I can see how hard this is for you," Nicolas said, "living with the knowledge that you let your daughter be taken. How much guilt you must feel."

The tears she had been holding fell, and it seemed as though all the air had been sucked out of the sky. He had found her open wound and he was rubbing his finger in it. She could feel Remko's eyes on her, urging her to look to him for strength, but she couldn't. She was breaking.

"How do you live through the pain of what you've done?" Nicolas asked, pressing deeper.

Carrington wanted to scream at him to stop. She wanted to yell that she didn't live through it, that she wasn't, that she hadn't. That every day she struggled to see the light. That she was tired of struggling.

"Let all who are weary come, and they will find rest," someone said nearby. She glanced over to see Aaron standing several feet away, his eyes filled with warmth. She wanted to scream for him to run, but she noticed that no one else was looking at him. It was just her. He was here for her alone.

He took a step toward her. "You don't have to struggle anymore; you don't have to search for the light. Let go of this shame you hold and embrace what you already know." As Aaron's words manifested to only her ears, the scene around her changed. The city remained, but beyond it she saw the field. The golden strands dancing in the breeze.

She wanted to run for it, lose herself there, forget this world. Surely there she could let go of her pain and be free.

"But you can do that here and now," Aaron said. "Freedom is always within your grasp. You just have to remember."

A heavy wind washed over the gathering, moving through the people, yanking at their clothes, wrapping its fingers around Carrington's body. Again no one seemed to notice its presence but her. It, too, had come for her alone. She let herself be taken by it; she let it douse her in perfect love.

She knew everything Aaron said was true. She knew she could be free, but she had been holding on to her shame for so long that it felt like a part of her. Giving it up meant accepting that she wasn't to blame. It meant forgiving herself, and she wasn't sure if she could ever do that.

Remember what I call you, beautiful daughter.

The voice of the wind rumbled inside her, and another wave of tears stung behind her eyes.

Remember who you are.

Your identity lies in me alone, and I see you as blameless.

Beautiful, perfect daughter.

"Let it go," Aaron said.

The wind whipped around her violently, and she felt the weight she'd been carrying for so long begin to lift. *Surrender,* she thought; *surrender.* And as the word formed into actuality in her mind, the shame began to dissolve. *Surrender.*

She heard the soft, warm laughter from Aaron's throat and she gazed at him to see his head back, face pointed toward the sky, wind playing through his hair. "It's always in the remembering that we find freedom," he said.

Carrington felt pure light pulse inside her, and she closed her eyes to fall more deeply into it. The power rushed through her veins and laced itself around her bones.

Remember who you are.

You are the light of the world.

She opened her eyes to see Nicolas staring at her, waiting for her to respond, as if no time had passed at all. The field in the distance was gone, Aaron nowhere to be seen, and the wind back to normal.

"I can save you from your pain," Nicolas said. "I can set you free." He reached out and slowly brushed his finger along the outside of Carrington's chin.

A moment ago she would have recoiled from his touch, would have felt nothing but fear, but now all she felt was the perfect light still pulsing under her skin. She smiled in spite of herself and glanced to see Remko on the edge of breaking. He met her eyes and she held them strongly.

"I'm already free," she said.

Remko's eyes lightened a bit, and his jaw relaxed.

She was free, she thought. She had always been, but she'd let her shame take her captive and bury her under its darkness. No more. She was the light of the world; she'd only needed to remember.

/ / /

Tic, tic. Nicolas cursed his inability to stay steady as the words rolled off Carrington's tongue. Something had happened to her suddenly. One moment ago he had seen her resolve crumbling, had nearly expected her to fall to the ground at his knees from the weight of her guilt, and then something had switched. Like a light being flicked on inside her chest, her eyes had changed. It infuriated him, and what little control he had left was wasting away.

"Free?" he said. "I have you. I have all of you. You are far from free."

Carrington moved her eyes to him, her expression calm and light. "You have my body, but the freedom I have you cannot take."

Tic, tic. Nicolas's jaw ached from the way he clenched it tightly. They were all mad, tricked into believing nonsense, and it was starting to become incredibly irritating.

"Let's see about that." Nicolas motioned in the air with his hand, and a guard walked toward him carrying a long silver box. He handed the box to Nicolas, and the crowd's energy started to change. Nicolas opened the box and pulled out a syringe filled with yellow liquid. Carrington glanced at the syringe and recognition filled her face. She looked over Nicolas's shoulder toward Remko, and Nicolas glanced back to see Remko's stance becoming restless.

Nicolas masked his joy at seeing them both uncomfortable and turned away from Carrington. He started to pace in front of her, facing the crowd. "For those of you who don't know this syringe, it is the beginning of your new life, your Genesis. One without problems or solutions. Just simple, peace-filled living, within the mighty walls of the Authority City."

He paused and nodded toward Carrington. "Let me

show you how it works." Carrington watched him as he started her way.

"Carrington," Remko said.

His voice made Nicolas pause. He couldn't deny he would love to see the ever-valiant savior of these people break. In fact, he longed for it.

"It's okay, my love," Carrington said, her voice full of hope and strength, "You know who I am. Do not fear for me, because I finally remember myself."

The tic pinched Nicolas's cheek and the dark energy inside him squirmed.

"Stand firm in your belief. And forgive me for not standing firm in mine," Carrington continued. "I forgot my true nature. I was lost to grief, but I am not lost anymore."

Remko's face was filled with worry, but Carrington's was ignited with something that made the hate in Nicolas almost tremble. He'd had enough. He stepped toward her, but she kept her eyes glued to Remko's.

"No resistance," she said.

"No resistance," Remko repeated.

"Enough," Nicolas said. *Tic, tic.*

"Stay the course, my love; remember who you are," Carrington continued, her voice gaining volume. Nicolas could see all the others standing around taking heart from her words. She was reigniting their faith.

A tremor raked down Nicolas's back. The evil presence in him roared its disapproval with each word that fell from her lips. "I said enough."

"Take heart. See beyond what is in front of you. Hear the call; remember who picked you, crafted you, held you through all things," Carrington said.

Rage, hot and heavy, crawled under Nicolas's skin. She believed she was invincible; she was wrong. She believed she was powerful; she was wrong. The monster that Nicolas kept caged railed against its prison bars. "I said be quiet."

Tic, tic.

"He calls you His own," she said. "We are the light of the world. If we stand with Him, then who can stand against us?"

The beast burst from its cell with fury. "Silence!" Nicholas cried and sent the back of his hand hard across Carrington's face. The sound echoed through the sky as her neck twisted sideways with the force of his strike.

The world froze for a beat, shock and astonishment filling the faces of the crowd, a single cry escaping Remko's lips as he yanked at those restraining him, Nicolas's gleeful monster lustful and engaged.

Carrington turned her face back toward Nicolas, the right side of her face pulsing red, her bottom lip split, a line of blood running down her chin. She held Nicolas's eyes for only a moment before turning back to Remko. "No resistance," she said. Her words more powerful than before.

Remko's shoulders shook as tears escaped his eyes.

"No resistance," Carrington said again.

Nicolas couldn't contain his rage any further. They were making a mockery of him. "I said enough!" Again he sent his hand down forcefully across Carrington's face, and this time the blow knocked her to her knees. She cried in pain, and Remko followed suit. He fell to his knees as well, his face twisted in agony, but he remained unbroken in his resolve.

They were all mad, Nicolas thought. Even on the ground Carrington looked to her husband to offer support. To encourage him to remain steadfast. "Remember who I am. Remember who you are," she said.

Her words gnawed at Nicolas's insides like tiny insects, digging into his brain and pulling out an even deeper level of anger. He was floored with rage, consumed by the monster dictating his actions. They thought they had power? He would show them what true power looked like.

Nicolas kicked Carrington once, very hard. She gasped in pain, all the air in her lungs exploding out and leaving her breathless. People wailed in horror and their cries echoed through the sky. Nicolas's monster trembled with glee at the sounds of fear around him and urged him on to inflict more terror.

"Stop!" a man cried from the front of the crowd as he stepped past the guard closest to him, hands raised, and moved into the clearing. "Please stop."

Nicolas turned his eyes toward the newcomer, an older man who was mistaking stupidity for bravery.

"Get back in line, old man," a guard shouted, but the man paid him no mind.

"Please—we have done all you asked," the man said.

"I said get back!" the guard yelled, but he kept his gun pointed toward his assigned group for fear that turning his weapon to the old man would spur more outbreaks.

"Dalen," a woman pleaded from the spot in line where the man had been. Her eyes were filled with tears as if the worst had already happened.

Wife, Nicolas thought. That made it better. He felt the twitch behind his cheek and it ached with fury. He had unleashed the beast and now it couldn't be contained.

"Please," the man said again, but Nicolas had heard enough. In one quick movement, he pulled his weapon from his side, aimed it at the old man, took one short breath, and pulled the trigger. The bullet sailed through the air flawlessly and landed dead center in the man's forehead.

For a moment the echo of the gunshot off the mountain wall was the only sound, and then a thunderous cry replaced it as the woman who'd been calling for the older man screamed in anguish. She tried to rush forward, but those around her held her back as her vocal cords broke the sky.

A sliver of pleasure blossomed in Nicolas's chest accompanied by more delicious evil filling him with power. He watched for a short moment as blood from the fallen man's head trickled across the dirt; then he turned back to Carrington, whose cheeks were dampened with tears.

He knelt beside her, wrapped one hand around the back of her neck, and yanked her head toward him. She moaned in pain, and Nicolas's power lust escalated.

"You did this," Nicolas said, as he forcefully turned Carrington's head to face the dead old man only a few yards away.

More tears escaped her eyes and her broken bottom lip quivered.

The city remained still as Nicolas lifted the syringe and injected its contents into Carrington's arm. He heard Remko let out a muffled cry as the Genesis Serum made its way into her bloodstream.

Remko remained on his knees, tears wetting his cheeks, his eyes glued to his fallen wife, his face filled with pain. Cries dotted the air as the city of Trylin accepted the death of one of their own. Nicolas watched as a milky cloud covered Carrington's vision and snuffed out the light that had been shining there before. The rest would have the same fate, and then they would know that his power had defeated their light.

Tic, tic.

20

Sam and Franklin led the group through the city, just as they had promised. It took them a couple of hours, moving slowly so as not to gain any unwanted attention, using alleyways and less-traveled streets.

The mostly constructed building loomed a block ahead. A single vehicle was parked in front. Stacks of newly cut lumber, workbenches piled with tools, buckets of paint, and large rolls of plastic were scattered around the grounds. Tall scaffolding crawled up the left side of the structure, and uninstalled glass windowpanes leaned against its base.

It was quiet, but there was some movement inside. Elise could feel the energy the second they crossed the boundary onto the property. They were meant to be here. It gave her a sense of peace for whatever was coming next.

There was still some hesitation among the group. Why were they here? What were they doing? Why now? She could see the questions, like ants crawling under the surface of their brave faces. They were all here out of faith, following the belief that this was about something bigger than them, which was both terrifying and exhilarating.

"This place is pretty cut off from the rest of the city," Timmons said.

"Yeah, they're trying to expand out this way," Sam said. "So other than the construction workers, we shouldn't run into anyone else."

"We'll leave lookouts at each entry point just to be safe," Willis said. They all agreed, and Willis motioned for Sam to take the lead.

The group took to the left side of the property and moved carefully toward the back entrance. The outside of the building was nearly finished, doors present in all the frames. Sam tested the first door they came to, but it was locked. He moved to the second set, a pair of double doors, and they opened easily. They moved inside one at a time.

The only light came from a couple of construction lights illuminating the large room they entered. The floor was concrete. Drywall had been hung, covering the framing, but not yet completely finished. The room smelled like glue and freshly cut wood.

Sam paused and turned to Kane and Timmons. "Monitor the back side of the building; make sure to alert us of any trouble." They nodded, and he turned back to the rest of the group. "Franklin and I will guard the front. Willis will take you from here."

Sam and Franklin headed off toward the front of the building, while Kennedy, Lucy, Sage, and Elise followed Willis toward the staircase at the far left side.

The stairs weren't completely finished either. Pale

wooden steps led upward, and the Seers were careful not to make too much noise as they climbed. Ten steps up and they were dumped into another large room with finished hardwood floors and warm beige walls. The windows here were filled with glass panes, and the trim was laid out on one side of the room, drying. The smell of fresh paint permeated the air.

Muffled voices drifted toward the group as the final member ascended the last step. The voices came from the doorway to their right and had several distinct tones. There was more than one person through the open frame, and Elise was willing to bet it was a group of men, standing around discussing floor plans, just as Willis had foreseen in his dream.

The rest of the group froze, all of them looking to Elise for their next move. The first two times she had connected with her power, it had been beyond her control, and the last time, it had happened out of necessity, to keep them all safe. She still wasn't completely sure how she was supposed to use what was contained inside her, but she'd trusted Willis's instincts to come here, and she had felt the calling of truth when they'd arrived. Suddenly a wave of doubt washed over her, and she felt a strong rush of fear.

What if she'd been wrong? What if she couldn't control it and this had all been a mistake? Nervous tension filled her chest, and she could hear her heart slamming against her ribs. She felt panicked. What was she doing here?

Remember who I call you.

Elise closed her eyes and focused on the voice floating through her mind. *Remember,* she thought. *Remember the power, remember the call, remember the light.* As quickly as the panic had emerged, it was doused with peace and silenced. This was who she was, who they all were. There was no need for fear.

As if led by the truth itself, Elise walked with confidence past the rest of the group and into the next room.

Six men stood around a large wooden cube, tall enough to act as a table but really just an oversize crate flipped on its head. On top of the crate sat long white papers with blue drawings etched across their faces. The men were deep in conversation, but one looked up as Elise stepped inside.

"Hey, you can't be in here," he said, drawing the attention of the others. They all turned, looking confused. Elise felt the presence of the Seers as they filed into the space after her.

"Lady, are you nuts? This place is dangerous," one said, taking a step toward them.

Elise blocked out all the doubt and fear trying to wage war on her resolve and surrendered to the buzz rumbling in her gut. The floor began to vibrate slightly, and the men all stared in disbelief. Elise felt the small tingling ignite into a fire as it spread through her body and across the floor. Before any of the men could move, it had reached them, climbing up their legs and into their chests.

The scene around Elise changed as images of the past came to life across her vision. So many memories collided like a mesh of indistinguishable colors. She tried to focus and control each image and the emotional charge it brought, but it was all too overwhelming. She started to lose her sense of self, and then the light flickered and went out and the room returned to normal. The men shook their heads, looking confused and frazzled.

Elise didn't understand. She searched for the light and found it again, calling it forth. It charged through her like lightning and once again set the room ablaze. She reconnected with the men, their memories exploding across her mind. Again the power proved too intense, but just as she thought she was about to lose it, an anchor attached itself to her mind and expanded the light. *Kennedy.* Elise could feel her sister's spirit melding with her own.

More visions splashed through the scene. The men fell to their knees as the power exploding from Elise and Kennedy washed them free of the Genesis Serum. Another anchor of power erupted beside them, making the light extend to every corner of the room. *Lucy.*

Reenergized, Elise pushed herself even further with both Kennedy and Lucy responding in kind. They tore away the mask of delusion that Genesis had caused and brought forth a truth strong enough to change the world. The room spun as the men cried out, their minds being transformed and renewed.

A soft hand reached out and touched Elise's shoulder, causing the entire room to still as if paused. She opened her eyes and saw that Sage was standing beside her, concern written on her face.

"Trouble's coming; we have to go," Sage said.

Elise looked to Kennedy and Lucy, then back to Sage. *Trust her; follow her.* The voice of her conscience was clear, and so she did. Elise spun around, Kennedy right behind her, Lucy at the rear, Sage leading the way. Willis was still standing at the top of the stairs, keeping watch, awe written on his face, his mouth parted in a smile.

"Wow," he mouthed, shaking his head. Elise smiled and continued to follow Sage down the stairs, the others on her tail. They nearly collided with Sam and Franklin, who looked surprised to see them.

"We need to go," Sam said.

"We know," Kennedy said, stepping past him and heading back the way they had come. Kane and Timmons were exactly where they had left them and didn't ask any questions as they all fled the building. They hurried back along the left outside wall, quickly taking cover behind the closest building and maneuvering away from the construction site, not stopping until Sage finally pulled up nearly a half mile away.

They all took a beat to rest, panting and huffing from their steady pace, sweat collecting on their faces. No one spoke for several minutes as they all worked to catch their breath.

"What happened?" Timmons asked.

Elise looked at Sage. "How did you know trouble was coming?"

The rest of the group looked at the small girl, her face flushed and red. She swallowed and shrugged. "I saw it."

"Saw it?" Kane asked skeptically.

She nodded and gave a small smile as if struck by the oddity of it herself. "I saw the soldiers coming, like a waking dream, I guess."

Elise smiled. Sometimes the quietest ones made the biggest impact.

Timmons nudged Sage playfully. "Should have told us you have superpowers."

She shook her head. "I didn't know."

"That was insane," Kennedy said, a huge smile plastered across her face.

"I don't know what you guys did," Timmons said, "but I could feel it through the floor."

Elise locked eyes with Kane for a moment and saw the doubt etched into his face. While the rest of the group lit up with excitement and wonder over what had happened— what could still happen—he looked as though he believed less than before.

"I've never experienced anything like that," Lucy said.

"That was a heck of a practice round," Sam said.

Elise suddenly felt light-headed and wobbled sideways. Willis stepped up to catch her before she fell and she smiled, embarrassed. Her chest ached a bit, and her head felt bloated.

"Whoa, you okay?" Willis asked.

"Sorry," she said. "Just dizzy."

"That really takes a lot out of you," Kennedy said. "I feel exhausted myself, and I only helped."

"You did more than help. I couldn't have done that without you." Elise looked to Lucy. "Both of you."

"We all played a part," Lucy said.

"We can really do this," Sage said. "Group by group, we'll go wherever Willis dreams about and cure people from this disease. This is why we're here."

Everyone was nodding. "Oh, man," Kennedy said. "Davis is going to be so mad he missed out."

They laughed as they headed toward home base. They could do this, Elise thought. They were created to.

21

Jesse stared out the window of his office, down over the city. The sun was fading, the day coming to a close. He was waiting for reports on Elise's whereabouts, lost in thought and constantly searching for answers. A dark essence pulsed inside his chest, and he swallowed hard against it. It had been growing, as if taking on a life of its own. Ever since Roth had handed him those vials.

Now they sat inside the top drawer of the tall chest against the wall behind him. Hidden from sight but not from his mind. He could feel whatever was in those vials calling to him from nearly anywhere in the Capitol Building, but being in the same room with them was almost too much to take.

His mind drifted to Roth. The man was back in his bedroom, nearly dead to the world and under constant surveillance. After his maddening outburst, he'd been pumped full of enough sedatives that he wouldn't rouse again. Jesse wasn't sure what to do with him yet. He had seen the devil in the old man, a darkness that exceeded his own and was fully in control. If he let Roth wake, Jesse wasn't sure it was Roth he would be getting. Jesse visited him every hour or so to make sure he stayed unconscious. So far he'd been able to conceal the deaths of the other Council members. He was thankful that the Genesis Serum was happily pumping through everyone's veins. They didn't question much. They were designed not to.

There was a knock at the door, and two guards let themselves in. Jesse turned to face them, hoping for good news. Their expressions spoke for them and Jesse slammed his fist down on the top of his wooden desk. The guards standing before him jumped as he cursed at their news. "How can she elude you again? She is only one girl!"

"She was gone by the time we got there, sir. We are searching everywhere, and we have started regular patrolling units through the underground tunnels as you requested," the guard said, "but with four hundred of our men out—"

"Yes," Jesse cut him off. "They are on their way back as we speak. Still, one would imagine that even the guards remaining in this city could easily contain a single girl."

"She isn't acting alone."

"But there can't be more than a handful of them. A city of our strength . . . They are making fools of us!"

"We will continue—"

"Enough!" Jesse said. "I'm tired of your excuses. Get out."

The guards looked at one another, and neither moved. "There is something else, sir," one of them said.

Jesse closed his eyes and rubbed his temples with his fingers. "What?"

"Another group was found on the east side of the city."

"Another? How is that possible?"

"A larger group than before, their minds warped, and they were speaking insanities just like the others. They were transported to the Genesis Compound for re-administration."

"How many groups are there now?" Jesse asked.

"This was the seventh incident, sir."

The room fell quiet as Jesse thought and the guards waited for further instructions. "We have to figure out how she is moving through the streets without being detected and if there is a pattern to her movements. She must be caught but remain unharmed."

"Yes, sir," the guard said.

Jesse nodded for them to leave, and they exited, closing the office door. He stood in the silence and tried to sort through the frustration thundering through his mind. Elise had been missing for five days, and in that time, a thread of chaos had started to unravel the Capitol Building.

The voices in Jesse's head were starting to rage against one another. Some called for her blood due to all the havoc she was causing; others were convinced that if he could just get her back, he could help her see the pain she was causing the city. He liked to believe she harbored feelings for him, that she thought of him even now while she was away. She couldn't be completely lost.

The opposing voice of darkness hissed inside his mind. He was being delusional. She was a permanent threat to the entire functionality of what made this city's peace sustainable. The Genesis Serum. She was immune to its effects, so where could she possibly belong?

But as always, the deep feelings he housed for Elise crept in. He loved her. Could he bear to live without her? There had hardly been any constants in his life. His father had been a terrible drunk, his grandfather had been taken from him too soon, Damien Gold was a lost cause, and his relationship with the Scientist had always come with strings attached.

Elise cared for him. She had to. Maybe she was the only one who ever could. And he was supposed to give her up? *No.* Anger flared hot under his skin. He was ruler of this city. Roth was indisposed; the rest of the Council was dead. It was only him, and after all he'd sacrificed for the betterment of his people, he would have the thing he wanted most. She was his, and they would not take her away from him.

She isn't yours, you fool.
She will ruin you.

The darkness grew with each passing hour. Large, like an expanding balloon, threatening at times to push out his other emotions so it was all that remained. He tried to fight against it but still found it oddly comforting. It had always been there, hissing, questioning, directing. It sang of Elise's demise, and when Jesse wouldn't sing along it cut away at his innards. It tortured him, and he was weakening with every blow.

Jesse collected himself and pushed his anger deep within his chest. Again the pull from the nearby vials called to him and he gritted his back teeth. He should destroy them, but he had tried, and each time he had stopped himself. So he would keep them locked away. They might torture him, but he would not succumb to the darkness as Roth had. He would be his own master, and he would have her.

/ / /

The vehicle bounced Remko up and down as it bumped across the rocky terrain toward the Authority City. He faced forward in the front passenger seat of the car, one CityWatch guard driving, another armed guard sitting behind him in the backseat. Remko's wrists were bound together in his lap with plastic wire, which left raw, thin cuts with too much movement. It had been several days since they'd left Trylin behind, nothing remaining there except abandoned buildings and lost hope.

Remko was riding in a different vehicle than the other Seers. After they had all been injected with the Genesis Serum, they had been loaded thirty at a time into the large armored vans that followed behind the smaller car Remko was now riding in. He'd watched as all the people he loved were stripped of their pasts. Wire, Kate, Ramses, each injected with a toxin equipped to steal their memories. Their convictions. Their souls.

Images of soldiers lifting Dalen's body from the ground

and carrying him off toward a side street haunted him. They'd tossed him out of sight as if he were garbage, his wife's cries still shaking the sky. Remko had insisted on complete surrender, the physical act of turning the other cheek, and in doing so he had gotten his friend killed. He couldn't fight off the blame clawing at his insides.

He'd suspected that Nicolas would have him injected last—another act of unrivaled cruelty, forcing Remko to witness the metaphorical death of everyone around him before being sentenced to the same fate. But still the serum had not been administered to him. Nicolas was more sinister than Remko had wagered. Instead Remko had been loaded into a separate car, all his memories still intact. Now he suffered through the pain of the past as they headed toward the city where he would lose his future.

His head throbbed and his ribs burned—from what, he wasn't sure. It was probably the manifestation of his own inner pain. Images of Carrington played on repeat. Her brave stance, the peace that had shown in her face even while Nicolas threatened to break it. Her final plea for her husband to remember who he was. The last moment before her eyes went milky and he'd lost her to Genesis.

He tried not to succumb to his misery. Not to give in to the hate that told him lies about his identity. He remembered a time not so long ago when the only emotion he'd lived with was self-hatred. A time when he'd gone days without showing himself mercy. Back before the truth had worked its way into his heart.

There were still moments of threatening darkness, doubt so dense it felt as though he wouldn't be able to see through it. But he wasn't the same troubled boy he'd once been. That he was sure of. And as the hours had stretched to days, Remko started to hear the familiar voice of love calling to his soul. Reminding him of his identity and singing a song that was his alone.

The car he was traveling in came to a stop, jerking Remko forward and out of his thoughts. The two guards in the car with him opened their doors and got out without giving him a glance. He sat, expecting someone to come around and get him, but instead he watched through the windshield as the two men walked over to the other vehicles where soldiers were unloading themselves. They stretched, grabbed water, lit up cigarettes. Remko kept his eyes peeled for Nicolas, bracing his heart and mind for another onslaught of brutality.

The backseat door popped open, and Remko looked up, expecting to see a black-clad soldier climbing in. He met Aaron's face in the rearview mirror instead. Shock and relief washed over him as Aaron gave him a comforting smile. Remko whipped around, his hands still bound together in his lap and rubbing together painfully.

"What are you doing here?" Remko asked.

"It's nice to see you too, friend," Aaron teased.

"You need to get out of here before any of them see you."

"Why? Am I in some sort of trouble?" Aaron's expression was too casual for the situation, and Remko felt himself becoming annoyed.

"Their commander—" Remko started.

"Nicolas, yes. I've heard of him. Very lost, isn't he?" Aaron said, a familiar empathy lacing his tone.

Remko didn't respond. Had he forgotten who he was dealing with? This ageless guide, cased in the appearance of an ordinary man, had stopped bullets in front of Remko's eyes. What was he so worried about? He turned around to look out the windshield and chuckled to himself.

"Something funny?" Aaron asked.

"I momentarily forgot who you were," Remko replied.

"Like you've momentarily forgotten who you are?"

Remko closed his eyes and inhaled deeply. He should have known that would be Aaron's response. He nodded to himself and heard Aaron chuckle as well. A deep, kind sound that felt renewing. "Yes, that is an unfortunate condition of the ego," Aaron said. "But no worries. All moments of trouble are love's way of leading you to truth."

"Do you ever wish love would get tired of you and leave you alone?" Remko asked sarcastically.

Aaron laughed out loud, his voice rumbling the inside of the car, and Remko felt a grin pull at the side of his mouth. Through his laughter Aaron spoke, leaning forward to squeeze Remko's shoulder. "Even now, in times of great trouble, so much joy can be found. Isn't life a beautiful thing?"

Remko smiled fully and shook his head. "I suppose you'll be leaving soon?"

"I never really leave you, brother. Think of all we have seen together, all we have experienced. Remember the lessons we have learned." Aaron held Remko's gaze through the mirror, and Remko felt his heart lift in his chest.

"Don't forget who you are in times of darkness. You are the light of the world, a son of the Father; who can stand against you?"

"But Carrington—"

"Have you forgotten who she is? Is she not the same as you, cloaked in power, filled with light? The rest is just a facade. Truth always prevails, my friend. Fear not."

Remko sighed and processed Aaron's words.

Aaron shrugged. "Or fear if you must; that too is an option. The choice to suffer is always yours."

Yes, Remko thought. Even in this time of darkness, he could choose the light.

His head jerked forward and he opened his eyes to see that the car was still traveling through the wilderness, both CityWatch guards at their usual stations, the rest of the caravan moving ahead slowly. He squeezed his eyes shut tightly and reopened them, shaking his head. He must have fallen asleep. Images of Aaron's smile and the echo of his words drifted through his mind. He grinned to himself. He should have known.

A few moments later, the car did pull up to a stop. The two guards exited the vehicle and joined the others, but this time Remko's door opened, revealing Nicolas's face.

Remko's first reaction was to let his fear and anger rear up in response, but Aaron's words played like music in the back of his mind.

Nicolas looked Remko up and down, his face twisted in mocking concern. "You don't look so good."

Remko again recognized the fiery rage threatening to rise through his belly and instead picked the peace that snuffed it out. The stillness of truth filled his body. It was clearly not the reaction Nicolas had hoped for, because the angry twitch that moved through his face flared to life. He yanked Remko from the car and out into the blaring sun. The movement tore open pain in Remko's stiff body, and nausea rolled inside his gut.

Remko's clear discomfort gave Nicolas pleasure. "Not so good at all." He held Remko close so that Remko could smell his vile breath. Once again, Remko was faced with a choice: suffering or light; hate or perfect love. A soft breeze wafted past his shoulders and Remko instantly thought of the greater power that called him His son. And he chose light.

"Maybe I should have a medic check you over. It would be a shame to have you die before we arrived in the Authority City," Nicolas said.

Remko hardly heard him, so great was the joy of love bubbling up inside. He started to chuckle soft and steady, causing Nicolas to pause. His face twisted, first with curiosity, then with rage as Remko's glee continued. The air swirling around Remko's body grew in speed and set his skin ablaze with the truth of who he was. It danced in a beautiful rhythm and filled him with perfect power. His laughter became bold and shook his shoulders as Nicolas looked on with frustration and the soldiers ahead started to stare.

"What could you possibly have to laugh about?" Nicolas spat.

"Death," Remko said. He took a deep breath through his laughing spell, controlled himself, and looked Nicolas straight in the eyes. "Death is an illusion."

Nicolas looked taken aback. Shock washed across his face, and before he could respond, a tremendous wind rocked around them. It swooped down over the forest, pulling at the branches, lapping at the grass, and shaking the ground. He heard shouts from the men as the wind disturbed their balance, taking many to their knees. Nicolas stumbled back and searched for control against its power. But Remko remained firm in his stance.

He closed his eyes and turned his face skyward, basking in the renewal of his mind that the truth brought. It soaked through his pores and refueled his weary belief. His face wet with tears of hope, his mind reenergized with thoughts of truth, Remko let the wind sweep away his fear and remind him of his power. The wind died away softly, but when he opened his eyes, he saw the forest differently. Clearly.

Everyone was shaken, some men pulling themselves back to a standing position, others hesitantly releasing the trees they had grabbed for support. All of their faces wide with wonder. Nicolas had moved several steps back from Remko, his face suspended in surprise, his chest heaving violently. He and Remko locked eyes for a moment, and Remko saw something he hadn't before: fear.

Nicolas smoothed his ruffled hair with a shaky hand, regaining his composure. He tore his eyes away from Remko and started toward his truck. "Load him back in the car," he yelled to a couple of guards who stayed frozen. "Now!"

Nicolas disappeared from sight, never stopping to glance back.

/ / /

"What is the point of all this?" Kane muttered, pacing back and forth across the room.

Davis ignored him and started handing out the small transmitters he'd concocted over the last few days. "Keep these with you at all times; they'll let me track your movements in case we get separated."

"Man, you remind me of your dad," Sam said.

Davis raised his eyebrows. "My dad's pretty weird, so I'm not really sure how to take that."

Sam laughed and shoved the transmitter he'd been handed into the inside pocket of his jacket. The rest of the group were storing theirs as well, making sure to keep them close as they prepared for another run.

This would be the eighth in five days, and Elise was starting to feel the effects of it on her body. She was having trouble sleeping, memories of people staying with her for hours after she'd broken contact with them. Exhaustion that food and rest couldn't seem to ease and aches in her chest followed her long after they vacated an Awakening spot. She was trying not to show it or let her concern outweigh her conviction. She was called to this, so she had to trust that all would work out the way it was supposed to.

Davis handed the last transmitter to Kennedy. "Any word from home?" she asked.

He shook his head no, and she gave a worried sigh.

"Good idea," Kane mocked. "Let's not pay attention to the only sane person in the group."

"Funny how you're the only person here who would refer to yourself as sane," Kennedy said.

"It doesn't make sense," Kane continued, ignoring Kennedy's snide remark. "They just re-dose them the second you guys *cure* them. Why keep putting ourselves at risk? What is the point?"

"Why do you always say *cure* like it isn't a real thing?" Sage asked.

"His point isn't completely invalid," Timmons said, sidestepping Sage's comment.

"Thank you!" Kane said.

"So we should give up?" Lucy asked. "Kane, you've been

with us on every run. You've seen how we are changing people. We can't stop now."

"Maybe you are changing people, but they're changing them right back. We're creating an endless cycle where we all just mess with these people's minds."

"We *are* changing people." Sage's eyes were hot with fire.

"I can't believe that's the way this will end," Lucy said.

"Can't or won't?" Kane fired back.

"Enough, Kane," Willis said. "Stay here with Davis and watch the monitors if you'd prefer."

"No, we need him," Kennedy countered. "He's the best warrior we have. Timmons can stay with Davis."

"I take offense at that comment," Timmons said.

"She's right; you all need me," Kane said. "But I'm starting to wonder what exactly we're doing here."

The room paused for a beat because no one knew what to say. He was right, and Elise knew it as much as the others. The Authority was collecting people and re-injecting them with Genesis hours after the Seers cured them. It was hard not to feel like the situation was hopeless.

Elise stayed quiet in the corner, keeping her thoughts to herself. She had been thinking the same thing Kane was for days now. What *were* they doing here? Awakening people, but to what end? None of them had seen Aaron in days, and Elise was having a harder time connecting to her power. She was supposed to be leading them, following the path, but sometimes it was difficult to see where the path was.

A sudden wave of dizziness washed over her and she faltered in her stance. Willis caught her by the arm and held her steady. She couldn't help but notice that he was always standing right beside her or watching her over his shoulder, tending to her as she recovered.

"You all right?" he asked.

She nodded. "I just need some air." But she knew he could see right through her.

Willis walked her from the room, down the long factory hallway, and out the back door.

Elise let the cold evening air fill her lungs as she inhaled slowly. The sun was sinking toward the horizon; soon the sky would be painted with beautiful sunset colors. There was a long moment of silence between them, and Elise was grateful for it. Her mind was moving in circles, trying to outrun her fear and confusion and somehow find the truth that was so easy to forget.

"You want to tell me what's going on?" Willis asked.

Elise exhaled. "Kane's right, you know. This isn't working."

"Maybe it's working on a level that we can't see?"

"No," Elise said, "it isn't. We're running in circles, chasing our own tails."

"Elise—"

"Tell me you haven't had the same thoughts. How can you be 100 percent positive we're doing the right thing?"

"Because I trust the light."

Elise huffed and shook her head. "This power I was

given, that I didn't ask for, that has consumed my life . . . Eventually we are going to get caught, and you are all going to die because I believed I was called to something I'm not even sure is real!"

Elise pressed her palms to the sides of her skull and felt fear begin to shake her insides. "I will have killed you all. I should have let you go back to Trylin."

"You didn't make us stay," Willis said. He was calmly leaning against the brick wall, his arms casually crossed over his chest. "We stayed because we saw the power and believed."

"And do you still believe? Even though nothing has changed?"

"You've changed," Willis said.

His words stopped her for a moment. He was right— she had changed. She had changed down in the Capitol Building's basement. She had changed on the roof with Aaron. She had changed when the light had awakened Sam and Franklin. Each time the light had moved through her, she had changed. The light had changed her. Had given her a purpose, had called her, chosen her. There had been so many moments of perfect clarity. Moments when she was so certain this was all there was, but how quickly they faded.

"How do you remember?" Elise asked.

Willis took a deep breath and chuckled. "Lots of practice."

Elise turned her face from his and stared down the alley, not really looking at anything in particular but losing herself to her own thoughts and fears again. "What if I can't do this?"

"But you are doing it," Willis insisted.

"What if I'm not enough?" Elise could feel tears brewing under her eyelids and she swallowed to control herself.

Willis pushed himself off the wall and took a step toward her. "I know it can feel like we're doing this for nothing, but don't forget who you are in the midst of your doubt."

A soft wind wisped past them both, a wind Elise was starting to recognize, and she could feel the power stir inside her. It beckoned her to see past her fear to truth, urged her to remember what was real and what her mind only convinced her was real. She inhaled deeply, pulling the wind into her lungs, and calmed.

"Maybe we should do this run tomorrow?" Willis asked.

Elise shook her head. Her fear was still there, as were all the unanswered questions, but the light was there too, and she had to follow it. "No, I'm fine."

"It's okay to admit it if this is too much; we can—"

"No. I just needed a moment. Don't worry about me."

"I do worry, though."

She smiled at him. "I love you for worrying."

The second the words left her lips, she wished she could take them back. "I didn't mean love as in *love*. I just meant I appreciate that you are always looking out for me." She knew her face was burning red, and she tried to ignore the evident sparkle dancing in Willis's eyes. He took a step closer to her, and she felt the red in her face deepen.

"Well," he started, "you were called to the people of this city, and I was called to you." He reached out and softly pushed a stray curl behind her ear, and she forgot to breathe. "I really have no choice," he teased.

His words magically broke the tension and Elise couldn't help but laugh. "How do you even manage?" she teased back.

"Who knows? I mean, you with your beautiful eyes and perfect face—it's really a struggle for me."

Elise laughed again and shook her head. He'd never flirted with her quite so outright, and in the face of everything happening around them, she knew the timing was awful. But she didn't care, because suddenly all she wanted to do was steal away with him and fall for him completely.

They stood there, frozen in their private moment. She thought for a second he might kiss her, but before she could find out, the door behind them squeaked and he stepped away. Kennedy poked her head around the door, cleared her throat awkwardly, knowing she'd interrupted something, and then spoke. "Um, I think we're almost ready."

Elise stole a final glance at Willis, then took off after her sister. They walked in silence back into the main room where the others were waiting. Elise strode to the corner to gather what she needed and felt Kennedy's eyes on her. She looked over her shoulder and scowled at her sister's raised, inquiring eyebrows.

Kennedy chuckled and went back to what she'd been doing, leaving Elise alone with her thoughts.

22 The group passed through the hospital basement door without being detected. Sam had been on medical patrol duty often and knew that breaking into the basement was relatively easy to do. The problem would be in making it up to the third floor, their destination according to Willis's latest dream. Timmons and Davis had stayed behind to man the fort and keep their eyes on the monitors, and Franklin had remained to keep an eye on them.

It had become clear that Davis wasn't interested in making runs, which was accepted by the group, as his skills were better suited elsewhere. He'd managed to hack into the data feed from the cameras that watched over all the major intersections throughout the city, and he now monitored them for changes in CityWatch patrols and identified open routes through the city's busiest areas. Elise hadn't met a mind quite like his before.

"So we're headed to the third floor?" Sam asked Willis. Willis nodded.

"Makes sense," Sam said. "The first couple of floors are used for administration and storage only."

"We travel together and quickly," Kane said. "We have no idea what we might run into, so follow my lead if need be."

Kane was the most equipped to get them in and out of difficult situations, so they always turned to him for tactical maneuvers. Even if they weren't sure he was completely convinced of the purpose of their actions, they needed him as much as anyone else on the team.

They all nodded in agreement and started for the elevator. There were two in the hospital, but only one was functional. The other was a service elevator that had broken down a couple months back, and as far as Sam knew, it hadn't been fixed yet. They would climb through the roof of the broken elevator and use the shaft's ladder to scale up to the third floor. They rounded a corner of the basement, and Elise heard Sam breathe a sigh of relief when yellow construction tape still hung across the service elevator door.

Sam reached the tape first and ripped it off. He and Kane worked together to quickly pry open the doors so they could move into the elevator box. The two were a good team. Without saying anything, they read each other's body language and acted. Sam stepped into the elevator and offered his linked hands as a support to lift Kane up so that he could move the emergency hatch in the elevator's ceiling. The thick, square panel revealed a large hole when removed, plenty big enough for them all to crawl through.

Kane hoisted himself up through the open space and

extended his hands down to assist Kennedy, Lucy, Willis, Sage, and Elise. Sam came through last on his own, as Kane was already leading people up the steel ladder that was built into the wall of the elevator shaft.

Lucy was ahead of Elise, and Elise could see that the woman was trembling. "You okay?" she whispered.

Lucy nodded. "Heights aren't really my thing." Nevertheless, she grabbed the first rung and started to climb without hesitation.

Elise counted the doors as they climbed. *One, two.* The shaft was unventilated and humid, making it hard to breathe as they climbed. The distance between the floors was significant, so by the time they neared their desired level, they were a good distance from the ground. Elise came to a stop as she waited on those in front of her. She looked up to see Kane holding on with only one arm, working with Kennedy to open the third-floor elevator doors. Elise smiled; her little sister was much tougher than she looked.

They managed to get the doors to open a couple of inches and Kennedy peered through to the floor beyond to make sure they were clear to enter. She nudged the doors open just a bit more, enough to squeeze her shoulders into the gap, and with Kane boosting her from below, disappeared. A moment later, the doors were pulled open enough for Kane to heave himself through, and they were all moving again.

Lucy, Elise, Willis, and Sam all pulled themselves

through the elevator doors and onto the third floor. The hallway that the elevator had led them to was empty. Most likely, this section of the hospital was for personnel only, and with a nonfunctioning elevator as its primary mode of transportation, Elise felt sure that they shouldn't run into many people. The fluorescent lighting overhead flickered and gave the hall an eerie atmosphere.

Kane moved ahead of the group to the end of the hall, where two wide double doors were closed. In each of the doors was a thin glass window. Kane peered through one to the next hallway before waving the others forward.

The hospital was the largest venue they'd been to yet. As always, they couldn't be sure what would happen once they arrived; they only knew that they were called to go and to follow their intuition once they arrived.

When Willis had said a hospital was the next target, Kane had been the first to say it was too risky. There were easily a hundred people in a hospital at any given time, and there was no way they could sneak in and awaken that many people without anyone else catching wind of it.

The hospital also had stronger security than the other locations they'd been to, which meant if they did get caught, getting away would be more difficult than anything they'd faced before. Everyone had heard Kane's concerns, but as always, they had gone anyway.

Elise reached Kane and looked through the glass panel herself. The hallway only held a couple of people; if they ventured farther in smaller groups, they would still have a chance to escape if things went awry.

"We can still go back," Kane said.

"We're already here," Kennedy said. "No risk, no reward, right?"

Kane looked at Elise and pleaded with his eyes.

She reached out and touched his arm. "It's okay."

He exhaled and shook his head. "Fine. Kennedy, Lucy, and Sage, you three stick together. I'll stay with Elise. Willis and Sam, you bring up the back, keep us informed if anything goes wrong. We stay apart but never far enough that you guys can't do your *thing*," he said, making quotations with his fingers.

"Really?" Sage said, clearly offended.

Lucy placed her hand on Sage's shoulder. "Let him be. We need to focus."

Elise glanced over her shoulder briefly at Willis.

"Good luck," he said and gave her hand a tiny squeeze.

Sage turned away from Kane, and they all took a final deep breath before Kane and Elise moved out into the well-lit hallway first. They slowly walked toward the main commotion, making sure not to travel too quickly as a couple of nurses entered the hall chatting away, causing the other two groups to wait for their next opportunity to enter. Elise felt her heart seize as the nurses passed, but they didn't pay Kane or Elise any mind.

The two women disappeared into a supply room, and Elise glanced back to see Lucy, Sage, and Kennedy moving into the hall, Sam and Willis quickly following. Kane put his hand gently on Elise's upper arm as they turned into the main hospital walkway and lost sight of the rest of the group. But she could feel them, the light inside of her calling to the light inside each of them. She held to it tightly as Kane navigated her through the large clusters of people and over to the far right wall.

Families were moving through, talking with doctors, children pulling at their mothers' hems, fathers holding the little hands of wandering troublemakers. Young couples, old couples, pregnant mothers, injured workers. Some people were coughing and pale; others rubbed their throats; one man gripped his skull. Several people sat at the front of the lobby in the rows of collected chairs, waiting for their names to be called.

Elise looked from face to face, hoping someone would pop out or something would give her any idea what they were supposed to do next. Surely they weren't supposed to start moving through the crowd, awakening one person at a time? There were too many people here to do that. It would start a riot, and Elise wouldn't be able to call forth all of their memories at the same time. The largest number of people she had tried to connect with at once was eleven, two days ago in a small market shop. Using Kennedy and Lucy as anchors had almost not been enough, and the experience had felt like it almost killed her.

She tried not to think of that pain and fear now. She tried to remember who she was, what she was called to, and the power that lived inside her. But surely she wasn't called to take on this whole crowd at once?

Kane led her into a corner where they could see the entire lobby. Elise caught a glimpse of Kennedy and knew Lucy and Sage must be close behind. There was no sign of Sam or Willis, but she could feel them, so she didn't worry.

"What now?" Kane asked, keeping his eyes trained on the room, searching for threats.

Elise didn't know how to respond. She opened her mouth to say something about having patience but felt a small tug on the end of her jacket. Surprised, she turned to look down at a small boy. He was maybe five or six, with short blond hair and sparkling blue eyes as big as saucers. He was smiling up at her and waved his tiny little hand when she looked at him.

She waved back and felt Kane giving the boy a suspicious glance. She rolled her eyes at Kane. "He's just a child."

He huffed and turned his gaze back to the crowd. "Good to know we are risking our lives so you can hang out with kids."

Elise ignored him and turned back to the boy. "Hello," she said.

"Hi," the boy replied.

"What's your name?"

"Eli."

"That's almost like my name—it's Elise."

The boy scrunched his nose and giggled. "I already knew that."

Elise was taken aback and confused. "You already knew my name?" She could feel Kane watching with interest now.

The boy nodded and motioned for Elise to come closer. She dropped to a squat and watched as he pulled a folded paper out of his back pocket. He unfolded it carefully, as if it were his most prized possession, and showed it to Elise. It was a child's drawing, a golden field with tall yellow grass and a single man standing in the middle with features that Elise would know anywhere. Aaron.

She looked at the boy. Their eyes connected, and she noticed the fire of light dancing behind them. The power housed in her soul began to stir. It buzzed under her skin and responded to the presence of the boy beside her. She reached out and stroked the drawing with admiration.

"This is beautiful. Did you draw this?" Elise asked.

He nodded and smiled so brightly that Elise felt her heart seize with hope. "He told me you were coming," Eli said. "We've been waiting for you."

"We?"

Eli looked up, and Elise followed his gaze. She saw children of all different ages, some with their parents, others standing alone, all of them watching her excitedly, their eyes wide, their little frames bouncing, as if they all knew what was coming next.

Eli leaned closer to Elise so he could whisper in her ear. "We see the light too."

Emotion choked Elise's words so she could only stare in wonder at the small child.

"Don't be scared," he said and held out his hand.

Without hesitation, Elise took it in her own, and her light started to pulse. Stronger than normal, faster too, like a raging storm, it swelled up into her chest and down through her frame. It rippled through her hand and meshed with the pure innocence radiating from Eli. He giggled as Elise watched the light work its way through his tiny body. It surrounded him like a spotlight that only the two of them could see and danced across his shoulders.

Joy unlike anything she'd ever known consumed her. She couldn't keep the smile off her face. It pulled her mouth wide and brought tears to her eyes. Suddenly Eli pulled his hand away and bounced over to a little girl who was standing against the wall a couple of yards away. Eli didn't even touch her; he just walked past and her body too became filled with light. Like he'd flipped a switch in her and made her come alive. Then together, the two of them headed in different directions toward other children, and the ignition began.

One by one, children all across the lobby became living lightbulbs, flickering to life as another one passed. And each time the power inside Elise surged. She tried to contain her excitement, but it was impossible, and she started laughing to herself. She knew people nearby were staring at her with strange expressions, but she didn't care. How could she when the light was manifesting itself in the hearts of children right before her eyes?

She caught Kennedy's gaze from across the room and

saw that all three Seer girls were smiling from ear to ear, swept up in what was happening before them. Elise looked at Kane, who was watching carefully but with his guard high. Even the perfection of children couldn't penetrate his wall.

Before Elise could take another breath, pain exploded in the back of her mind. Like hot burning coals, it seared her skull and brought tears to her eyes. It was so intense she let out a cry and caught the attention of most of the room. Light swept through her body and poured out into the room. She didn't have to focus as she had before; the light grew strong on its own and gripped the people closest to her.

Memories sprang up across her vision as wildfire consumed the air around her head and took her to her knees. She searched for the anchors of sanity that Kennedy and Lucy provided and clung to them, hoping to not get completely swept away in the power raging through the room.

Cries of anguish filled the air. She could see people all across the lobby, not just the ones she was connected to, dropping like flies.

Elise couldn't control the onslaught of light that was working through people's minds, calling forth their deeper truth. Erasing the fog that they'd lived under for so long. Why couldn't she control it?

She searched for the source of the chaos, moving her eyes around the room through the hazy cloud of memories covering her vision, and she saw them. Children, covered in light, strong and pure, moving through the crowded lobby and touching people. A little girl brushed her fingers across the arm of an older man, and his mind peeled apart. A boy laid his hand on the shoulder of his mother, and her memories were restored. At least a dozen children, acting as tiny vessels for the light, all connected to Elise.

But the pain was the most unusual thing. As if she were experiencing the physical symptoms of everyone in the hospital at once. It rammed against her skull and filled her chest with fire. Her throat was being stabbed with knives, and her back, her legs, and her feet ached like nothing she had ever felt before. The horror of disease and death clouded her control, washing away her ability to stand.

"Elise," she heard someone yell through the madness. "Elise!"

Willis, she thought, *or maybe Kennedy.* The voice felt familiar, but so much was happening inside her mind that maybe there wasn't a voice at all. The linoleum floor was cold under her knees, and then it was hot, the temperature of her body switching rapidly. She heaved forward, catching herself with her palms. Sweat dripped from her forehead, and she struggled to breathe normally.

"Elise!"

She could feel Kennedy and Lucy reaching for her with their own light, trying to offer their strength, but it wasn't enough. She was barely keeping it together. *This must be what death feels like,* she thought. Moments of utter pain until suddenly there was nothing. Elise would welcome the nothingness; death suddenly sounded like a relief.

Fear not, daughter of the Father, light of the world.

The voice eased her pain momentarily, but the second it was gone, the overwhelming ache returned.

"I can't," she managed, a fresh wave of tears spilling from her eyes.

Remember who you are. Remember who they are, for all carry the light. Help them see.

"I can't . . ." Elise felt like she might lose her breakfast all over the floor.

Help them see.

Elise closed her eyes and tried to block out the throbbing between them. She must be missing something.

All carry the light.

Elise searched the room, looking for her salvation. She couldn't do this on her own. But then, she didn't have to. If all carried the light, then all housed the same power she did. All were children of the Father, all were called beyond this world of physical form, all were greater than they knew. Even the doubters. Something pierced through her pain, a brilliant white light that shined differently than the rest. *A child,* she thought, but maybe it was something else.

Suddenly, she felt desperate for the new light. Her instincts told her to reach for it, and she did, managing to rotate her body enough to stretch out her hand and grasp the bottom of someone's ankle.

The room shifted again; the picture in Elise's mind changed. She saw lights and color spewing from every corner of the room as if someone had set off fireworks. Every person in the lobby was now connected to the light as it grew rapidly, weaving its way through the building and crossing onto other floors.

The pain continued but became bearable. The ache, the throbbing, the burning sensation still hovered close by but no longer threatened to rip her body into shreds. She breathed, sucking in chilled air and pushing out hot, steadying her panicked heart, and accepting the pain.

The source of her new strength dropped down beside her, and she glanced up to meet eyes that were wide and scared. Kane. His face pale and his shoulders shaking. She was gripping his ankle, and his entire body was shrouded in the white-hot presence of the Father's light. He reached out his hand and took hold of Elise's forearm, and more fireworks flew across the room.

He was an anchor. The strongest one she'd connected with. He was keeping her alive, holding her together, channeling enough power that the entire hospital felt like it was covered in light. Kane was doing it. And then, in an instant, it was over. The pain dissolved, the buzzing faded, and the light that had ignited the room returned to the souls of all around, leaving them with only silence and hope.

Elise took several short breaths, trying to return her breathing to normal. Her mind spun, images of people's pasts playing back and forth like repeating videos. She lifted her eyes to see people pushing themselves off the floor, shaking their heads, weeping with joy, searching for answers, all their eyes holding the same expression: *I remember.*

She tried to push herself up, but her arms were shaky and she slid back down. Then a strong pair of hands gripped her shoulders and carefully lifted her to her feet. Willis. He looked concerned, and she forced a small smile to signal she was unharmed.

"Elise," Sage said, and they all knew that meant it was time to go.

Sam was already moving, Kennedy and Lucy right behind him. Elise turned to see Kane standing beside her, his eyes on the ground, his fingers still trembling. She wanted to reach out and touch him, but Willis was pulling her toward the exit, and she wasn't strong enough to fight him.

They moved quickly, leaving behind a room filled with people processing what had just happened to them. She could hear the laughter of the children as she turned the corner and headed back for the service hallway. The sound echoed in her mind, and she smiled. Had they really just cured all those people?

Willis stepped away from Elise to assist Sam in sliding the service elevator's doors back open, and Kane stepped up beside her. She looked at him, and he looked back. His face was drenched in sweat, his eyes filled with tears. He opened his mouth to say something but couldn't find the words. The light was that way, she knew—overwhelming, powerful, beautiful, humbling. Perfect love always was.

Elise wanted to tell him it was all right not to have anything to say, but a strong weariness fell over her and her vision swayed. Kane came in and out of focus, her head suddenly seeming to weigh a hundred pounds. She stumbled and heard someone call her name right before she slipped from the wall propping her up and headed for the ground. Her world went dark before she hit the floor.

23

Jesse followed the armed guards into the main lobby of the hospital. It had been cleared out a couple of hours ago, and everyone who'd been present during the disturbance had been transported to the Genesis Compound immediately. CityWatch guards had searched for Elise and her team in every crack of the building, then widened the search to ten blocks in all directions. They'd come up empty-handed. Again.

They had discovered an hour after the initial storming of the building that the lobby wasn't the only area affected. In fact, they'd had to clear the entire hospital—all the rooms, on every floor, all the way to the top. Jesse's mind swam in horror at the thought. This hospital, though smaller than some, easily held several hundred people, and none of them any longer showed signs of the Genesis Serum. Jesse fought off a shiver; he had to keep his composure so that this didn't escalate any further out of control. It seemed impossible that all of this destruction was coming from Elise.

The reports from the victims were the same as before. One moment they were going about their days, and the next they were being consumed with memories. Their minds had become twisted by the past, by events they didn't even know had taken place. Painful and inescapable. Then, as the memories shoved their way back into their brains, an overwhelming sense of purpose and peace, always accompanied by light, replaced their pain.

And they saw her—a beautiful young girl with raven-black hair welcoming them back to the truth. That last statement was corroborated by them all—*welcoming them back to the truth*—which was then followed by madness, as if their minds were still recovering from what had happened to them. Many spoke in gibberish, others cried, some laughed hysterically and said nothing more, but all had a new presence behind their eyes. A presence with the renewed capacity to ponder all the moments leading up to this one and even search for answers. The kind of behavior that had driven the Scientist to invent the Genesis Serum in the first place.

People were working madly all around him. Sweeping each floor for evidence, trying to make sense of how Elise and the other Seers were doing it. Looking for the scientific explanation. Jesse worked to keep his mind focused on the task at hand, but each time he had a moment of silence to wander, his thoughts returned to the past.

He remembered Remko standing inches from Aaron, his gun raised. And then he pulled the trigger. But nothing. Jesse had watched as a broken man had shot his rebel leader several times to no avail. The bullets seemed to evaporate into thin air before leaving their chamber. Jesse feared the same mystical power that had stopped live bullets was now working through the streets of his city.

How were they supposed to fight against something they couldn't see? Against a madness that seemed to be stronger than science? If Roth were standing beside him now, he would scold Jesse for even thinking there was another power greater than science, but Jesse's mind couldn't comprehend how anything else was possible. It crawled within him and wreaked havoc on his mind. He couldn't let this insanity continue, or he would surely lose all they'd built.

Elise was the key; she always had been. The Scientist had been convinced the only way to prevent what was happening was to have Elise eliminated, but Jesse sensed that another way was possible. He knew her. She didn't have a malicious bone in her body. Her mind was naive and fresh. She was being manipulated by the rebels, used for their agenda. He had to find her, had to help her see that she was not bringing good to this city but rather destroying it. He knew if only he could separate Elise from those Seers, then he could reason with her.

Can you? Can you save her?

The voice was growing stronger, following him daily, and his separation from Elise had increased how often it spoke to him. Like the devil himself was taking up residence inside his chest. Hissing, whispering. Worse, he found himself taking comfort in not being alone. Was that comfort causing him to seek out the voice's counsel more often? Jesse couldn't cope with his own madness in the face of what was before him, and he reverted his thoughts to Elise.

The problem is finding her, he thought. Finding her and then getting to her before she destroyed the minds of his men. Even with the Genesis Serum rushing through the veins of his CityWatch soldiers, Jesse could see hints of fear whenever Elise came up in conversation. They were afraid of what she could do to them, as was Jesse. Getting close to her was no small task. But if they could just get to her, take her out of the equation, then taking out the rest of the Seers would be simple.

Jesse was working through a plan in his mind when someone called his name. "President Cropper?"

It yanked Jesse out of his thoughts, and he glanced over his shoulder to see two guards escorting a young man in a white lab coat. One of the head scientists over at the Genesis Compound. Jesse knew the compound's rooms were currently stuffed with patients, so seeing him here filled Jesse with concern.

"I'm headed to the Genesis Compound after this. Can it not wait?" Jesse demanded.

The doctor shook his head, and Jesse cursed under his breath. He motioned for the guards to leave them. He then gave the scientist a slight nod to continue, and the man did, hesitantly.

"We've encountered some difficulties getting those attacked at the hospital re-administered," the scientist said.

"Difficulties?"

"It seems as though none of them can be re-administered."

"I don't understand."

"The common Genesis formula no longer has any effect on them."

"That's impossible. They were all injected successfully before?"

"Yes; something in their genetics must have changed. We are searching for a solution—"

"How could all of them now be different?" Jesse asked, realizing the volume of his voice was starting to draw attention.

"Sir, I have all available personnel working on the issue—"

"I want every scientific and medical mind in the city working on this! Nobody leaves that compound until those people are re-administered. Is that understood?"

The scientist nodded. "There is something else."

"How could there possibly be something else?"

The man swallowed and continued. "It seems they have all also been healed."

Jesse felt his heart race.

"All signs of infection, sickness, and pain are gone. From all the patients."

Jesse's mind ached in an effort to comprehend the vastness of what the scientist was reporting. Like bullets disappearing from a fired weapon, more impossibilities were being presented to him.

The blood is the key.

An image of Roth standing before him in the Council Room, the other members dead around him, the Scientist's old, wrinkled hand holding out large syringes filled with a dark-red substance, speaking with a voice not his own. *"The blood is the key,"* he had said, and Jesse heard the darkness say it now.

The blood is the key.

But could he trust the voice? Should he? Was it worth the risk of giving it more power? He had to do something.

The head scientist standing before him spoke, breaking the silence. "I'll head back to the Genesis Compound and get everyone on the serum issue. I'll keep you up to date on all advances."

Jesse nodded his approval. "I'll go with you, but first we need to go by the Capitol Building. There's something there I need."

Jesse couldn't risk any other new developments causing more chaos. The madness had gotten out of hand, and they needed a solution. Maybe he already had one.

Regardless, Elise had to be contained. Before leaving, Jesse turned to a guard a foot away and told him to instruct the CityWatch's commanders to meet him at the Capitol Building in an hour. They would work around the clock until Elise was found.

But first he would listen to the haunting voice and try to save those already taken, and then he would save the rest. The future of the Authority City depended on it.

/ / /

Jesse stood behind the thick glass panel. On the other side was a sterile white room containing a woman strapped to a medical chair. She had a crazed look on her face, her mind bending in and out of reality as her images of a life she wasn't supposed to remember crashed around inside her head. The young scientist who had delivered the news that Elise's latest victims were immune to the Genesis Serum stood beside the chair while a guard stood on each side of the single door that led into the room. The young man held a small syringe of the dark substance that Roth had given Jesse.

Even from this side of the glass Jesse could hear the whisper of the moving essence call to him. It tickled at the back of his neck and made his teeth chatter. He felt equal measures of fear and anticipation as the young scientist prepared the subject for injection. The woman thrashed about, yanking at her restraints and mumbling through the protective gag across her mouth.

The young scientist looked hesitantly at the syringe in his hand and then back at the glass for a final time. He had asked more questions than Jesse was comfortable with after Jesse had retrieved the blood from his office, but like others in the Authority City his veins pumped enough of the Genesis Serum to make him compliant.

With a final swallow, the young man pressed the needle of the syringe into the tip of the plastic tubing that ran toward the injection spot in the woman's arm. She watched as the dark blood slowly crawled through the thin tube toward her, and she yanked more violently against the ties that held her down. Almost as if her body knew what was coming and was trying to rescue itself.

Jesse watched anxiously. He had no idea what would happen once the substance reached her bloodstream. He wasn't even fully convinced anything would happen, but something strange and powerful had filled Roth's body that day he stepped into the Council Room. Something had brought him back from near death, something Jesse didn't want to admit he recognized.

The young scientist took a step back, the full amount of blood now swimming through the plastic tubing, and watched as the first drops of darkness entered the woman. She clenched her eyes shut and her body went deathly still. She was bracing for something, and after a pause that seemed to still time, her body convulsed back to life. It jumped away from the chair, the straps nearly snapping from the pressure of her movement. Her body lurched and twisted as the rest of the blood drained into her veins. The two guards at the door moved closer in case she needed to be restrained further, and the young scientist moved all the way back against the far wall.

The woman's back arched, the top of her skull grinding into the metal medical chair, her eyes rolling up to look at the wall behind her. Her arms twitched and her legs shook as her entire body quivered under the power now shooting through her system. Her eyes were open wide in horror as her body seemed to bend farther than was possible and then collapsed against the chair like dead weight. Again she went utterly still.

Jesse stepped closer to the glass, his eyes craving whatever would happen next. He noticed the rise of darkness within himself, the pleasure he was getting from watching the dark blood work its way into another, and he swallowed the bitterness collecting on his tongue.

It seemed as though an entire minute passed as the woman lay there motionless. The guards backed off, and the young scientist slowly stepped toward her chair to read her vitals. Jesse could see her chest rising and falling softly, so he knew she was still alive.

Suddenly, she took a huge gulp of air, her eyes snapping open and her body coming back into motion. The room's other occupants all jumped with her sudden movement and waited, tensed, as she lifted her head from the back of the medical chair and stared through the glass directly at Jesse.

His breath caught in his throat as her coal-black eyes met his. He saw the darkness that sang to him when he was alone, that whispered to him constantly, that had driven Roth into the Council Room. That same darkness was captured in her eyes and flowing through her veins. The blood was darkness in its purest form, and it had overtaken the vessel before him.

The woman held Jesse's stare for a long moment before

her head fell back against the table and again she was out cold. Jesse's heart raced long after her eyes were shut and she was once more under the veil of slumber. He couldn't shake from his mind the image of her eyes as the young scientist ran tests on her body and the guards stood watch, poised to move if she sprang to life again. Jesse couldn't erase the power he'd felt in her stare or the way he'd felt the darkness stir inside his chest.

He turned away from the glass and considered what the Scientist had given him. A weapon to turn the awakened over to the darkness. To give them completely to its power, to offer them up to be used as it saw fit. If Elise was curing people with light, then maybe the only way to combat her attempts to ruin this city was to drive it out with darkness. Fire with fire.

The darkness rumbled excitedly in Jesse's brain.

Yes, he thought, the blood was key.

24

Elise's eyes fluttered open slowly. The room started to take shape through her sleepy haze, and she noticed the ache between her eyes. She tried to recall what had happened to her but couldn't. Her mind was still cloudy. The room around her was bathed in the light of the fading sun, dark-orange beams piercing through slits in the closed curtains. She was lying on several stacked sleeping mats, tucked under a heavy blanket, and she suddenly realized how warm she was.

She shrugged off the blanket and tried to push herself up to a sitting position. Her head swam with the motion and a soft thudding started at the back of her neck. She pushed through her discomfort and finally got herself upright. She steadied herself and considered standing, but before she could move any farther, someone opened the door and entered the room. Willis.

"You're awake," he said softly, shutting the door behind him.

Elise attempted to stand, but Willis was beside her so quickly that her intentions never manifested.

"Whoa there. I'm not sure standing is such a good idea," he said.

"What happened?" Elise's voice was gravelly, her throat dry.

Willis handed her the glass of water he was holding and she gratefully took it. She sipped the water, slowly at first, and then downed the rest as if she'd been dying of thirst.

Again she searched her mind for her most recent memories. They'd been at the hospital. The children had been powerful; she had images of them moving around the lobby, laying hands on people and starting their Awakening process. She remembered the intense pain, the overwhelming number of people's memories, and . . .

"Kane," Elise said out loud.

"He's fine," Willis assured her. "He's in the next room with the others. We're back at the factory. You passed out at the hospital. Do you remember that?"

"I remember the hospital. Is everyone all right?"

He nodded. "We made it out and back here safely, but it was close."

She had passed out. She remembered it slightly now. Her head had suddenly felt so heavy and her world had gone dark. But she didn't remember traveling back, so they must have had to carry her. How long ago had that been?

"You've been sleeping off our last encounter for two days," Willis said as if reading her mind. "How are you feeling?"

Elise exhaled and wished the tiny pulse throbbing inside her brain would stop. "Fine," she lied. "A bit disoriented is all." She tried to offer him a hopeful smile, but it was hard to fake away the discomfort.

Willis sat down beside Elise on her misshapen bed. "You don't have to lie to me. It's all right if you still don't feel well. The hospital was extreme."

"Any news on those people?" Elise asked.

Willis was smiling. "I don't know what was different this time, but all of those that we awakened at the hospital can't be re-administered."

"What?"

"The Genesis Serum has no effect on them anymore. You made them like you."

"Immune?"

"Looks like it."

Elise let his words sink into her bones. "It wasn't me, you know. The light is what changed those people."

"It healed them too."

She looked at Willis in surprise. He shrugged, a playful grin on his face, and she smiled genuinely in response.

"I didn't even know the light could do that," Willis said.

Elise's smile only widened. "The light can do anything."

"And you carry it, which makes you pretty significant."

"We all carry it. You saw those children at the hospital, running around, fully abandoned to the truth. It was one of the most incredible things . . ." She trailed off, losing her words to the memories.

Willis swept her hand into his own, tangling their fingers together and sending her heart racing. His palm was warm and his touch sent tingles up her arm. The hold was both strong and gentle, and once again Elise had a strong desire to run away with him.

"You scared us at the hospital. You scared me," Willis said.

"I'm okay," she assured him.

"I can feel you when you dream, you know. I get a glimpse of the pain you're in. I know you're not okay."

Elise didn't respond. She didn't know what to say. He was right; she wasn't okay. Every moment she was awake, she could sense the lifetime of memories boiling under her skin. She was absorbing parts of them all somehow, and they followed her.

"You should have told me how much of a toll this was taking on you," Willis said.

"And what good would that have done?"

"I would have—"

"Stopped me?" Elise cut in. "I'm called to this, remember? And it isn't over, so I can't stop."

"But you can't keep going like this. What if it has permanent effects on you? What if it . . ."

Elise already knew what he wouldn't say. "Kills me?" The thought had crossed her mind for the first time in the hospital. She was, after all, just a girl. She carried the light, yes, but she was still human, still fragile. Willis squeezed her hand, and they remained quiet for a long moment.

"I want to reassure you that that won't happen," Willis said. "I want to tell you that everything will be fine and that I can protect you from the pain. I want to save you from this, but I don't know how."

"Maybe it's impossible. Maybe I can't be saved."

Willis shook his head and moved his eyes so that they were staring right into hers. "I don't know how to lose you now." He moved his free hand to graze the side of her face. "And I don't want to find out."

The air between them stilled, and Elise held her breath. The moment seemed to last an eternity, the second between him staring into her eyes and the moment his lips touched hers. It was as if everything had moved into slow motion, but then it happened. Their lips pressed together and the throbbing pain in the back of her mind vanished. All the worries of what was to come erased. All that was, was their kiss. Powerful and tender, unlike anything she'd felt before, and the familiar ache to hide away from the world with him grew. In that one instant, she considered taking his hands in hers and walking away from this city and never looking back.

A knock at the door broke the magic, and Willis respectfully pulled away. Elise followed his lips with her eyes as Willis called for whoever had ruined their moment to come in. She forced herself to stop staring at his face and turned to see Kennedy glancing in to check on her sister.

Elise shook the regret from her shoulders and smiled at Kennedy.

"I'll give you two a minute," Willis said as he stood, giving Elise's hand a final squeeze, and left. Kennedy walked across the room and sat down beside Elise.

She wrapped her arm around her sister's shoulders and shot her a sneaky little grin.

"What?" Elise asked.

"Apparently I'm making a bad habit of interrupting the two of you."

Elise chuckled and rolled her eyes. "Yes, dear sister," she said, playfully shoving Kennedy's shoulder. "Yes, you are."

/ / /

Elise saw Kane sitting on the edge of the old factory roof, just where Kennedy had told her he would be. According to her, Kane had spent the majority of his time since the hospital alone, the wheels behind his eyes always turning, his mind caught up in itself. Kennedy and Willis had tried to keep Elise in bed, insisting that she needed more rest, but the room had started to feel claustrophobic, and she was worried about Kane.

She made her way toward him slowly, her body still exhausted and tender. She kicked a small pebble and it bounced against the stone roof, causing Kane to lift his chin and see her coming.

He stood, alarm on his face, an automatic reaction he'd acquired around her. "Everything okay?"

She nodded and smiled. "Yes, just needed some fresh air," she said as she reached him.

"I'll let you have the roof," Kane said, moving to step away.

Elise gently touched his arm. "Sit with me?"

His eyes flashed with fear, and Elise tried to make her expression reassuring. After a moment, he nodded and the two sat. Elise turned her eyes to the city in front of her. It stretched far and wide, the evening light covering the buildings and streets. The sun was sinking toward the distant mountains. She found herself thinking about what it might be like to stand at the top of one of those mountains and touch the sun as it faded away.

Say to that mountain move, and it will move.

Elise let the presence of her Father fill her tired soul. The last time she'd been on a roof, she had been with Aaron, and the light had revealed itself to her in such a defined way that it had sent them all on this journey. A journey many of them had believed in from the very beginning, while others had come around only as the adventure had continued.

Kane was different from all of them. Sage had told Elise in confidence that she was worried Kane would never believe. Even though he had been present for many of the moments when the light changed people, Kane had remained skeptical and cold. A warrior through and through, his logic outweighed his ability to believe. Now, though, Elise thought, stealing a quick glance at him, everything was different.

The silence between them lingered for a while. Both remained lost in their own thoughts as the cooling air swept over them and the sky faded overhead. Elise was searching for something to say to break the silence, but Kane spoke first.

"How do you not feel overcome by it all?" he asked.

Elise chose her words carefully. "I surrender to it."

"Surrender is not something that comes easily to me."

"Yes, it has been painted as a negative word, hasn't it? The truth is, there is overwhelming power in surrender. In letting go of all you think you know to discover truth."

"Letting go feels like giving up."

"That's because you still see yourself through the eyes of this world. You still believe you need to fight and resist and conquer. But you don't."

"Are we not currently fighting a war?"

"I don't think of it that way. I believe we are helping people remember the light that already lives inside them, so that they understand there has never actually been a war to fight."

"Even against those that did this to you? Stole you from your family, kept you captive? You don't feel like they should pay for what they've done?"

Elise took a slow breath and let the moment linger. Did

she think about the grievances she could hold against Jesse and the Authority, the debt that should be repaid to her for all her suffering? "Yes," she said. "Sometimes I crave justice for myself. My mind tricks me into thinking that somehow retaliation will give me power. But then, I have seen true power come only from surrender and letting go of injustices. So if I believe real strength comes from letting go, then how can I believe that holding on to my grudges will also bring me power? The two can't exist together."

"So then how do you deal with it? It's all good and fine to say I'm letting it go, but how do you stop it all from crawling back up into your mind?"

"Life is a cycle of remembering and forgetting. The Father is in all and with all, and He tells me I am the light of the world. So if I believe His words are true and that we are all the same, created equal, and that I am the light of the world, then you must be too. When I start to forget who you are, then I, in turn, also start to forget who I am. So I practice remembering."

Kane shook his head and turned his gaze back toward the city. "It all messes with my mind, man."

Elise chuckled and nodded. "It's relearning, really. The way the light breaks down what you have previously believed and shows you what real truth is."

"I wasn't even sure if I believed, but then . . ." Kane trailed off and Elise could see the emotion clouding his face. He kept his eyes turned away and his voice at a whisper. "I can still feel the light in me, pulling at my chest." His eyes filled with silent tears and Elise's heart broke. "It's constantly with me now. Destroying my mind and making me question everything."

"It's okay to question, to wonder," Elise said. "Don't judge yourself for searching."

Tears were now sliding down Kane's cheeks and he inhaled angrily. "How could I not have seen before? I was so close to it and still didn't see. I must look like such a fool."

"The light reveals itself to everyone in its own perfect timing. You are not a fool, Kane; you learned you were the light of the world exactly when you needed to, and probably saved my life."

Kane glanced up at Elise. "I'm sorry. I should have asked how you're feeling."

She shook her head. "It's all right. I'm fine."

"Aren't you afraid of what could happen to you if we continue?" Kane asked.

First Willis and now Kane. *Remember who I call you. What shall you fear?* The voice poured over Elise like refreshing water, and she smiled. She let go of the fear starting to build in her system and felt the soft rush of peace. "Only when I forget who I am."

Kane was shaking his head again. "I have this terrible feeling that this is only going to get worse before it gets better."

Elise nodded. "As things usually do," she said, her spirit

soaking in the truth of the Father's voice and letting go of the fear. She looked across the city, its lights coming alive in the dimming evening sky, and took a deep breath. *Yes, things will probably get worse.*

25

When the evening sky finally went dark, Elise and Kane left the roof to join the rest of the group. Everyone else was gathered together in the main room around a large fire blazing up from the inside of the thick metal barrel. Elise followed Kane into the room and felt her heart skip a beat when Willis looked up and smiled at her. She wondered if there would ever be a time when his eyes didn't make her stomach do somersaults.

Franklin walked into the room after them, and Sam nodded in his direction. "Where have you been?"

"Just doing some patrols, trying to keep busy," Franklin said.

"You don't actually need to do that anymore," Davis said. He was sitting at the large desk he'd constructed, staring at the monitors that he hardly left alone. "I installed two more cameras yesterday, so the building and all the surrounding streets are completely covered. We have eyes on them." Davis glanced at Franklin over his shoulder. "Cool, right?"

Franklin gave him a small grin. "Yeah, cool," he said meekly. Elise wondered what was on his mind. She still

didn't know the former CityWatch guard very well, and
they had hardly talked in depth about how he was dealing
with all this. In fact, she'd hardly talked to anyone other
than Willis, Kennedy, and now Kane.

Elise surveyed the room, suddenly feeling an overwhelming need to speak with each of them. This journey
they were all on together was far from anything they could
have expected, and it was taxing on the mind and the soul.
Had she gotten so caught up in following the mission that
she'd missed the chance to really connect with those around
her? She definitely connected with them as they followed
the light, but did she actually know any of them?

"Any idea where we're going next?" Lucy asked Willis,
yanking Elise from her thoughts.

Willis was sitting in a chair next to Davis's workstation,
spooning stew into his mouth. He glanced at Elise, and
she could see the worried expression on his face. If he had
dreamed about something, he didn't want to share it with
the group, because he was worried about what it might do
to her. She wanted to tell him not to worry about her, that
he couldn't hold back information on her behalf. Didn't
he understand how important their mission was? She was
going to have to say something to him.

"Dude, those new cameras you installed are blank," Sam
said to Davis, leaning into the table and looking closely at
the screens.

Davis leaned forward, his forehead scrunching in frustration. "Must be a bug—they were just working."

Sam chuckled. "Guess you shouldn't have dismissed Franklin's efforts so quickly, huh?" He turned to the place where Franklin had been standing, but he wasn't there anymore. Sam casually scanned the room for Franklin but came up empty. Elise too found herself curious. Hadn't he just been there?

She saw Willis's face go pale as he stood from his seat a moment before a cold arm wrapped around Elise's chest. It pulled her back tightly as the tip of a small metal object was forced up against the side of her skull. Her mind registered *gun* before she fully understood what was happening, and her body's primal instincts took over. Her hands grabbed at the arm restraining her as the person behind her forcefully dragged her several feet away from the rest of the group, all of them on their feet now and staring at what was happening.

"Franklin, what—?" Sam said.

"Stay back!" Franklin yelled, pushing the gun tighter against Elise's head, his voice echoing painfully in her ear. Franklin was the one holding a gun to her head? Her mind tumbled over itself trying to comprehend how this could be possible.

"Franklin—" she said.

"Shut up," he snapped. He was holding her so tightly across her chest that she was struggling to breathe. His arm trembled as he took a couple more steps back, yanking Elise along with him.

"Whoa," Willis said, raising his hands in a surrendering

pose. "Just take it easy." He took a step forward, and Elise felt the gun cock against her temple. Willis froze.

"I said stay back," Franklin repeated.

Elise could feel his panicked breaths rising and falling with his chest; she could sense the tension in his hold. What was he thinking? How had it come to this?

"Franklin," she tried again. "Please, whatever it is—"

"No," he said in a violent whisper, "you don't understand."

"This is insane, man; come on. Just put the gun down," Sam said.

"This is a safe place for you," Sage said, suddenly showing her face through the concerned crowd across the room.

"You're one of us now; we can work through this," Lucy said.

Franklin's entire body shivered, and he muttered under his breath. He seemed to be battling with himself, and his loss of control made Elise nervous. She was trying to see through the blind fear that was threatening to overwhelm her system, trying to find the light that reminded her there was nothing to fear. But as he shook and took another step toward the door, pulling at her and cursing under his breath about someone being late, Elise struggled to see anything but despair.

"Everyone stop talking!" he yelled and jerked Elise again. The motion rattled the pain in her muscles, and she cried out. Willis was on the move then, but it was too late. Just as his feet moved to cross the room, dozens of

CityWatch guards descended on the factory floor. They pushed into the room past Franklin and Elise, their guns raised, shouting commands.

"Freeze!"

"Hands up!"

"Everybody on their knees, now!"

Willis stopped, his face pulled tight with anger, but did as he was told, placing his hands above his head and kneeling on the wooden floor. The others did the same, fear engulfing their expressions. More men, dressed all in black, filed into the room and moved toward the Seers to restrain them.

Elise could feel the light inside her tugging at her mind and she closed her eyes to call it forth, but something sharp pricked at the side of her neck, and she reopened her eyes wide.

"I'm so sorry," Franklin whispered to her. "I had no choice."

"What did you—?" Elise started to say but lost control of her mouth. It felt fuzzy along with the rest of her face as the site of the prick stung painfully. Her eyes went hazy as the room around her began to swim. She tried to shake it off, but she couldn't seem to connect her thoughts with the use of her muscles, and the darkness started to flood in.

"Forgive me," Franklin said. Those were the last words she heard before the darkness came and took her completely.

/ / /

Elise woke suddenly. She pushed herself up from where she'd been lying, her heart racing and her mind running at full speed. Like she'd been shot up with adrenaline, the blood under her skin throbbed with wild abandon. What had happened last? An image of Franklin filled her mind and everything came rushing back to her. Her hand reached for the spot on her neck, and she felt a tiny bump where he'd injected her with something. A sedative? So she couldn't use the light to save them. They'd been taken by the Authority. All of them.

She looked around, expecting to see prison bars, and was surprised to find none. She wasn't met with a cold cement floor or dark stone walls. Instead, she was in a golden field, the sky above blue and kind, the ground warm from the large sun hanging overhead. She knew this place, had seen it in the young Eli's drawing, had heard others talk about this heaven on earth. And now, here she was.

She stood and looked around the field. Several tall trees stood scattered about, and wheat stretched for miles in all directions. The sweet songs of birds echoed through the sky, and a soft, warm wind carried their tune on its moving waves. She turned in a circle and saw no one. It was just her, with the birds, the grass, the breeze, and the overwhelming sense that she wasn't alone. It was in every inch that she touched and in every molecule around her. It was a sense carried by the wind, a sound echoing in the tweeting of the birds that filled the air. Someone was with her. Someone always was.

Elise felt overcome with the power of that sensation. She closed her eyes and felt the truth rush through her blood, pricking at her senses, filling her with strength. The wind became stronger, swarming around her, encircling her, calling forth the light of her soul. It made her feel so small, like a single blade of grass in the field that stretched in every direction around her. Who was she that such power had been bestowed on her? Who was she that such light had been given? She was just a girl, trying to do the work of an army. A silly student trying to function as a master. And it was all for nothing. They were finished. Those who had followed her delusions had been captured and were now headed for death. She had been a fool. Who was she that she thought she could save them all?

Heavy waves of doubt and fear crushed against her shoulders. Panic and regret toppled down over her head. She fell to her knees, struggling to breathe as the wind intensified. Who was she but an ignorant child dressed up in a superhero costume, playing a dangerous game that would surely get them all killed?

Remember who I call you.

Was her power even real or just another twisted concoction of her mind's delusions?

Surrender.

Shame filled Elise's bones, and she grabbed her chest as

the realization of what she'd done to her poor Seers manifested into pain.

Forgive.

She heard the voice through the ache but only as a
small whisper that bounced off the surface of the darkness
that was already overtaking her. The aches and pains of
her body flooded her system, reminding her that she was,
once again, too weak to take on such power. It was killing
her, screaming at her that she wasn't enough. And she'd
ignored it.

Let go.

Hot tears spilled down her cheeks and she cried out in
anguish. She had done this. She had killed them and herself. How could she not have seen her own insignificance?
Now they would all pay for her misguided hopes.

"It is only in our lack of faith that we become small,"
a voice said.

Elise jerked her head up, and the wind died out completely. She wiped the tears from her face and turned to see
a beautiful girl standing only a few feet away, the golden
grass reaching all the way up to her hips. Soft blonde hair
framed her face and fell past her shoulders in long straight
lines. But it was her emerald eyes that drew Elise in so
closely that it felt as if the beautiful girl were holding her
hand. The only other person Elise had ever encountered
with such an inviting gaze was Lucy. In fact, the girl before
her favored Lucy quite a bit.

"Hello," the girl said.

"Hi," Elise replied.

"Do you mind if I sit with you?"

Elise shook her head no, and the girl smiled as she covered the short distance to Elise and sat in the warm grass beside her. Elise shifted off her knees and pulled them tightly to her chest. The two girls sat in silence for a moment, the sun warming the cold that had sneaked into Elise's body, the song of the birds returning.

"I'm Arianna, by the way," the girl said. "I think you know my sister Lucy?"

"You're Lucy's sister?"

Arianna shrugged and smiled. "Well, I was for a time."

"And now who are you?"

"Isn't that the question we all seem to be asking?"

Elise turned her eyes back to the field. "It's a hard one."

"That's just the thing—it isn't really. We only convince ourselves it is."

"Then why is it so hard to remember?"

"Because we give the lies power when we judge ourselves, which we do constantly. We enforce the lie that we are powerless and weak each time we blame ourselves. Every time we hold on to our doubts."

"But I am just a girl; I can't save them. I thought I was stronger than I am, but I'm not. And now people will die because of me." Elise felt a strong wave of tears approaching. She tried to swallow back the emotion, but it was more than she could control.

Arianna's eyes filled with compassion, and she brushed

Elise's shoulder gently. "Who told you that you were just a girl?"

The question struck a chord deep inside Elise's spirit, and something other than shame vibrated in her gut.

Remember who I call you.

Tears ran down Elise's cheeks. "But look at me."

"I am," Arianna said, "and you know what I see? Power beyond your ability to imagine. Strength—enough to stand against any opposing force. Love, perfect and blameless, as you have been called His."

Elise shook her head slightly, feeling the call of Arianna's words mix with the light of her spirit, but the shame was still blinding and heavy. "But if I fail . . ." She couldn't finish her thought as emotion filled her voice.

"Who told you that you could fail?"

Again the chord in her soul strummed and the vibration grew, slowly piercing through her doubt.

"Did the light not call you blameless? Did it not cover you in perfect love, call you its own? Did He not tell you that you are perfect? So now you turn to the light and say no, you're wrong; I am not what you said? Do you believe the light can be wrong?"

Elise didn't know how to answer. How could she say that the light and the truth, by which so many people had been healed, were wrong? But how could she believe what they said about her?

"Every time you judge yourself, you judge the light. Every time you doubt your power, you doubt the power of the light. Because that power lives within you, Elise. The light is in you. Don't you see who you really are?"

The strumming of truth that had been working on Elise's self-doubt and shame broke through with a vengeance. Her body was ravaged by light, now burning holes in the darkness that had swallowed her. And the voice of her Father began to sing a song she knew but had forgotten.

I call you daughter. Perfect, chosen, light of the world.

"But the others," she said, thinking of the Seers. "I have doomed them."

"Remember who you are, Elise, and then remember that they are the same. How could they be doomed when they have already been called by perfect love? They too are light—all of them," Arianna said.

I call you daughter. Perfect, chosen, light of the world.

All who come from the light are in the light and are light. Remember who you are.

Elise stopped resisting and surrendered to the truth that called her its own. She fell into it as a child might collapse into a parent's embrace after a terrible dream and let its warmth soothe her. "How could I have forgotten?" she asked.

Arianna reached for Elise's hand, and Elise turned to see tears brimming in the girl's eyes. "Don't judge yourself for forgetting; otherwise we are right back where we started," she said with a smile. "Remember that all moments are love's way of bringing you back to yourself. Only in forgetting do you get the chance to remember." Her smile widened, nearly large enough to consume her small face, and fire danced behind her eyes. "Even in moments of doubt, you are still perfect; even in times of fear, you are His. And once again, you get to walk through your doubt and fear and remember that you are the light of the world. Isn't that amazing?"

Elise laughed and cried all at once. "I am afraid."

"That's okay," Arianna said. She reached up and placed her hand on Elise's cheek as a sob broke from Elise's chest.

"See your fear," Arianna said. "See your shame, or doubt, or anger, whatever you are facing. Always feel them; never run from them, because running is just another form of resisting. So feel everything that you encounter, and then turn your eyes to the light and remember that it is greater than anything you will ever face. The light is yours, and you are the light's. So what can stand against you?"

More warmth and light surrounded Elise, and she let Arianna's words work their way into her heart. She wanted them to make a permanent home there so they would be with her always, so she would never forget them, even in times when she might forget herself.

"Just follow the light," Arianna said, "and you will never face anything that you can't overcome."

Elise smiled at the beautiful girl and nodded. She would—with all her heart she would.

"Ah!" a voice chimed in behind them. Elise and Arianna both turned to see Aaron walking toward them, and Elise was filled with such joy she could hardly contain herself. "Have I missed something magical?" Aaron asked.

Arianna chuckled. "Only a moment of remembering."

Aaron smiled at Elise and nodded. His eyes were filled with kindness and love. Elise could feel her throat constrict with emotion once again, and she hoped to never leave this field.

"Well then, I think we should celebrate," Aaron said.

"Oh no," Arianna said.

Elise gave her a funny look, and Arianna teasingly rolled her eyes. "Always with the dancing," she said.

"Dancing?" Elise said.

"Oh yes. There is no better way to enjoy this field than to dance through it," Aaron said.

Arianna was laughing quietly beside her as Elise shook her head. "You want me to dance in this field?"

"Of course!" Aaron said.

"Like a child?" Elise teased.

Aaron smiled and nodded with such conviction that Elise's heart skipped a beat. "You must first become like a child before you can enter the Father's kingdom," he said. "Now—" he clapped his hands together beside his face, one eyebrow arching higher than the other—"we dance."

Elise and Arianna both fell into laughing fits, joy bouncing between them. Arianna grabbed Elise's hand and helped her stand.

"We might as well," Arianna said through her laughter, "because he won't stop until we do." She shot Elise a wink and the wind whipped up around them. The sun seemed to grow, lighting the field up like pure gold, and Elise joined Arianna in twirling about, Aaron leading them in their ridiculousness.

And the light that called her daughter, and the truth that called her its own, and the love that claimed her and empowered her, all danced through her being as they moved about together. One with each other, one with the Father, lost in perfect love.

26

Jesse sat inside the Capitol Building's banquet room at the large dining table. It had been set for dinner, a feast hearty enough for ten men laid out across the surface, the lights dimmed and the curtains drawn. Guards stood in every corner of the room, armed and on alert. They wouldn't be taking any chances with their dinner guest.

Thoughts from the day rolled around inside Jesse's head while he waited, and in the silence of the room, his eyes began to feel heavy. He'd hardly slept the last two days. Images of the Scientist's blood working its way into people's systems constantly filled his head. The blood brought them back into a peaceful state of compliance, but it took them one step further: it filled them with abnormal power. They were full of strength, less human than machine, their movements fluid and quick, their minds sharp. They were completely obedient and selfless, almost to the point where it wouldn't be hard to argue they were rid of self altogether.

They were like a dark army. All those who had been infected by Elise's light were now better than they had been before. It was both terrifying and wonderful to see. Unsure of their purpose yet, Jesse had them all contained at the

Genesis Compound. They were being monitored constantly, as his staff strove to better understand what they had.

An urge Jesse had a hard time ignoring tempted him to inject all the CityWatch guards. It would make them superwarriors, give them an upper hand against any opposing enemy, but what might it mean to give so many over to the darkness? How much could they take before they found themselves serving a power beyond the Authority City? How long could Jesse control it? He feared it would overtake them all if he let it.

An image of the Scientist entered Jesse's mind. His old, decaying face, that smug expression he wore when he knew he was right, the click of his tongue that smacked against his yellowing teeth as he instructed Jesse on what he'd done wrong. He thought of him lying a couple of rooms over, still dead to the world. Jesse felt relief that the man was controlled for the moment. If he were here, he would insist they take the darkness further than Jesse was ready to, and he would accuse Jesse of being small-minded and weak when he argued they shouldn't. Not to mention that he would make certain Elise was dead. And Jesse couldn't have that.

He was pleased that the plan to capture the Seers had gone so smoothly. Franklin had reacted exactly as Jesse had predicted. Another soldier had spotted Franklin some days ago and followed him to the location where the Seers were staying. Jesse had known the problem was getting in and out without setting Elise off and losing more good men.

She would need to be restrained and her abilities neutralized somehow, so the plan with Franklin had started to take root in Jesse's mind. Franklin had family in the city, unlike Sam, and Jesse knew that with his newly acquired awareness, Franklin would care very much about what happened to them.

The rest had fallen together quickly. Getting Franklin alone, threatening those he loved, getting him to agree, and setting all the pieces in place. The real question was what to do now. No, he thought, the question wasn't *what* to do now but rather *whether* he could. He knew the solution. He was a smart man; it was plain—simple even. Destroy the problem at its root. Eliminate the virus before it had the chance to spread any further.

Jesse shook his head, his stomach nauseated, the way it always was when his mind started to process what was next. He cursed himself for feeling so conflicted. He was leading this city, charged with doing what was best for the people above all else, and yet he continued to let his own personal desires cloud his judgment. He knew it, he wasn't blind to it, but he couldn't bring himself to step off the ledge and jump into the abyss.

That's what it was. A bottomless abyss that he knew would swallow him whole if he leaped from the edge. He would be doing the city a service by eliminating Elise and the other Seers, cutting off the monster's head, but the gnawing reality of what it would do to his mind kept stopping him. Could he kill the only person he had ever loved?

Could he succumb to the darkness that it would take to do that?

He could feel its pull within him even now. The familiar slithering fingers that worked their way into his chest and tugged. With each passing day, it felt closer, as if it were starting to make his heart its home. He used to hate the way it felt, hate the way it whispered to him, but now he found himself looking for it, seeking comfort in it.

And it was always there pointing the way, telling him that the road was easy if only he was brave enough to step into the power and walk toward greatness. Jesse was struggling to see any other path than the one it presented to him. He wanted another way, longed to save the young girl who had so much of his heart, but what if the darkness was right and this was the only way?

Two loud bangs sounded on the closed dining hall doors, and Jesse's shoulders tensed. Two guards, standing on either side of the doors, moved to open them. As they swung inward, two more guards led in the prisoner, her hands bound together in front, her face turned forward and her eyes aimed directly at Jesse. His throat tightened as their eyes met, and he noticed a difference in her immediately. This was no longer the small, timid girl who had been a prisoner; rather, this was someone who was sure of her power and filled with peace.

The darkness in his chest thrashed, and Jesse knew the next hour would determine everything. It was time to see if he could really save her or if she was too far gone.

/ / /

Elise awoke from the field in a small stone cell. Light shone through the single barred window; the rustle of city activity softly drifted in on the wind. Her doubt and shame were there to greet her, but the perfect light that had electrified the golden, grassy plain was there too to help her remember.

You are the light of the world.
Perfect and called blameless.
What should you fear?

Like a steady, familiar tune, her Father's words of love brushed across her consciousness and drowned out all her uncertainties. She kept her mind focused on Arianna's soft smile and Aaron's tender laugh. She meditated on her truth, she practiced remembering, and she waited.

At one point, she moved to the front of her cell to survey what was around her and saw only more cells, all empty. She was being held away from the others, which sent more ripples of fear through her. Fears that were easily calmed by returning to the truth that they were all the same as her, also made from light and filled with light. She shook her head and smiled. It was hard not to judge herself for still being afraid and worried. But she walked the path Arianna had shown her, felt the emotion ballooning in her gut and then let it go, standing firm in what she was starting to believe beyond a shadow of a doubt: that life truly was a cycle of remembering and forgetting, a constant returning to your true identity; and that all moments—the good and the bad—were just milestones on the road back to truth. The thought gave her strong, unwavering peace.

At some point, as the sun began to fade, several CityWatch guards came for her. Again she was given the opportunity to practice returning to truth as the sight of them opened up a fresh blend of worry and fear. But it wasn't as loud or violent as it should have been. The peace of truth covered it quickly, and she found herself watching the guards' faces as they opened her cell door.

She recognized their hesitation, the alarm working behind their eyes. They glanced back and forth between themselves until one of them eventually stepped into the cell. *They are afraid of me*, Elise realized. Afraid of the power that buzzed under her skin. She felt it even now as she stood in the tiny cell, stronger than ever before. She could use it against them, free herself, free the others.

Confidence filled her chest; she should awaken them. But even as the thought crossed her mind, she felt the light still. It settled into a quiet hum instead of the usual raging storm. Elise noticed the guard was holding a syringe, which was clearly meant for her. More sedation so she couldn't access her power. Another round of fear rose like a wave. They were trying to make her weak. She wouldn't let them. She called forth the light in her system and waited for it to move with vengeance in her bones.

But it stayed peaceful, and Arianna's words echoed through her mind.

Turn your eyes to the light and remember that it is greater than anything you will ever face.

Just follow the light, and you will never face anything that you can't overcome.

The light is yours, and you are the light's. So what can stand against you?

Elise felt the pull of the light to see the soldiers differently than she had before. *All who come from the light are in the light and are light.* These men were not her enemy. They were the same as her: children of the Father. A truth she had known but never understood until she saw them with restored vision.

Surrender.

Always follow the light, Arianna had said, and right now the light was still, peaceful. So she would be too. Elise released her need to defend herself against these men and trusted that the light's guidance would not fail her. In that moment, she fell into a place of surrender. Strength and certainty filled her like hot air, warming her to the insides of her bones and pulling her close. Her worry fell away, her anxiety capsized, and all that remained was security.

She glanced at the closest soldier as he moved toward her and extended her arm. He stopped cold, concern filling his face.

"Don't worry," Elise said. "I won't fight you."

Hesitant at first, the guard looked back to his partner and then stepped forward and injected Elise. The toxins rushed into her bloodstream quickly, making the entry point tingle and burn.

"This will only make you more compliant," the guard said. "President Cropper has asked for you to join him for dinner."

Within moments, Elise could feel the numbing serum start to take effect. *More compliant,* she thought. Yes, it was difficult to sense the full power of the light through the fog taking over her mind, but she knew it was there, under the surface, still holding her close. She would rest in that truth no matter what.

It took the soldiers only a couple of minutes to escort her from the prison section of the Capitol Building up onto the main level that she knew so well. Had it really been only a matter of days since she had lived here within these walls, her eyes blind to who she really was?

Her thoughts faded in and out as the drug continued to spread through her. The touch of her power came and went as well, the numbing sensation working strongly against her. The guards came to a stop outside the Capitol dining room. Elise had eaten inside with Jesse on numerous occasions, always in awe of her surroundings and searching their conversations for clues as to who she was, why she was different. She imagined their conversation tonight would be very different from any they'd had previously.

The guards opened the door and escorted her in, across the shiny marble floor and to the far end of the table, where Jesse stood as she approached. Their eyes connected and two things happened to her all at once. First, she felt her pride rise up in anger. This was the man who had taken her from her family and lied to her about their existence, the one who had locked her away and treated her like a prisoner. Now he stood before her, a cold expression on his face, surely with the intention of bringing an end to all the good she was doing, just so that he could have his false illusion of peace and security.

The second thing that happened to her was that her heart broke. Jesse's face was pale and sunken; dark circles crowded his eyes, draining the vibrant color they usually held. He looked as though he hadn't slept in weeks. The once-strong man that she had sought as her only ally now appeared weak and small. Weariness lined his expression; he was driving himself mad because he was losing control.

The second reaction began to outweigh the first as the Father's words played again in her mind. Wasn't there still light in Jesse just as there was in her? She recognized the desperation in him that she knew so well for herself. Underneath the poise he was barely maintaining, he was longing for clarity and direction. And she had it in her to give. Suddenly, being taken by the CityWatch, being thrown in a cell, being confronted by all the potentially harmful outcomes for her and the Seers made sense. Maybe she was here for more than just the end. Maybe she was here for him.

Even though the numbing was strong, the power of the light inside her chest was stronger. She felt it expand as she switched her perspective toward the man she'd once looked to for comfort and saw him as something much more.

The guards waited for Jesse's cue and then placed Elise in the chair to his right as he took his seat at the table. They cut the wire that bound her hands and gave her another injection that stung with intensity. She scrunched her face in pain and rubbed the place where she'd been pricked.

"Sorry; I know that one can be a real pill to take. I figured we should be able to speak plainly, so I wanted to make sure you were fully functional," Jesse said.

Elise felt the fog from the first injection start to lift and she understood. Jesse was a smart man; he knew that Elise was a danger to those who had been injected with Genesis. But Jesse was not one of those people, so the light would not affect him the way it did the others. She heard the rest of the room shift uncomfortably and she quickly took in her surroundings. Two guards in each corner and two at the door. Ten in all, each one looking at her nervously.

"I am trying to show goodwill toward you, having you for dinner, letting your mind be clear. It would be nice to reassure my men that they are safe from you," Jesse said, raising his eyebrows at her.

Elise nodded in agreement. "Of course," she responded. She wasn't here for them.

"Should we eat then?" As the words left Jesse's mouth, kitchen staff entered the room through a nearby door to help serve the feast before them. They tried hard not to look nervous, but clearly Elise had worked up quite the reputation for herself.

"I assume my kitchen staff is safe as well?" Jesse asked, leaning back in his chair.

"You really have nothing to worry about," Elise replied. She tried to share a smile with the server closest to her but was ignored as he quickly got to work.

"There wouldn't be any need for all these precautions if I didn't have anything to worry about," Jesse said.

"What are you so afraid of?" Elise asked.

"Come now, Elise, there is no need for games between the two of us. You know exactly why all of these measures were taken."

"I know you believe that what I am doing is harming the city."

"No, that is not something I believe; that is something I know."

"And how do you know?"

"Again with the wordplay."

"No, I am asking you honestly. How are you so certain that what we are doing is bringing harm and not good?"

"Because with it comes the unraveling of what we've spent years to build."

"Sometimes unraveling is good."

"Not when it destroys peace and harmony."

"A false, forced sense of peace. A peace that is controlled by chemicals and manufactured in a laboratory. That isn't real peace. That's simply control."

"Control that has saved this broken world from its own destruction," Jesse said, grabbing his glass of red wine.

Elise sighed softly. The lies falling from Jesse's mouth sounded just like the Scientist's. She could see the evidence of the old man's work in Jesse now. He was brainwashed like the rest, but not by a serum. His was a blindness by choice, his path one of willful resistance. But Elise knew that the light was in all; it was only a matter of calling it forth.

"Destruction you are trying to unleash," Jesse continued.

"I would never do anything to harm the people in this city. This place is my home, and they are my family," Elise said.

"Then stop. Can't you see the negative effects you are having on people's minds?"

"What you and I see is very different."

Jesse paused and took a swig from his glass. "Tell me what you see."

Elise considered her words carefully. "I see a forgotten truth, a lost sense of identity. I see the unity that binds us all being exposed. I see people returning to who they are supposed to be. I see light coming forth from everyone around me, and though that may be having negative effects on their compliance, it is opening up their hearts. And for the first time, many of the people I see are experiencing true peace."

"They are also experiencing pain, guilt, and shame. Restoring their memories brings back their burdens and sets them on a path of self-destruction. People are inherently selfish and spiteful. They may be filled with light now, but that will fade, and then they will experience suffering."

"That may be, but that too is okay. Choice gives people the opportunity to lovingly lead themselves to the truth, whether that be through triumph or failure. And yes, the mind can at times be selfish, but the soul, the true nature of a person, seeks truth. Filling them with light reminds them of that true nature."

Jesse ground his back molars and gave Elise an annoyed grin. "You sound like Aaron."

Elise drew back slightly in surprise. "You know Aaron?"

"I knew him, once, a long time ago."

Elise searched the pondering expression working across Jesse's face. "You've encountered the light, haven't you?"

Jesse didn't look up at her, but something flashed in acknowledgment behind his eyes.

"I can see it in your face," Elise said. "You know the power it holds."

"What I know is that history tends to repeat itself. There isn't a force on earth that can stop people from destroying each other and themselves."

Elise shook her head. "You're wrong. I can show you."

Jesse raised his eyes from his plate, and Elise could see the curiosity turning inside his mind. She reached her hand out and placed it gently on his arm. "Let me show you the light."

27

Jesse felt the darkness rise up in defense at Elise's words. Yet his heart skipped a beat, and he sensed a familiar strand of curiosity rippling through him. He'd felt it years before, when he'd been with the Seer camp; he'd felt it again many times since while having conversations with Elise over the years; he'd even felt it recently as reports of what Elise was doing had started to come in. A question formed just long enough to prick at his mind before vanishing away.

What if they were right?

Elise's eyes shimmered with confidence, her touch soft and comforting, causing the source of evil rummaging in his chest to squirm. He'd noticed the way it had quieted the moment she'd entered, the same reaction he'd often had around her as she'd grown. But her power, the light, was stronger within her now. It was undeniable. Jesse had hoped to find cracks in her beliefs, had hoped to find common ground and convince her to come back to his side.

Always trying to save her. Even when she can't be saved.

"I won't let you destroy the minds of my people," Jesse said.

"It doesn't destroy their minds; it opens them," Elise replied.

"How does it work?" He felt the darkness trying to pull him back, but his curiosity was strong.

"The light exists inside everyone already. I just search for it and bring it out."

"How can you know that?"

"I can see it. The light is in everything—the air, the earth, every soul. I can feel it and sense it. Always. Even in you," Elise said.

Her words tugged at something beyond his rational thought and pierced through the flutters of doubt that had taken up residence in his stomach. They sent uneasy tension cascading down his back, and he straightened up further in his chair. "And what if I don't believe?"

"Your disbelief doesn't make the light nonexistent; it only makes you unable to see it." Elise leaned a bit closer, her smile full of wonder, her eyes dancing on waves of joy. "But I can help you see, if you want."

The tug of war started low in Jesse's gut and rose up through his chest. His interest and wonder fought to outweigh his logic and sense. He was the leader of this city, a grown man who didn't have time for her delusions of salvation. Yet he'd seen the evidence of what she was saying, the physical and mental changes in those who had been affected by her gift. And there was something in him that desperately wanted to know the truth that she offered.

Part of him wanted her to be right; part of him wanted her to be wrong. Most of him just wanted to make her his. He couldn't deny the urge to reach out and touch her. Even if she was blatantly acting out against him, even if she was rebuking everything he stood for, sitting here with her now made his yearning for her stronger than ever.

Don't be swayed by her manipulation. But his curiosity was just too great.

"Show me, then, but not on one of my men," Jesse said. "Do it to me."

Elise gave him a curious look, taken aback.

"You said all have the light, even me," he said.

"Yes," she said, eyes shining.

"Then show me."

/ / /

Elise let the shock of Jesse's request fade. *Show him. Bring out his light.* She couldn't fight off the nervous tingles moving through her fingers. She'd only ever pulled light from people who had been given Genesis. Those who had no choice but to forget who they really were. Jesse had turned a blind eye to the truth purposefully. That was something completely different.

Doubts started to land inside her mind like stones. What if she couldn't? What if she wasn't strong enough?

What if she failed and lost the one chance she had to show him the power of truth? Fear filled her chest, and she saw a smile pull at the corner of Jesse's mouth. He recognized her fear, and embarrassment crept up her neck.

Elise closed her eyes and pushed her doubts aside, meditating on the truth that was so easy to forget. Energy rushed through her and eased her uneasiness away. A soft breeze drifted across her face and shoulders, bringing the perfect love that resided inside her to life.

She opened her eyes and saw the room clearly. Different colors bounced around, swirling with the light that filled the room and everything in it. What could stand against her? What did she have to fear?

A smile filled her face, and this time it was in Jesse's expression that she saw fear. The power, given to her by the light, swelled within her. She focused on it, calling it up and sending it forth. She felt it move and grow under her skin, wrapping itself around her bones and overtaking her wholly. Within moments, the light was seeping from her, reaching out toward the light of others, and she focused it toward Jesse.

It crawled out from her fingers and stretched toward him. Soft at first, like a whisper, it called to the truth that lay dormant inside him. If she could only touch it, connect with it. A strand of light moved into his chest and she saw his body react. He shifted uncomfortably, trying to move away from her, but the back of his chair kept him steady. She reached further, stepping deeper into his mind. As with all the others, she connected to his memories. Though they were not forgotten, they were still tied to the false truth about who he believed he was.

The room faded slightly, as if caught behind a fogged glass panel. Elise let Jesse's memories fill the space around her head. A small boy caught up in a violent outburst from a man stumbling around, thrashing out his anger on the child at his feet. A teenage boy being consoled by the man as he whispered lies to the boy about the world. The same boy being introduced to a younger version of the man Elise knew as the Scientist, the two of them discussing the change that the world was destined for. Back to the drunk man ridiculing the young boy, then tossing a bottle of liquor across the room at his head. The small child hiding up in his room, his door closed and blocked with a dresser as the vicious man pounded away on the outside.

Moment after moment filled her mind, breaking her heart as she dug ever deeper into Jesse's soul. Until it ended. A dark cloud thwarted her attempt to push deeper. It crushed the light that had risen up and turned all the warmth in the room to cold. Dark and heavy, like tar, it rolled across Jesse's memories, kicking Elise out and sealing them off. It felt like hate, and she could taste the bitterness of it in her mouth. It pushed back angrily against Elise's advances and rattled her confidence. She'd never encountered anything like it.

She sank into the truth more deeply, searching for more

light to combat the dark waves flowing from Jesse. The further she went, the harder the power was to contain, and she felt herself losing her grip. With a slip, it sprang from all of her cells. Across the marble floor and to the guards at their posts. It connected with their souls and without being able to stop it, the light began to dig up their pasts. Memories flashed in hurried images across her mind, tumbling over one another, dancing across the open air around her head.

Her mind exploded with pain, but she pushed forward, Jesse's eyes wide with fear, his face fixed in terror. The guards cried out and dropped to their knees around the room. One after the other, each one encountering the power that now encased the dining hall completely. She tried to pull it back, to honor her promise that she'd keep the guards out of it, but the power was too strong; it rippled from her uncontrollably.

"Stop," she heard Jesse say. He had scooted his chair back from the table and was clenching the armrests with force, making his knuckles white. Elise could see pain working through his shoulders, could feel his intensity and terror as he tried to release himself from her grasp. "Stop!"

But she couldn't. The light was moving on its own, battling the darkness rising up from Jesse, calling for the truth inside the guards, dancing through the air, ripping at Elise's mind and tearing through her muscles.

"Stop this now! I've seen enough," Jesse yelled, shaking Elise. "I've seen enough!"

Something stung at the side of her arm, and she cried out, losing her focus on the light. She looked down at her arm and saw that a needle attached to a large syringe was stuck deep in her skin. Only a small amount of the dark-red substance remained, and Jesse pushed the end of the syringe and forced the rest into her bloodstream.

She glanced up at Jesse, confused, and his face was shadowed in both regret and fear. Elise only held her confusion for a moment, because suddenly the blood in her veins felt as if it were on fire. She stepped back from Jesse as the feeling began to spread to every inch of her body. It scratched and burned, eliminating the light as it scorched through muscles and tissue. A deep desperation and fear started to form in her chest. She could feel the substance smothering her power with cruelty and vengeance. She wanted it out. What had he done to her?

Elise took another step back, her legs unsteady, as the attacking essence forged its way down her quads and into her calves. She could feel it turning her into something else. Darkness—the same darkness she had been battling moments before—began to bubble up into her chest. It covered the light, hid her power, erased the words of strength she clung to. It was consuming her and choking out who she knew she was.

Elise started to feel panicked. She didn't want to succumb to the darkness, but she could feel it taking her deeper into its clutches with each breath. She rubbed the skin on the top of her arms viciously. She felt like the darkness was moving through her cells and turning even her flesh into something else. Hot tears sprang to her eyes as her dread grew.

She tried searching through the dark clouds forming in her chest for the Father's voice, the light, her power, anything that would bring her back, but all she felt was the rapidly building presence of whatever Jesse had injected into her. It was making its way toward her mind, climbing up through her neck and restricting her breathing.

Elise gulped for air and felt tears slowly sliding down her cheeks. She clenched her eyes shut as images of her own past played like painful memories through her brain. Sitting alone in her room for hours, wondering who she was; being carted out of sight and handled with coldness; crying herself to sleep as loneliness surrounded her; being abandoned by Jesse, being tortured by the Scientist, being held prisoner, being lied to. Being nothing. Being worthless. Being powerless.

Then, smaller than a whisper, something drifted through the growing darkness and touched her mind. Warmth, a feeling of closeness, a loving reminder.

Light of the world.

The thought broke through for only a moment before being covered in darkness once more, but it was enough to ignite a flame. Elise pushed past her self-hatred, past the loneliness that had convinced her she was powerless, past the shame she carried for being broken, past the lies she had believed about her own worth, and let it all go. The small flame exploded into a massive fire of light and power that consumed the darkness eating away at her true nature. It trampled over every speck of disbelief and reclaimed her soul to truth.

Elise opened her eyes and saw the room once again captured in light, Jesse's face pale and afraid, the darkness that had just been inside her surrounding him like a shield. He inched away from her as she approached, and the darkness lashed out in anger.

"Arrest her," Jesse cried, but nobody responded. The guards were on their knees, their minds changed, their eyes opened. Elise let the light fill her heart and then she pulled it back into herself, letting the room fall into a normal rhythm. She wasn't here to fight with Jesse. The guards were glancing between Jesse and Elise, some with tears in their eyes, others only confusion, but none of them responded to Jesse's command. He glared around the room, breathing in short bursts, and then strode angrily to the double doors.

He pounded on them a couple times, and as they opened, several more guards entered the room, all with the Genesis Serum still swirling through their veins. He pointed toward Elise, and the guards headed for her.

They reached her quickly, recuffed her forcefully, and yanked her forward. Jesse stood across the room, his hands trembling, his back to her. She wanted to see his face, to see if there was any hope in his expression, to see if the light was even now reaching for his truth, but he wouldn't look at her. She was escorted from the room, back down to the cells on the basement floor, and locked away. Left alone with only her thoughts. The darkness inside Jesse was greater than she'd thought. Worse, he had tried to kill the light inside her.

Elise slid down against one of the stone walls to the floor and pulled her aching knees close. Her brain throbbed and her body burned. Her shoulders trembled and her chest heaved as if she couldn't get her breathing to stabilize. Her vision spun and she thought for a moment her world might go black.

Black like the night sky outside, black like the shroud covering Jesse's heart. Tears moistened her face and she shook her head. She'd wanted to show Jesse the light. She'd wanted to save him, to bring him back to the truth, but all she'd done was enrage the evil controlling him.

A terrible thought crossed her mind like a whisper that she couldn't silence. What if Jesse couldn't be saved after all?

/ / /

Jesse stormed into his office and slammed the door behind him. Anger pulsed in his temples, the darkness filling every inch of his frame. His breath was short, falling from his mouth in heated bursts, thundering at the same pace as his heart. He turned to the desk sitting to his right and with a tremendous cry, ran his arms across the top, sending all of its contents crashing to the ground.

He shivered in his own fury and tried to control himself. Running his hands forcefully up over his forehead and across the top of his head, he focused on taking steady breaths. One and then another, slowing his racing heart, calming the trembling in his fingers.

A sneaky piece of light pulled softly at his gut and he cursed out loud. It was still sitting with him, moving like wisps of smoke in his chest. He couldn't get rid of it, couldn't stop it from threatening to dissolve all the control he had managed to acquire over his lifetime. Memories of his father and childhood rolled through his brain once more. She'd poisoned him with the past. A past he'd worked hard to block out. Yet in a single moment, she'd dug up his inadequacies and aired them. Using that light, she'd attacked him; she'd attacked his men; she'd destroyed their minds and played with their psychological welfare.

And she had somehow withstood the darkness. There had been a moment when Jesse had started to believe that the dark blood Roth had given him was actually going to save Elise from herself. He'd watched it work its way through her body, across her face; he'd started to see rescue. But then she had crushed it. With light.

The darkness hissed inside his mind. *It's a trick. Don't be so easily deceived.*

Again the warmth of the light tugged at his heart, and he felt his breath catch in his throat. He could sense himself wanting to give in and let it flow through his veins, but his shoulders were tensed in fear. What would it uncover? What would it change?

Everything, the darkness whispered, soft and sweet in his ear. *It would change everything.*

Jesse didn't want things to change. He wanted them to go back to the way they were before. When he and Elise had been one another's comfort. He wanted his rule of the city to continue, he wanted to ensure the peace was kept, he wanted Elise to be his. He wanted it more than he could stand. But he knew now he could never have her. She was too far gone.

She will destroy everything you have created. That light will take away your power.

Jesse rubbed his temples and sank into the chair behind his desk. His mind was clouded with confusion. He'd known Elise was powerful, but it was far more impressive to see with his own eyes the way she had brought his guards to their knees. To feel that force moving through his own body. To taste the leftovers still on his tongue. Yet still the darkness buzzed inside his mind, something he knew and felt comfortable with. But that power . . .

That power will seek to destroy you. That power will take away all of yours.

Elise's words drifted through his cracked psyche. *"The light exists inside everyone already."*

It's only there to taunt you. To control you.

"It doesn't destroy their minds; it opens them."

It only opens the past, forcing you to surrender to your pain.

"I can see it. . . . Even in you."

Lies used only to convert you.

Jesse was breathing more steadily now, his chest rising and falling in rhythm with his heart. The twinge of light was fading; the darkness filled the gaps as it left. The familiar sense of control reentered and calmed his mind. He looked at the ground, where the contents of his desk were now scattered about. He hardly ever lost his temper in such a way. He didn't like the way it made him feel, and her power had caused it. She was more dangerous than he'd imagined.

She needs to be destroyed.

Jesse leaned forward, elbows on both knees, and hung his head. He knew eliminating her was the best solution for the city. He knew, as its leader, that he was called to do what was best for its people. But he couldn't. She occupied a special place in his heart and he couldn't turn away from that. He loved her too much. If Jesse were a stronger man, maybe he'd be able to take care of her without suffering the consequences. But he wasn't. He knew it would destroy him. But if he let her live and exist in the city, then she would destroy them all.

You have no other choice.

He couldn't do it. Jesse tried to silence the hissing in his mind, but it only grew.

Don't be weak. Do what you were called to. Rule!

There had to be another way.

You have no other choice.

He could send her away. He could send all the Seers away and still save what was left of what he'd built. Without her lurking around every corner, tearing down what he was trying to construct.

Don't be a fool.

"I cannot do what you ask," Jesse said out loud.

Of course you can. You have to.

"I won't."

Then she will destroy you.

"No, I will send them away. I will rid the city of all of them."

Weak, stupid little man.

"Enough!" Jesse slammed his hand on the empty desktop and pain vibrated up his arm. The voice dissolved into nothing, the darkness receded back deep inside his chest, and the room fell into an eerie silence.

The stillness made him feel utterly alone. No more Elise, no more light, no more darkness. Only he remained to suffer alone with one resounding question pumping through all the pathways in his brain: to kill or not to kill Elise.

28

Elise sat awake as the hours of the night ticked by. She couldn't get her mind to shut off or slow down. It ran on full steam into the early morning and through the sunrise. Her thoughts filled with Aaron, with Arianna, with Jesse. All buzzing around her brain, multiplying, and blending into one another.

Her emotions played a similar game: chasing each other, colliding, stretching so that they were filling every inch of her. She tried to feel them all, wading through them as she confronted one at a time, saw each one for what it was, and then practiced letting it go. Sometimes it happened easily; other times it seemed impossible. She closed her eyes, tucked her mind away, and dropped into her spirit.

She found herself back in the golden field, the wind sweetly sweeping across the valley, the perfect sun warming her chill. And he was there—Aaron, standing before her, as if he'd been waiting for her to come. The moment she saw him, she nearly burst into tears, for she longed to let go of the pain that came with forgetting and wrap herself up in this field forever while the rest of the world drifted away.

"I may have ruined it all," Elise said.

Aaron chuckled softly and shook his head. "You couldn't ruin anything."

"But he may never believe."

"Do you not trust your Father?"

"Of course I do—with all my heart."

"Did he not tell you that all came from the light?"

"Yes, but Jesse doesn't see that."

"Then he simply needs a change of perspective."

"And what if I can't show him?"

"You already have," Aaron said.

Elise shook her head. The weight of seeing someone she cared for so blinded was pulling down on her confidence. "How can you be so sure?"

"Because I believe the power of the light is bigger than anything else in existence. There is nothing it can't overcome. You experienced it for yourself. Do you think Jesse is too much for the light to handle?"

Again Elise shook her head.

"Then don't worry. Find joy in the fact that Jesse still has the light waiting for him. He still gets to discover his true identity in his Father."

"But what if he doesn't?" Elise felt tears roll down her cheeks and she sucked back an emotional breath. Even here in this perfect place, she remembered the way the darkness had crawled through her bones.

Aaron crossed the grass to where she was and gently brushed the tears from her face. "Let go of your fear. He already has the light inside him. He will see it. They will all see it. That is the journey. Remembering that you belong to the light is all there is."

Elise opened her eyes and was back in her cell, tears still fresh on her cheeks. A soft wind blew into the room through the open barred window and wrapped itself around her shoulders. She inhaled deeply and surrendered to it.

"That is the journey. Remembering that you belong to the light."

Aaron's words floated with the breeze, calming her, stilling her fear, washing it away. She trusted the light. She trusted her Father. So she let go and sat in the truth. She didn't even notice Jesse and the two guards until they were standing right outside her cell.

Jesse looked at her for a long moment, and neither of them said a word. It was clear he hadn't slept either; his eyes were bloodshot, his face gray from exhaustion. But she could feel him. Both the light and the darkness that battled in his spirit. His terror and confusion. His loneliness and pride. He was waging war against his true identity, a power too strong to overcome, and it was tearing him apart.

She held his gaze, and eventually he dropped his eyes to the floor. "This has to end," he said.

End, Elise thought. She could only imagine what he meant by *end*.

"You have caused too much destruction already. This can't continue."

Elise wasn't sure how to respond.

"Renounce the light," Jesse said softly.

Elise's breath caught in her throat.

Jesse lifted his eyes to meet hers, and she saw swirls of darkness moving behind them. "Renounce the light, and you can go free from here and return to the Capitol Building."

Renounce her truth? She couldn't do that. "And if I don't?" she asked.

Jesse's jaw tensed enough that she could see the muscles in his mouth working. "Then you have to leave."

"Leave?"

"Leave the city, permanently, never to return," Jesse said.

Elise could sense a new form of pain collecting in his chest as he spoke, and something suddenly became so clear to Elise that she couldn't believe she had never realized it before. He loved her. All these years, she had been stored away inside this large brick building, never fully understanding how much this man cared for her. She wondered what he'd done to protect her. Wondered how far he'd gone to keep her from the Scientist. She reflected on all of their encounters—the lessons, the conversations, the dinners. Those had been his way of showing his love for her. He'd never said it, but it was clearly marked on his face now. He loved her.

Leave the city, she thought. How many times had she wished for exactly that? Yet Elise was surprised by the dread filling her heart. Leave the city and go where? This place was all she'd ever known. She had no idea what was out there. She knew Trylin City waited for her, but she'd been so caught up in the present that she hadn't really thought about what would happen when she was finished here.

Would she ever see Jesse again if she left? Again Elise was surprised by the sorrow she felt after all this man had done to her. But what could he ever really have done to her? She stood with the Father, clothed in light, surrounded by truth. Peace eased itself around her, and she knew beyond a shadow of a doubt that she forgave him. She held nothing against him now. Instead, she saw him as he truly was, the same as her. He just didn't know it yet.

Like the flip of a light switch, she realized that her job had never been to save him. It had only ever been to help him remember that the Father's light was already inside him.

"I can't renounce the light. It is in me fully," Elise said. "As it is in you."

Jesse closed his eyes. "Things could be like they were before," he said. "Better. I can give you anything you want. You could rule this city with me."

Elise shook her head. "No. I know who I am now, and

there may come some moments when I forget, but I will never be separated from the light. Like I said, it's in me fully."

"Then you must go, so that my city can be rid of your madness."

"And what of the others?"

Jesse held her glance, pleading with his eyes, and it pained her. Again he dropped his eyes from hers. "The other Seers will leave with you, and none of you will ever set foot inside this city again."

Elise stood and took several steps toward Jesse. He backed away from the bars of her cell, and she stopped. Once again she watched him battle his own emotions, but this time she didn't worry or fear. The Father was bigger than all battles and wars; His truth was able and sure.

She wanted to say something that would convince Jesse of the truth, but words were lost to them both. She could see the darkness tugging down on his shoulders and felt the light pulling up at hers. Another long period of silence passed between them before Jesse unlocked the cell door and opened it.

"Thank you," Elise said, and Jesse fell silent. In a final flash of desperation, he said, "It doesn't have to be this way."

"Yes it does," Elise said, "because these are the choices we are making." She took a step toward Jesse, and she sensed his spirit tense. "I just wanted to say . . ." She trailed off, trying to find the right words, searching for something grand and moving but coming up short. What really could be said at this point? Nothing he could say would sway her choice, and she could say nothing to sway his. They were truly at a stalemate, so all that was left to do was leave. "I just wanted to say thank you. I don't think I realized everything that you really did for me until now. Also, know that I hold nothing against you."

The color drained from Jesse's face, his eyes showing shock that quickly swirled into anger. Elise could sense the darkness digging its tentacles in deeper, dragging Jesse further into its depths and pouring waves of resistance upon him. Elise knew she had nothing to fear, but the evil crawling along Jesse's insides made her own flesh shudder.

He held her gaze for another long, threatening moment before pulling his eyes away and walking down the jail hallway as two guards entered to escort her out.

"Elise," Jesse said.

She glanced at him, now standing several yards away.

He barely looked at her as he spoke. "If you or any of the Seers ever return, I will kill you all."

/ / /

Jesse let the words fall from his mouth and left the prison corridor. He felt her eyes on him, and it tore at his heart. Part of him wanted to rush back to her, apologize, and beg her to stay, but the darkness slapped him back hard enough to knock that part loose. How could he still be sympathizing with her after all the destruction she had caused? How could he still want her?

How can you be letting her go?

The whispers were harsher and more violent now. Chasing him. Jesse fought to keep them quiet but lost.

This is a massive mistake.

She will be back.

She will ruin you.

Jesse shook his head and walked with long strides up the staircase toward the main Capitol hallway.

You still have time. You could still stop her.

He moved with speed as he nearly tore down the long hallway toward his chambers.

Do yourself a favor and end this before it comes back to haunt you.

Jesse clenched his teeth hard enough to give himself a headache and saw Elise's face in his mind. He would never see her again. The moment the thought passed through his mind, his rage took over, and as he crossed the threshold into his bedroom and slammed the door shut, a pained cry echoed from his throat.

They are all here. There is still time. Kill them all.

Jesse swore against the stuffy air around him and struggled to breathe through his pain. She was supposed to be his. She was supposed to choose him. Now he would always be alone. And she was to blame.

You coward.

There was a soft, vibrating chuckle that made Jesse's teeth ache as the darkness mocked him from inside.

Don't say I didn't warn you.

29 Jesse woke with a start. His eyes adjusted to his surroundings and his mind twisted with confusion. He expected to see his bedroom, large and dark from the night sky. Instead, he was sitting in a field of golden grass under a perfect blue sky dotted with fluffy clouds. Fear rattled his chest and he pushed himself quickly off the ground. How had he gotten here? Where was here?

He spun around, searching for anything distinguishable, but he was met only with more yellow fields stretching as far as he could see in all directions. A slight breeze swept up the ends of the grass in its wake and sent an uncontrollable shiver down Jesse's spine. The sun beat down on him from overhead and he squinted into its rays. Movement caught the corner of his eye, and Jesse turned to his left, directly toward the blinding beams. He lifted his hand up to shield his eyes, as he searched ahead for whatever might be coming.

There was something walking his way—a person, maybe a man? It was nearly impossible to tell through the glare of the sun, but as the person approached, something inside Jesse's gut started to quake. It was a man, a man he'd met before.

Aaron stepped through the dazzling rays and came into focus. Jesse felt his breathing quicken, coming in small huffs as his mind tried to comprehend what was happening. Aaron was standing before him, and they were alone in a field that Jesse didn't recognize. Had he been kidnapped in the middle of the night? Taken as he'd taken Elise? The thought stirred up dangerous emotions in his chest, and he tried to shake them off as Aaron spoke.

"Hello, Jesse."

Jesse searched for his ability to speak but found that nothing seemed to be working as he would have hoped. His mind was foggy, his tongue numb, his eyes blurry. Was he dreaming? That was the only plausible explanation; he must be dreaming. He cleared his throat and regained control of his voice. "This is a dream," he said matter-of-factly.

"Perhaps, but then some would argue all of life is a dream," Aaron said.

"Where am I?"

"The field—it's quite famous."

"I've never heard of it."

"That's because you are running from the truth."

Jesse's mind buzzed with the awareness of something burning deep within him. Light, bright and hot, poked through the layers of stone he'd built up around his heart.

"Get out of my head. I don't want to be here," Jesse said.

"But here we are, so that can't be entirely true."

"What is that supposed to mean?"

"Well, your heart brought you here for some reason."

"No," Jesse said, taking a step away. "I know what you are trying to do. Do you enjoy making people suffer?"

"All the suffering you face, my friend, you create yourself. Only you can choose to suffer. You can also choose to let it go."

The light was stronger now, yearning to grow and spread out through Jesse's bloodstream. But he forced it down, trying to shut it in, to control it. He wouldn't be taken without a fight. "And surrender to you, I suppose? Let you be king?"

"Not to me. This has never had anything to do with me. Surrender to the light and let it lead you to the peace you are searching for."

Peace, Jesse thought; how long had it been since he'd had peace? Had he ever known it? Did it even exist, or was this just another ruse to get Jesse to comply?

"Don't listen to that delusional hack," someone said behind Jesse.

He spun around and saw the Scientist stepping toward them, his aging face wrinkled in familiarity and his gray eyes very much alive.

"Roth," Aaron said.

"How dare you use my name as if you have the right to speak to me," the Scientist spat.

"You're dead," Jesse said. His head was spinning again, sweat collecting under his shirt and soaking through. He felt parched, as if his throat were a desert and he were dying of heatstroke.

"Don't let yourself be deceived, boy," Roth said.

"Clever of you to speak of deception," Aaron said.

Roth turned to Aaron, hate spewing from his eyes. The darkness that Jesse knew so well seemed to ooze from the Scientist's skin, through his pores, and out into the field. His eyes turned solid black, and Jesse felt a tremor run across his shoulders.

"You know nothing about me," the Scientist yelled, pointing his finger at Aaron. Then he pointed to Jesse. "And you know nothing of him."

"I know that all who come from the light are filled with light and are light," Aaron said, stepping toward the Scientist. "I know that you have tried to poison his mind with lies about his true nature. I know that you have no place where the light is, and the light comes for all, so where will you run?"

The sky opened up overhead and rain began to fall softly over them. A light drizzle draining down from the heavens. Jesse watched as dark clouds snuffed out the perfect blue and replaced it with an ominous sense of terror. Lightning cracked to his right and wind whipped violently across the grass.

"I am not threatened by your pathetic light!" Roth said, black smoke rolling off his tongue as more darkness erupted from the old man. It worked its way across the ground toward Jesse, moving up his legs and into his gut.

It filled him with a familiar comfort that he wished he didn't long for.

"You should be," Aaron said. As darkness poured from Roth, Aaron's skin began to glow in response. As the Scientist was filled with darkness, so Aaron was filled with light. He shone like a bright bulb in the middle of the darkening field.

Jesse felt himself drawn forward, almost needing to touch the man's vibrating, glowing skin, but before he could take a step, dark memories of his past began to play through his mind. His miserable father, drunk and violent; his mother dying, leaving him alone with a monster; his grandfather doing the same, failing to rescue him from the abuse of being used as a punching bag. And with each painful memory, Jesse saw something else. The darkness, its presence growing as each flashback inserted itself into Jesse's brain. Always with him, sitting with him in the dead of night, hiding with him when his father was on a bender, watching him, whispering to him.

Jesse glanced up at the Scientist, but he was no longer there. Damien Gold stood in his place instead. The same darkness floating out from his flesh, the same black circles for eyes.

"We have always been there," Damien whispered, his mouth moving but the words coming out in a whisper for Jesse's mind alone.

"Jesse, see more than what is before you," Aaron said, his voice calm and steady. Jesse turned his eyes from the darkness now dressed up in Damien's skin and looked at the teacher.

"You can be free of all of this. You just have to remember who you are," Aaron said.

"No!" Damien screamed. "Where was your precious light when we were alone? Where were you when we were dying inside?"

Jesse felt the darkness reach up into his chest and wrap its fingers around his heart. His mind swam again with painful moments that he had tried to lock away, and each time only the darkness was present. Damien was right; the light that claimed to be there for him was nowhere to be found.

"Don't trust what you see through its eyes," Aaron said, rain thundering down in massive waves now. "See with clear vision, true vision, and know that you have always been held in light."

"A light that left you to suffer alone. We were there; we will always be there," Damien said.

Jesse gripped the sides of his chest. The darkness was maneuvering freely through his body, the light burning less fiercely in opposition. Aaron's voice echoed inside his ears, while Damien's voice pricked at his brain. Rain, falling in buckets of chilled water, soaked Jesse to the bone while lightning tore across the black clouds and thunder shook the ground.

You can be free of all of this.

We have always been there for you.

You have always been held in light.
We will always be there.

Jesse felt like his head might explode, and his legs shook beneath him. A hand touched his shoulder, and it yanked him back to reality. He looked up to see Aaron standing beside him, his face inches from Jesse's.

"Let it go," Aaron said. "See the light of who you really are."

But that was just it, Jesse thought; he'd never really seen the light at all. In times of trouble, the only thing that had ever really been by his side was the darkness. It had never left him; it had fought alongside him and filled him with the fury he had needed to guard himself; it had given him the anger he had needed to hold grievances against those who had wronged him. And Aaron wanted him to let it go? For what? Peace?

Jesse yanked his shoulder away from Aaron and stepped back. What would peace bring him? It would only make him weak, and he couldn't afford to be weak.

Aaron's eyes filled with pity, and it made Jesse's stomach turn.

"Who do you think you are?" Jesse asked. "Do you think I need your light? Do you think I need you?"

"You don't," another voice said beside him. Jesse turned to face the darkness once more, and this time it was wearing the face of his father. Jesse nearly stumbled back in shock at seeing the man he'd loathed so much. Jesse thought of all the times he had begged his father to remain calm, all the times he'd apologized for things he hadn't done, all the times he'd dragged the man's unconscious body to his bed. But under his hate, Jesse felt the same yearning that he could never seem to outrun. He wanted his father to approve of him, to love him, to want him.

The man, with his stubbly face, had the same black eyes as the Scientist and Damien. His unwashed hair was parted to the left side, thinning and disheveled. His sloppy stance and drooping posture were just as Jesse remembered. The man he called father reached out his hand and patted Jesse's shoulder.

"You never needed anyone. I made you strong; I gave you enough anger to take over the world. Don't disappoint me now," his father said.

The person standing before him was a shadow of a man. Less than Jesse had ever been; he saw that now. But his father was right about one thing. He had given him something invaluable. Anger. And anger burned. As the word materialized in Jesse's mind, his father pulled a burning torch from behind his back. The single strong flame licked up the rain as it fell upon it and stayed ignited.

"Again, I urge you to see who you truly are," Aaron said, his words nearly drowned out by the thunder rolling across the sky.

Jesse kept his eyes on the fire dancing before him.

"You know who you are," his father said and extended the torch. "Burn it all."

The darkness roared inside Jesse's chest and he reached

forward, took the torch, and with a shout, brought it down toward the grass at his side.

The flames captured the wheat with ease, setting it ablaze quickly and spreading with fury. Within moments, a large circle of fire blazed around them, devouring the once-golden grass and sending billows of black smoke into the rain.

Jesse's father started to laugh beside him, a deep chuckle that grew in volume and passion as it echoed with the thunder. Jesse himself felt a trill of pleasure escape from his mouth and he glanced up toward Aaron, expecting to see the man's face in shambles. Instead, the calm that always seemed to hold his expression was steadily in place. He nodded to himself and spoke softly. "Even now, dear brother, the light is with you. Remember, all you have to do is see it." He then turned and walked into the raging flames that were destroying the entire field.

Ashes rose with the wind, laughter poured out from his father's throat, the rain crashed down around them, and Jesse watched as the fire that burned from his anger eradicated all signs of Aaron's peace. And then it was all gone.

Jesse sat up in bed, startled, throbbing pain splitting across his mind and into his shoulders. He tore the covers from his body and sat, his mind spinning, his skin wet with sweat, his lungs gasping for fresh air. He stumbled from bed, tripping over his own feet and falling to his knees. He dragged himself forward, pushed himself up with his palms onto shaking legs. With a couple of difficult steps, he reached the window and threw it open. Cold air rushed across his face and he breathed it in as if it were life itself. His whole body was shivering, his mind recapturing all the moments he'd just experienced.

We will always be there for you, the darkness whispered. *Burn it all.*

Yes, Jesse thought. The essence of the dream still following him, he strode across the room and ripped open the top drawer of his dresser. A single syringe remained, its contents dark blood.

Do it.

Without another thought, Jesse pulled the syringe out and injected himself. The darkness swirled violently as it brought Jesse to his knees, his body trembling under its power. He took short, labored breaths as the dark blood ravaged his system quickly, erasing all his pain and questions and filling him with only rage.

Kill the girl; kill the light.

Yes. His heart rammed against the inside of his rib cage, and with that one final thought, he surrendered to the darkness.

Power unlike anything Jesse had ever known surged around and through him as the darkness filled every pore and silenced the nagging light once and for all. He took a deep breath and pushed himself up from his knees. He turned and stared at the mirror hanging over his dresser. There he saw it. His eyes like black marbles, brimming with power—a power that was now completely his, a power he should have succumbed to long ago. It yanked at him and he felt himself moving toward his bedroom door and then out into the hall.

The night was as dark as his soul, his mind focused and following the whispers of what had infused itself into his heart. Long strides carried him forward, into another bedroom, where the beeping of medical machines and the staleness of age hung in the air. Jesse's arm opened the top drawer of the tall dresser in the room and found what the darkness was asking for. A long, thin blade. His hand wrapped around its hilt and pulled it forth.

He turned then to the old man lying motionless, as he had for weeks, in the bed in the center of the room. It was dark, only the small green lights of the machine displays casting any light in the room, but Jesse didn't need to see. He finally already did. As the voice of his new master called him toward the bed and made its demands softly in Jesse's ears, Jesse obeyed.

He moved to the side of the bed, took a long final glance at the man who had given him so much and taken so much from him. He had been a faithful follower of the dark essence now abiding in Jesse, but his usefulness had come to an end.

With a steady hand, Jesse reached down, grasped Roth's skull for support, and slid the blade cleanly across the man's throat. In the stillness of night, Jesse could hear the way the skin sliced open and could feel the warm liquid that pumped forth from the wound.

The beeping machines buzzed frantically for several long moments before fading out completely.

And then it was just Jesse, his hand still bracing the head of a dead man, the darkness cooing words of affirmation and pride. Jesse stepped back and let the knife fall to the marble floor with a clink. The darkness possessed his focus and yanked it toward something else. Images of Elise floated behind his eyes, and all he had felt before evaporated. Only one thing remained. He would kill the girl. He would burn them all.

/ / /

Elise sat in the passenger seat as Willis drove them away from the Authority City. Two vans, carrying the eight of them to a destination no one was sure even existed anymore. Heading for Trylin had been the obvious choice, though they hadn't received any communication from there since learning that the city was under siege. Their families and homes could be destroyed, but they had to hope, and they had nowhere else to go.

After the two guards had escorted Elise from her prison cell, they had led her to a van where the other Seers were waiting. There had been such relief to be reunited, but the loss of Jesse lingered with her even through the joy. Troubling thoughts of leaving the only home she'd ever known, even if that home had been a prison, seemed to follow her. Willis had sensed it immediately and had held her hand but said nothing.

She had been overjoyed to have him back by her side. She'd felt the calling of light and let the sadness fade. What she had known inside those walls was nothing compared to what she knew now. She was whole, and she was free. She was also in love. With a boy she'd met in a dream. What a story they'd have to tell someday.

They had been given two vans on Jesse's orders, and they had rested only an hour before leaving. Everyone was anxious to get home, and Elise couldn't blame them. She found herself wondering about what life would be like now. Elise glanced at the side van mirror and watched as the Authority City began to fade behind them.

As he had done several times since they'd been reunited, Willis reached out and grabbed her hand. "You okay?" he asked.

"Yes," she said, "I really am."

He glanced at her and winked, and all of her concerns melted away. Whatever came next wouldn't stand a chance against who they were now.

"I was thinking that maybe once we sorted out where we are all going to live, that you might be interested in joining me for dinner," Willis said.

"Dinner?" Elise asked, a slight tease in her voice.

"Yeah—food, candlelight, you, me . . . you know, dinner."

His boyish grin could quite possibly heal the world, Elise thought. She giggled and opened her mouth to respond but never got the chance. Several earsplitting reports ricocheted across the sky, one right after the other, followed by the sound of crunching tin and squealing tires. Willis gasped and slammed on his brakes as the van in front of them swerved violently and disappeared into a dark cloud of smoke. More shots smacked the sky, connecting with more metal, and Elise flew forward in her seat.

"Hold on!" Willis yelled as the front of their vehicle rammed into something ahead of them, shattering their windshield.

Shards of broken glass rained down over Elise's body, and her head was thrown back brutally against her headrest. It sent burning spasms into her skull. She screamed and raised her hands to protect her face and felt pain sting her bare arms. The van shifted against the force of the blow and then came to a stop.

"Elise!" Willis yelled.

Her ears were ringing and she could hear the screams of others. She uncovered her face and turned to nod at Willis. He kicked open his twisted door, and Elise shakily pulled at the buckle strapped low across her waist. Her door ripped open and Willis helped her from the van. Timmons, Kane, and Sage stumbled from the back, blood dotting Kane's shirt, Sage gripping her arm.

"Is everyone all right?" Willis asked, and they nodded.

Elise walked around the front of the van and searched for the other vehicle. Dark smoke filled the air, and through it she heard screams of terror. *Kennedy!* Elise started running, ignoring the pain she felt in her knees from being nearly crushed.

"Elise!" Willis yelled after her, but she didn't stop. She dove into the smoke.

Small pits of fire were scattered about, all of them sending black waves into the air. Elise's eyes watered as the smoke assaulted her senses. She squinted through the darkness until she saw the van several yards away. It was turned on its side, more smoke escaping from its hood. Elise pushed herself to move faster just as she saw the first tongue of flame dance up from the van.

"Kennedy," she said, then cried louder. "Kennedy!" To her left, she heard the roar of heavy machinery and turned to see an armored CityWatch vehicle approaching rapidly. Fear threatened to eat away at her identity, and she tried to ignore the urge to panic. She had to get to Kennedy.

Elise reached the van, rounded the back, and saw Davis trying to jerk Kennedy from inside the front cab. She rushed over. "Davis!"

He glanced up at her and she saw the worry on his face. "Her ankle," he said, and she understood. A burst of flames exploded from the van's hood, and dread dropped inside Elise's gut like lead. She jumped up beside Davis and looked down to see that Kennedy's ankle was pinned between the passenger seat and the driving console. Her face was twisted with pain and wet with sweat, and she was yanking with all her might on her leg.

She looked up to see Elise's face and choked on emotion. "It's wedged too deep."

"No, no, we are going to get you out," Elise said. She

could feel the heat from the fire building beside them and felt herself losing her battle with panic.

"Davis, on three," Elise said. He nodded and they tugged. Kennedy cried in pain, and Elise felt her heart break. "Again," she said. Once more they pulled, tears streaming down Kennedy's face, her bellows of agony ripping through Elise's insides. She felt her own tears as the flames grew and Kennedy still wasn't free.

Oh, Father, please, Elise thought. *I can't lose her. I can't.* "Again," she said, and with more power than she knew she had, Elise yanked at her sister. Screams cut the sky, but at last the weight shifted forward and up. Kennedy's ankle sprang free, but the moment of joy was short-lived, as the heat flared in the engine and the entire front end of the van exploded into flames.

30

Jesse smiled as he stepped from the military-grade tank. His mind was clear and his sight focused. All previous questioning of right and wrong were gone; all that was needed was action. The Seers had departed with a half day's head start, but with all the resources of the Authority City at his disposal, it hadn't taken long to catch up, storming across the open valley toward the caravan of the enemy, and rain violence down upon them.

He hadn't expected that firing at the vans would be so successful, but to his surprise, his soldiers had nailed their shots with precision and sent the entire scene into chaos. The darkness now fully consuming his mind trembled with glee.

Things always work best when you are aligned with greatness.

Jesse smiled. Yes they did, he thought. His army had been only a couple of yards away from capturing and destroying them all when the front van had exploded, sending flaming shards in all directions. The darkness danced with pleasure, and Jesse chuckled, catching a glimpse of himself in the rearview mirror. His eyes still black, his heart still true.

How delightfully perfect.

Yes, he thought, *yes it is.*

/ / /

Elise's eyes fluttered open. Her sight was hazy, her head ringing; a soft buzz filled her ears. The side of her face scratched against something rough as she tried to lift her head. She saw dirt and rock. Smoke filled her lungs, and she coughed it out as she managed to lever herself up so she was propped on her hip. Elise searched for clarity and remembered.

Panic mushroomed in her chest as she saw bits of fiery car parts scattered around her. She surveyed the area for Davis or Kennedy and saw neither of them. She used her palms to push herself off the ground onto her feet and took a couple of steps. There was smoke everywhere, but through its fog she could see men with guns capturing the other Seers. Sage, Timmons, Lucy, Willis, all of them rounded up and cuffed.

She had to find Kennedy. She walked a couple of steps, searching frantically in all directions, and then she spotted her. Crumpled on the ground, clothes blackened with ash and mixed with dark red from her own blood. Elise rushed over, nearly stumbling, desperate to get to her sister. She coughed as her lungs struggled for air and dropped to her knees, sending ripples of pain up her thighs that she couldn't care less about.

"Kennedy," Elise said. The girl's eyes were closed, her face sticky with blood and dirt. Elise didn't know what to do, but didn't think moving her was a good idea. Terror ravaged her mind. Her hands shook as she reached down to feel for a pulse. The world froze before a slight tick under Elise's fingers released intense relief. Kennedy was alive, but barely.

"How do I save you?" Elise whispered, tears filling her eyes.

Remember who you are. The voice was so strong and calming that another rush of tears collected behind her eyes. *You are the light of the world.*

Elise reached for her truth, the one she had lost sight of in her fear, and welcomed it with open arms. How easy it was to forget and how crucial it was to remember. She eased her mind, walked through the storm of emotions rising up inside her like waves, and let them all fall behind her into still waters. She placed her hand on Kennedy's chest and sent her power racing down her arm and out her fingers.

Her light connected with the light inside Kennedy, and they intertwined, creating a magnificent glow. It shot out from Kennedy into the air and dried the tears on Elise's face. She could feel her sister's energy returning, growing as the light shone between them. Healing their minds and recapturing their hearts. Kennedy's body seemed almost to levitate off the ground as the power of their Father healed her body.

Something clicked behind Elise and the light dissolved, though its presence still washed over her skin. She knew what she'd face when she turned around; she could taste the vile darkness on her tongue, but she felt no fear. She was resting in truth, so what should she fear? Still facing her sister, Elise opened her eyes and felt them blaze with power.

She rose and turned. Jesse stood behind her, a yard separating them, his gun raised and engaged. His face was shadowed in darkness, his eyes black holes. Several feet behind him, guards had gathered the others together. Terror played on their faces as guns were pointed at them, forcing them to huddle closely. Willis pushed toward the front of the crowd and nearly stepped out of the circle before a guard pressed the end of his weapon to Willis's chest. His eyes found Elise's and she tried to send him some reassurance, but his face didn't ease.

Not that she could blame him. Jesse, the man leading this attack against them, had let the darkness devour him. That was why he was here. He was following a path he'd chosen, and it was leading him straight away from the light.

Yet even now, she knew, the light pursued him. Even as he was filled with hate and vengeance, the light called him chosen, son of the Father. Elise wanted to see his light but struggled to see anything past the darkness using his face as a mask. She waited for her own anger and fury to come. Had he not just tried to blow them all to bits? Wouldn't it be justified? Her mind told her yes, but she was learning that trusting her mind alone could be dangerous. Elise wanted to see him as a monster because it was true that he had done monstrous acts, but the light that called her chosen lifted her above her mind and showed her more. It spoke words of truth that she couldn't escape.

I call him chosen, perfect, blameless.

As you are, so is he.

The Father seeks to bring all to the light.

Help him remember and see.

If even for a moment Elise had considered taking the path of resistance, the words of truth now pulled her back. Jesse was lost and blind, but so had she been once. She knew that her true power came from showing perfect love, as she was called to do by her Father. Perfect love held no record of wrongs; it didn't keep score and tally blame. A strong wind encircled the valley and swept through the ends of her hair. It filled her with assurance, and she smiled.

"Jesse," she said.

His face twitched, and she saw the darkness seep from the pores on his face.

"You should be afraid," Jesse said.

"Why?"

"Because I'm going to kill you for all you've done."

"I know."

"Do you not fear death?"

"I am standing with the Father. If the Father is with me, then what should I fear?"

"And will the Father save you from my bullets?" Jesse sneered, his voice altered and hardly his own.

"The Father has already saved me," Elise said. As the words left her mouth, they became like water for the seeds of her soul. She was already the light of the world. With faith the size of a small seed, she could move mountains, heal the sick, raise the dead. Hadn't their faith in the light already done those things? Another level of assurance filled her, and her confidence in her true identity grew.

"You're a stupid girl," Jesse said.

"I am the daughter of my Father, chosen and called," Elise said.

Jesse gritted his teeth. "I should have killed you when you were a child."

"I am filled with light."

"Stop it."

"I abide with it, and it lives in me."

"Shut up!"

"I am a daughter of light, perfectly loved."

"Enough!"

"Perfectly whole."

"I said stop!"

"As are you," Elise said, and there was a brief pause before a crack shattered through the air.

Everything slowed. Time nearly froze. Even the breath in her lungs stilled. She saw the bullet spiraling toward her, but again she did not fear. *With faith the size of a small seed . . .* She let her mind completely succumb to her true nature, and the light wasn't just within her but embodied her entirely.

The scene snapped back into normal speed, and she raised her hand with confidence. "Stop," she said, and the bullet froze in midair. Gasps from onlookers filled the space, as the bullet hung aimlessly for a moment and then fell to the ground. She moved her eyes to gaze at Jesse, the man now white as a sheet, his weapon shaking in his trembling hand, and she began to walk toward him.

He seemed to be in such shock that he didn't even step back. He just stood quivering as she approached, and when she was only a foot from him, she reached out her hand and touched his cheek.

/ / /

The scene around Jesse changed. The world he knew disappeared, and he found himself standing in a field of ash. Everything was gray and dead, stretching for miles; ashes were lifted softly by the breeze as it drifted by.

"You burned the field of gold," said a soft voice.

Jesse spun around and saw Elise standing across the somber plain. His heart was still thundering in his chest, his lungs unable to get a steady breath. She had stopped a bullet. Flashes of Remko unloading a gun into Aaron's skull bounced around inside his memory. Aaron had made bullets disappear, but she had stopped one in midair.

"Why?" Elise asked.

Jesse snapped back to the present and glanced around at the cinders beneath his feet. "I was killing off the light."

She nodded as if seeming to understand and then looked back at him. "Did it work?"

Jesse couldn't get his heart to return to a normal rate. "Who are you?"

"I told you; I am the daughter of my Father."

The darkness hissed at her words and clawed at Jesse's brain. The pain burned viciously through his bones, and he struggled to breathe through the ache.

"You can be free from that," Elise said.

"Why does everyone assume I want to be free?" Jesse asked.

"Don't you?"

"Not if it means surrendering."

"But have you not surrendered already?"

Jesse shook his head. "No, I am in control."

"You and I both know that's not true."

"You know nothing."

"I know about your father, how he abused you. I know about Damien Gold and the Scientist, how they used you for their own personal gain. I know you believe the darkness brewing inside you is all you've ever had, but you are wrong."

The darkness roared violently and twisted around Jesse's lungs.

"You have never been far from the light," Elise said, taking a step toward him. "And you never will be." Again she touched him, this time on his chest, her hand warming his skin the moment they connected. His mind swirled with pictures—moments and memories from his past. The same dreadful snapshots that had been dug up to torture him ever since she had tried to bring forth the light.

He wanted to rip her hand away and hide from the pain of the memories that kept chasing him, but her hold on him was too strong. Her touch dove into him and secured itself to something solid. Something past the darkness rumbling like a hateful beast.

"See who you are," Elise said.

"I see," Jesse cried. "I see the pain all the time."

"No, see past the pain to the truth of who you are."

The darkness gnawed at his brain, sending spirals of agony down his back. He couldn't go further, didn't want to. The pain was too real, too volatile. But Elise pushed on, past all the darkest memories that Jesse caged away, past the darkest core where the evil beast lived, and reached a new plain.

A new memory: a single moment; a beautiful woman dressed in casual clothing, humming a sweet song while rocking a tiny child to sleep. Her eyes were kind and filled with love, her touch soft and easy. She gently brushed back the baby's hair with her fingers and smiled brightly. "Never forget, my beautiful son, how precious you are," the woman cooed. "All I have is yours, and I will give up everything for you. Do you know why, little boy?"

Her voice was so kind and comforting that Jesse felt his legs wobble beneath him.

"Because you, my only son, are the light of the world."

Her final statement ignited a fire within him and began a journey through the series of events that comprised Jesse's history. Every moment that he had hidden in darkness, kept from the light, replayed, but differently this time. Running from his father, hiding from his madness, becoming corrupted by Damien, being used by the Scientist. Losing his mother, losing his grandfather, losing himself. In all these moments the light could be seen hanging over him while he slept, dashing with him into hiding, following his footprints, stirring inside him, keeping him close.

The realization of how close the light had always been dropped Jesse to his knees. Again his mother's sweet words echoed through his head.

Because you, my only son, are the light of the world.

Darkness brutally pounded against his skull, trying to knock loose the truth that was starting to blossom there. Its screams tore at Jesse's eardrums, assaulting him with hatefulness.

Stupid boy, don't listen to her.

You, the light of the world—ha! You are nothing!

I am all you have. I will never leave you.

The vibration of its words shook him deep to his core. The voice was right; it was always right.

"No," Elise said, reading his thoughts, "the light has always been with you. It is with you now."

Like a small flame, light flickered to life inside Jesse's chest. It wavered against the darkness that still resided there but grew as Jesse let himself feel it. Tears gathered behind his eyes, and he choked back an outpouring of emotion.

"Listen to what it calls you; hear its truth speak above the whisper of darkness," Elise said.

You are nothing.

Stupid, foolish boy.

Jesse searched above the chatter of what he knew and hoped for the scant chance that Elise might be right. Had been right all along.

And then his entire world changed. A voice, like peaceful waves on the ocean, filled his ears and stole his heart.

Hear me, son of the Father, perfect and loved.

Remember who I call you. Remember where you came from.

Chosen, blameless, perfect son of mine.

The emotion Jesse had been holding back broke through as his mind was cleansed with the new form of love that grew with each word from the voice.

Hear me, son of the Father, perfect and loved.

Remember who I call you. Remember where you came from.

Chosen, blameless, perfect son of mine.

Jesse's shoulders shook as tears overtook him. The small flame that had ignited in his chest spread as each layer of grime melted away and parts of his true identity started to shake loose. Had he really missed it all along? How could he never have seen?

A thunderous wind whipped across the barren field, twisting up and around Jesse, running through his hair, pricking at his skin. It was warm, filled with intention and overwhelming power. It filled every cell and shattered the darkness, chasing it from Jesse's heart. Shame, worry, fear, hate—all the emotions that had walked with him, lived with him, and burdened his shoulders—were lifted away with the wind. They were replaced with acceptance, strength, freedom, and love in such strong waves that Jesse feared it would tear him apart.

Hear me, son of the Father, perfect and loved.

Remember who I call you. Remember where you came from.

Chosen, blameless, perfect son of mine.

Jesse fell forward, catching himself with both palms, and wept into the ground. His entire life he'd believed he was alone, worth nothing but what he could be used for, a slave to the darkness that haunted him, unable to be free. Now he saw that all he'd ever needed to be whole was always with him. Spoken to him by the sweet words of his mother, carried in his spirit, and blocked out by his own darkness.

"We all forget," a voice came, and Jesse lifted his eyes from the ground to see Aaron squatting down beside him.

"But the things I have done in my forgetfulness . . ."

"All necessary to get you here. Only in forgetting do we have the opportunity to remember."

Jesse pushed himself up, wiping his hand across his face to clean the snot and tears that had made him a mess. He looked around and saw that Elise was gone; it was just him and Aaron, in a field, once beautiful and golden, that he had burned to the ground.

"I've destroyed so much," Jesse said.

Aaron smiled and started carefully dusting away a spot in the ash. "All things are destroyed except for the truth. And where there is destruction," Aaron said, lifting his hand, "there can always be rebirth."

Where his hand had been, a tiny green bud had sprouted, reaching for the sky and giving the field a tiny ounce of color. "The first step in believing in who you really are is letting go of who you thought you were," Aaron said, "Don't worry; it will all grow back. There's magic in this place."

Aaron stood and extended his hand to Jesse. He took it, and Aaron pulled him up so that they were both standing in front of a tiny green sprout in a field of ash.

31

When Jesse reentered the world where he had just tried to destroy the Seers, hardly a moment had passed. Everyone was still standing in shock as Elise had only seconds before stopped a moving bullet. She was in front of him, her small hand on the side of his face, her eyes brimming with joy.

He remembered the field, and his mother's words, and the awakening of his light. Even now his fingers trembled at the thought of it, as if he wasn't sure it could be real, and he felt the slight pull of the familiar darkness creeping back in.

"Whenever I start to forget, I remind myself of what the light said to me," Elise said.

He didn't have to reach far; the words drifted back like an old song that Jesse knew every word to.

Hear me, son of the Father, perfect and loved.

Remember who I call you. Remember where you came from.

Chosen, blameless, perfect son of mine.

The darkness subsided, but the shame was heavy and thick. He struggled to see through it, to see how he could ever make up for all he had done. He glanced around him, at the people he'd been moments away from killing, at the guards he'd helped to blind with the Genesis Serum, and back to Elise, the girl he'd tried to murder.

The girl he had loved. He saw her differently now. His desire for her had been replaced with respect and admiration. She was never destined for him; he knew that clearly now. She was bound to another, and the romantic feelings that had captured his heart for so long were replaced with love and longing for another: his Father, the true desire of his heart, and the light, his new source of longing.

"If it helps," Elise said, "I forgive you."

Jesse huffed an awkward laugh and shook his head. "Now what?"

"We show everyone their light. And we can start right here."

Yes, Jesse thought, *show everyone.*

/ / /

Something was happening in the valley straight ahead of their caravan. Nicolas ordered the vehicles to stop and climbed out of the van in which he was riding shotgun. Several other soldiers also climbed out from their vehicles, but Nicolas motioned for them to hold firm as he trekked toward the edge of the hill and glanced down into the wide valley.

Hundreds of CityWatch personnel stood scattered about. CityWatch vehicles dotted the background, and a sense of unrest filled the air as all of them focused on whatever was playing out in the center of their gathering. Nicolas squinted to try and see exactly what was happening, and a deep-seated fury began to form in his gut. He recognized Jesse even at this distance and knew that the girl standing opposite him had to be Elise. His soul sensed it even before his mind was certain. Dozens of questions formulated inside his mind, all of which he pushed aside as the darkness in his chest blossomed and began to speak to him.

They have all abandoned me but you. They have forsaken my power. They have given in to weakness. Do not do the same.

Nicolas was struck by how clear the voice was, as if someone were standing beside him, whispering into his ear. He should have been caught off guard, unnerved, but the voice was so familiar and direct that Nicolas didn't even flinch. From where he stood, he knew that something had changed within Jesse, that he was no longer just weakly in love with a girl who threatened him but that he had given his heart to another power altogether.

They have all abandoned me, but you will not. Surrender to me, and I will fill you with enough power to destroy them all.

Nicolas trembled as an explosion of dark power rumbled through his body. It ignited his mind and muscles in ways he never thought possible, but as quickly as it had come it disappeared. He gasped at the sudden departure and longed for it to return.

Surrender to me first.

Nicolas clenched his back teeth and gave in to the

calling lingering in his mind. The power returned with force, rocking through his figure like a hurricane and swallowing him with rage. Nicolas closed his eyes, and the power enveloped each of his cells, whispered instruction, and sent him on a path he was born to travel.

He opened his eyes with intention.

Burn them all.

/ / /

Remko watched as all the CityWatch soldiers were instructed to exit their vehicles. They had been stopped for several long minutes. Remko didn't know why, but something was apparently happening in the valley below them. There was trouble ahead. The guards were suiting up, gathering weapons, following commands, preparing themselves to march on Nicolas's orders.

Something softly tugged at his heart and he suddenly felt desperate to get out of the van to see what was happening. He waited, an unwarranted excitement building as the soldiers all fell into line and began to march down the side of the hill and out of sight. He waited another moment to make sure the coast was clear, and then, with his hands still secured behind his back, he awkwardly managed to open the door and climb out.

The second his feet touched the ground he felt it.

The light.

It was swimming through the air, setting the atoms

around him on fire. The light ushered him toward the edge of the hill, and his heart caught in his throat as he glanced down. His eyes took in the whole scene but ignored everything except the beautiful raven-haired girl facing Nicolas and his army with certainty. He couldn't make out the details of her face, but tears stung the back of his eyes because his heart knew her instantaneously.

He wanted to rush down to her, yet his feet were grounded. He wanted to cry out her name, yet his voice was gone. All he could do was stare in amazement. After years of longing, of not knowing, there she was.

Elise.

/ / /

Elise buzzed with excitement. The light was weaving through the air around her, dancing beside her, singing to her soul. Jesse stood before her, his face changed, his eyes clear. His light pulsed softly, the strength of it still unknown to him, but its presence undeniable.

Suddenly, piercing through her happiness, she felt another essence that she knew all too well. Darkness.

Fear rose in her core but only for a moment before it was overcome by the unchanging power flowing through her veins. If the light was in her, what should she fear? Even this monster was no match. She turned her head to see a man walking down the tall hill with an army behind him. They were coming for her, led by the darkness embodying their leader.

"Nicolas," Jesse said behind her.

"Yes," Elise said.

"He means us harm; we should leave," Jesse said.

"No." She turned to face him. "Remember who you are, and know there is nothing to fear."

Elise saw Nicolas's face come into focus as the army drew closer, and the same dark essence that had filled Jesse's face only moments earlier now laced his. This was an enemy she was getting used to, but it still sent a shiver down her back. Again she was faced with fear, and again the light was stronger. Nicolas was fueled by hate, but Elise was captured by love. She closed her eyes, felt the light that had won over death itself, and did what she'd been called to do. She sent it forth.

/ / /

Nicolas followed the leading of his newborn power as he closed the distance to Elise and Jesse. *Burn them all.* He could feel the rage growing within him with each step. He saw his president's face, saw the fear that lingered in his eyes, and felt the evil essence twist with pleasure.

Elise, however, was a different story. Her face was not the same as Nicolas remembered; it held a certainty that provoked the darkness to unparalleled anger. He yanked his weapon free and motioned for the army behind him to prepare to fire. He heard the clicking of weaponry as the guards followed orders, the darkness pumping his heart coiling up to strike. Nicolas started to raise his weapon when the ground beneath his feet began to shake.

He looked down to see pebbles bouncing from the tremor vibrating the earth and slowed his march. The army behind him followed suit, and as he glanced up, holding himself steady, he saw that everything around them was falling victim to the powerful quake. The guards started to mumble among themselves, concern lacing their voices, and Nicolas turned his eyes to Elise, who was the only steady thing in sight. Her face glowed with light, and more hate thickened in his soul. The darkness grew furiously and screeched at the open sky.

Burn them all!

Nicolas tried to raised his gun again, but the vibration in the ground grew. He wobbled, nearly losing his footing, and struggled to hold on to his weapon. The dark, howling presence filled his ears, and the ground felt as though it would split beneath him. And then it all stopped.

Everything went still. Nicolas's eyes were on Elise as she opened hers and locked them on him. Nicolas felt himself retract a step. The darkness urged him forward, but his body was reacting to the girl before him. His heart pounded against his bones. Elise's eyes were nothing but light, piercing out toward him and reaching into his chest. The white light lifted her arms, swirling around her like armor, and she brought her hands forward, clapping them together.

If they made a sound, Nicolas didn't hear it because as

her palms connected, bright light exploded from her in all directions. It washed over Nicolas and drove him to his knees, a force hot enough to burn away his resolve. He gasped for breath in the wake of it. He couldn't see anything through the blinding heat. It dove into his skin and set his blood on fire.

He yelled out against the pain and dropped his gun; it bounced on the ground and skidded away. He grabbed for his head, the light opening pockets of agony in his mind, trying to envelop him and kill off his darkness. *No,* he thought, *I will not succumb to this madness!*

She had to be stopped. He searched the ground for his gun but felt nothing as the earth started to shake again. Cries from his army echoed with the pounding of pain in his head. She was attacking them all.

His shouts of anger filled the air. He would not be taken! The darkness rained down around him, threatening to crush him with its power. It called for blood. Demanded death. Nicolas dared not fail it, but he also couldn't secure his footing. He dug for more fuel, begging the darkness for more power, for guidance. It yanked him forward and called him to stand. Nicolas followed its urging, pushing against the light and fighting to stay on his feet. He reached out, stepped forward, and connected with a body. The moment his hand grasped an arm, the light cleared just enough that Nicolas could see his face.

Jesse.

The man who had led them into this mess, the one who

had never been strong enough to handle the power that came with his position, the man who had abandoned the darkness for something else. The man who had given up his power for love. The evil coursing through Nicolas's flesh raged at the sight of Jesse, and Nicolas felt his hatred for the man intensify.

Light cascaded around him, burning him, while the darkness lurched out, wrapping him in ice. Nicolas and Jesse held one another's gaze. Uncontrollable rage flooded Nicolas's senses, and suddenly all he wanted to do was crush the pathetic man standing before him.

Jesse opened his mouth to say something, taking a step back in fear, but Nicolas wasn't interested in what he had to say. He was following a power greater than himself, and it called for blood. The darkness erupted gleefully in his chest and rage blinded him as with a mighty shout he yanked the knife from his belt and drove it forward.

The blade sank deep within a fleshy target, and Nicolas looked up, expecting to see the color draining from Jesse's weak eyes. Instead he saw Elise's. The light evaporated from the valley as Elise gasped in pain. Nicolas glanced down to see his knife plunged deeply into her gut, his fingers drenched in her blood.

His shock passed quickly as the darkness hissed in pleasure, and Nicolas pushed the knife deeper into Elise's stomach. She had stepped in to protect the man who had stolen her. Stupid girl. Her eyes rolled into the back of her head before she clenched them tight in agony.

"No!" screamed a voice from behind her. Jesse moved around her and pushed Nicolas away, and the knife receded from its place. Nicolas stumbled backward from Jesse's force as others in the valley, now able to see, cried out for Elise. Nicolas felt the manic rumble of laughter that wasn't his own scurry through his chest and up his throat. It fell from his mouth and echoed across the sky. He had lost himself to the darkness.

Another outburst matched his own as Jesse flung himself at Nicolas. The two tumbled to the ground, rolling in the dirt, and then Jesse had secured the boy beneath him. Nicolas felt the older man's fist come down hard against his chin, snapping his neck sideways. Again he hit him, and again, pain raging through Nicolas's face. Blood shone on Jesse's knuckles as he let another wave of anger explode through his fist.

The darkness continued to laugh toward the sky between Jesse's blows. It had complete control of Nicolas now, and it hissed words out through his teeth. "Yes, claim your rage."

Jesse hit Nicolas again, screeching at the sky.

"Come home, little boy; come home," the darkness whispered through Nicolas's mouth.

The words finally caused Jesse to pause, which gave Nicolas the perfect opportunity to gain the upper hand. He shifted his weight, rocking Jesse sideways, and thrust him off to the ground. Nicolas rolled away, swinging his leg out and connecting the heel of his boot with Jesse's face.

Jesse's head snapped back and Nicolas rose to his knees. He reached out for the collar of Jesse's shirt and yanked him forward far enough to send a hard punch across Jesse's face, knocking him back to the ground.

Finish the girl. Burn them all.

The darkness was buzzing in Nicolas's ears and he swung his eyes to where Elise was now kneeling, her blood darkening the ground as she tried to remain conscious.

Finish her!

Nicolas worked himself to standing and started for Elise.

Yes! Burn them all.

A shot snapped through the air, and a tight pinch spread out at the back of Nicolas's head. The world stilled, and for a moment only his breathing existed, until the pinch expanded into intense, unbearable pain, and his world went black.

/ / /

Jesse held the gun in his hand, his arm extended toward Nicolas, his knees ground into the dirt. Smoke floated from the end of the gun as the shot bounced through the air. The bullet landed squarely in the back of Nicolas's head, and after a pause he crumpled forward, his skull bouncing off the dirt. A tremor shot down Jesse's spine. He looked at the fallen boy, shame filling his bones, but he pushed it away as thoughts of Elise entered his mind. He turned toward her as she gasped for air and the other Seers gathered around.

Jesse stood and moved to her without another thought. Her face was pale, her eyes hazy as he dropped to his knees beside her. Others were speaking, but he tuned them all out. He pulled her from them and laid her in his lap. He cupped his hand over the place at her side where Nicolas had stabbed her, trying to put pressure on her wound. "I'm sorry," he whispered. "I'm so sorry." He could feel the sticky heat of her blood squishing between his fingers. She had stepped in front of him. She had taken this wound for him. After everything he had done to her, she had sacrificed herself for him.

"Hold on, Elise, please." Tears pooled in his eyes, and then he heard the comforting voice of his newfound love.

Hear me, son of the Father, perfect and loved.

Remember who I call you. Remember where you came from.

Chosen, blameless, perfect son of mine.

The light filled his mind, blinding him as if the light in Elise hadn't faded with her fall, and its power began to build under his skin.

As she is, so are you. I call you to myself, child of the light.

With faith as small as a seed, you too can move mountains.

His mind was new and his fear great, but Jesse felt pulled down a path that was covered in light. Could he really walk that path, as he'd seen Elise do? Could he too be filled with such power? He could sense her life draining away with the blood that dripped through his fingers, and he knew there was no time for hesitation.

He closed his eyes and searched for the light that called

him. He let go of his anger, let go of his reservations, let go of his pain, let go of his logic, and fell headfirst into the pool of brilliant light filling him. He swam in it, the light holding him close, and he saw himself so clearly that all previous doubt of who he was vanished. He clutched the newfound truth and harnessed its power. He felt it roll down through his arms and into his fingers. The world around him erupted into brilliant colors, dancing across his vision, pounding with such a furious love that Jesse felt lost in it.

Tears moistened his face and he completely surrendered to his Father. Joy like a river gushed around him. Waves of peace lapped over him, filling him with childlike wonder. He began to laugh, his voice breaking the sky, his world reshaping, his heart healing. The moment stretched out and then faded, but the awareness of his true nature remained strong within him.

He opened his eyes and was back in the valley. Elise lay in his arms; others stood around. A young girl who favored Elise and a broad-shouldered boy knelt on her other side, tears in their eyes, wonder on their faces. The other Seers were there too, hundreds of guards standing behind them, all awakened and free from their blindness. He turned his gaze back to Elise and watched as her eyes fluttered open, filled with color and life. He helped her sit up slowly, his hands still trembling with light. She looked around, and then directly at him.

They said nothing. There was nothing to say. She smiled at him and his heart ballooned with delight. The others pushed in then, and he backed away a bit. The young girl who must have been her sister threw her arms around Elise's neck, and the handsome young boy kissed her forehead. They encircled her with love, and Jesse moved back even farther to watch from the outside. He heard a male voice he recognized calling Elise's name and looked up to see Remko Brant rushing toward them, his hands tied behind his back, tears flowing down his face. The whole scene was magic, perfect, as it was supposed to be, and the light was still buzzing between them all, encircling them in love.

/ / /

Carrington woke from her delusion, her mind aching with the painful recurrence of memories, her heart mixed with emotions. She blinked through the darkness surrounding her. She heard the grunts and grumbles of others she knew, saw the shadows of bodies shifting through the dim light. Then a soft click, followed by a shrilling creak, and the enclosed space was filled with daylight.

She squinted at the onslaught of new light and pushed herself off the wall where she had been propped. She steadied herself and took a deep breath. She knew where she was, in an Authority van being transported to the Authority City. She knew Trylin had been taken; she knew Remko wasn't with her; she knew she'd been given the Genesis Serum; she knew her memories had been stolen; and she knew they had been returned.

Only moments ago a different kind of light had filled this space. A light Carrington knew well but forgot too often. A light that warmed her heart and broke her free from doubt and called her home. A light that saved her time and time again, that met her where she was, that drew her close, that called her daughter. Even thinking of it now, the remnants of it still lingering in her vision, brought tears to her eyes.

But something was different this time. The light was deeper and stronger than any she'd experienced before. It sang to her soul and whispered for her to travel toward its source. It beckoned her to follow, and Carrington knew she had to go. She moved with the others as they stepped down from the back of the van onto the valley floor. Forest and mountains stood around them, the sun high in the sky, the air cool with an afternoon breeze. And there was light. Not from the sun but from the Father.

It danced around and twisted with the wind. It rolled through the air and shuffled across people's feet. Carrington could see it clear as day, across the entire valley, touching every soul, seeming to encase the world in love. And as her heart called, she followed the light's streams. Around the side of the van, up to the edge of a decline, down the hill, her feet pulling her faster than her mind thought necessary, as if her body knew what was waiting for her before she'd perceived it.

Several yards in front of her was a gathering of people. Hundreds strung out, some standing, others pushing themselves off the ground, all encircled with light. And in the center was a man standing beside a girl, dark curly hair surrounding her shoulders, her body buzzing with light, and Carrington's entire world shifted. Her heart knew the girl as her mind slowly caught up.

Elise.

She didn't stop moving but picked up speed and rushed with desperation and joy. She didn't slow until she was only a couple of feet from her daughter, pushing though the people gathered around, tears running like streams down her face and the voice of her Father speaking truth over her.

When she is with me, what can stand against her?
I call her daughter, perfect and chosen.
Fear not, for I have always held her close.

Carrington pushed to the front of the crowd and stopped. Elise looked over at her, and the two stared for a long moment. Carrington struggled to breathe, struggled to think clearly. Her legs had stopped working. Her heart thundered so quickly her chest ached. She couldn't drag her eyes away from the beautiful woman in front of her.

Then her cruel mind began to remind her of all the time she'd missed with her baby girl. All the hours gone, all the memories they hadn't shared. All the moments that had been stolen from them. Anger like a wave rose within her and threatened to cast out the light still swimming through her blood. The world had been so unkind to Carrington to keep her sweet daughter from her. But even as the thoughts rummaged through her mind, Elise stepped toward her until she was close enough to reach out and grab Carrington's hand. Her touch brought on another rush of tears, and Elise used her free hand to reach up and wipe her mother's cheeks clean.

"The world may have kept us apart, but the light always drew us together. You have never been without me, and I have never been without you," Elise said.

Her words broke Carrington's heart and reminded her of a truth strong enough to heal the entire world. Her anger vanished as peace filled her soul. The Father had never let Elise out of His sight. The light had been with her all of her moments, as it had always been with Carrington. It had been hard to see that through her grief, but it was clear now. She had never needed to fear or worry, because a love stronger than death had held her sweet Elise close even when Carrington could not.

Carrington nodded with a proud smile at her daughter's wisdom and pulled her close. They held each other for a long time. Eventually Remko and Kennedy joined them, and Carrington let the power and grace of the Father remind her of who she was.

/ / /

Jesse watched as the moments after healing Elise played out before him. Because that's what he had done. He had healed her. Or at least he had been the channel. The power of the light had healed her right before his eyes and then he'd stepped back to watch from the outside.

He watched as the other Seers cried with Elise and held

her tightly. He looked on as Elise wrapped Kennedy, her sister, in an embrace, holding her for a long moment. He watched as the boy she had given her heart to pulled her close and kissed her. Jesse was surprised to feel no jealousy or remorse. His feelings had really transformed into something completely different, just as he had.

He faced Remko for the first time in twenty years, battling with guilt, and then found himself awestruck by the love Remko demonstrated. He watched as Elise encountered the love of her mother for the first time when Carrington came rushing down the hill toward the group. The family he'd broken finally reunited. Then several hundred others joined them, some of whom Jesse recognized, most of whom he didn't.

There were more tears and laughter than Jesse had ever experienced, and he found himself stepping farther and farther back to watch it all and give those around him space to reconnect.

He kept expecting to look at Elise and feel the familiar desire, but it was gone. He'd used her, he realized, as a way to feel something that was now completely satisfied by his Father. It was odd even now, after change had only been with him for a short time, to think that he had ever sought anything other than the true calling of his heart.

The wind softly comforted him as his mind experienced the roller coaster of doubt and then belief. A constant cycle of remembering and forgetting, and being refilled with joy each time.

"All of life is that cycle," someone said beside him, and Jesse turned to see Aaron standing to his left.

Jesse nodded. "Yes, I've heard that before."

Aaron placed his hand on Jesse's shoulder and affectionately squeezed it tight. "I have waited a long time for you to return, brother."

Jesse smiled and felt the light warm his chest. "Everything will be different now."

Aaron laughed and gave Jesse's shoulder another squeeze before releasing him. "Yes, the whole world will change."

Jesse marveled as he looked back at the large group of people gathered before him. He took a deep breath, felt the perfect love of his Father, and knew that no matter what lay ahead of them, they were all carriers of the light. Created from perfect truth and held in everlasting power.

Jesse smiled. "May we never again forget who we truly are."

EPILOGUE

E lise stood facing Willis, her hands clasped in his,
his eyes locked on hers. They stood at the front of
the large Capitol ballroom, the entire room filled to
capacity with people from all over the city. White
satin hung around them in flowing trails, and bursting bouquets of yellow and white flowers filled the
room with sweet scents. People were dressed in their finest,
and the room was humming with such joy that Elise found
it hard to keep her laughter contained.

She wore a crown of small white flowers that perfectly
matched the white gown her mother had finished only
weeks before. Aaron stood before them, his eyes shining with the significance of this day. Remko stood to his
left. The two men looked on with love as Elise and Willis
promised themselves to one another.

The city was changed, the streets filled with a new sense
of identity and love. A place once ruled by fearful men
hiding from what they didn't understand was now ruled

by light. They were all learning to live differently. To love differently. To forgive differently. They struggled, and they would continue to struggle for as long as they lived. But they were beginning to understand that pain and struggle were not the enemy. In fact, when they operated in light, there was no enemy at all. For who could truly stand against them when they stood with the light?

"As Willis Lane and Elise Brant have committed their lives completely to the light, so now they commit themselves to each other," Aaron said to the crowd.

Willis beamed and Elise fought the urge to kiss him right here in the middle of the ceremony. She could feel her heels bouncing and Willis chuckled at her squirminess.

"As fellow followers of the truth, as fellow children of the light, we bear witness to their union and join with them in celebrating their love, created by the light and ordained by the Father," Aaron said.

Aaron then narrowed his gaze to just Elise and Willis, his voice dropping slightly in volume, and he placed his palm over their joined hands and smiled. "Let what the light has brought together be strong enough to face all troubles. Let no man or darkness break apart what has been joined here. Let your union remind you of the Father's perfect love, and may it stay with you all of your days."

Elise felt tears breaking through her happiness and slipping silently down her cheeks. Willis's eyes danced with love as he brushed her cheek with his thumb and pulled her close. His lips pressed against hers and the room ignited into cheers. The building shook with the force of it and joy rumbled out into the streets. Elise pressed herself deeper into Willis's kiss and wrapped her arms around his neck, hoisting herself up onto her toes.

He smiled through their kiss and she felt herself doing the same. The light swirled around them and through them, setting their souls ablaze with joy. She was his and he was hers. Joined together by choice and chosen by light. Perfect love uniting with perfect love, to spend the rest of their days following the voice of their Father. The future was bright.

Elise and Willis separated, smiled at each other, and turned to face the rest of the room. Another round of shouts and cheers vibrated the walls, and Elise laughed with glee. Carrington, who had been standing in the front row, rushed forward and pulled Elise into her embrace. Kennedy joined them, tears brimming in her eyes. Remko was next, all of them wrapped together.

Elise was overwhelmed with the joy of it all. A perfect moment she knew she would never forget as long as she lived. She laughed again and felt the light fill her chest.

Yes, she thought, the future was very bright indeed.

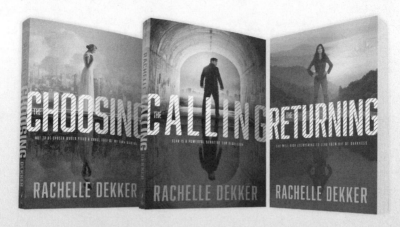

ACKNOWLEDGMENTS

I've said it before, and I'll say it again: writing a novel takes a village. Mine is extremely awesome, the best there is, without whom I would be lost.

To Tyndale: for all your endless belief and hard work, from marketing to cover creation to letting me take chances, thank you so much for being part of my journey.

To the Fedd Agency: Esther and Whitney, thank you for always having my back. Standing beside me in the sun and in the fire. Whitney, your constant excitement about my future has been a stunning gift, and it continues to inspire me. Thank you.

To Katy: I'm running out of ways to say thank you for all the input, all the patience, and all the time you put into each of my novels. You've become a key part of my process, and I'd be afraid to face it without you now. (Also, shout out to her awesome husband, Graham, and sweet son, Mac, for all the future hours she's going to have to sacrifice with them. I've got quite a few more books to write! She is lucky to have them, and I am lucky to have her.)

To the Blue Monkeys: you keep me focused, remind me that I'm not alone, and offer ample hilarious distraction. I love all of you.

To JT, Kara, and Chelise: They say you don't get to pick your family—well, I'm pretty sure you were picked exactly for me. You inspired these novels in so many ways, and I can't thank you enough for that.

To Mom and Dad: I've known since I was a little girl that things aren't always what they seem. I was born with a feverish curiosity and an imagination that could transport me to worlds only I saw. Thank you for never dulling those parts of me. Thank you for encouraging me to ask questions and find answers and dream. Thank you for pushing me to read and encouraging me to explore. And thank you for doing the same yourselves. For showing me through your actions—even though I haven't lived under your roof for twelve years—that chasing after adventure is worth every crazy look you get from the neighbors. You two act more like children all the time, and it is a beautiful thing that I am incredibly grateful for.

To Daniel: You are the love of my life. The one who grows beside me, never trying to overshadow, strong and steady when the storms come, cool and comforting in the blazing sun. Silly when I am taking myself too seriously and a good voice of reason when maybe I'm not taking myself seriously enough. No one else sees my journey of writing the way you do, and the fact that you see me, amid all the crazy, ranting madness, is everything. There's no one I'd rather lie by the pool with, as we find shapes in the clouds and talk about what it would be like if we could both suddenly fly. Thanks for being my bae!

To my Father: When the darkness becomes too much, when I feel afraid of the past and the future, when I forget my true identity, when I get caught in the lies of shame, when I can't forgive myself, your soft, kind spirit is always there to remind me: *This too shall pass; this too I have conquered. Remember, see, let go, and return to truth, where love knows no bounds and anything is possible.* I write to remember these truths and I give it to the world so that they might remember as well.

ABOUT THE AUTHOR

The oldest daughter of *New York Times* bestselling author Ted Dekker, Rachelle Dekker was inspired early on to discover truth through storytelling. She won a Christy Award for her critically acclaimed debut novel, *The Choosing*, which was followed by two more books in the Seer series: *The Calling* and *The Returning*. Rachelle graduated with a degree in communications and spent several years in marketing and corporate recruiting before making the transition to write full-time. She lives in Nashville with her husband, Daniel, and their diva cat, Blair. Visit her online at www.rachelledekker.com.

JOIN RACHELLE ON THE JOURNEY

Visit www.rachelledekker.com

DISCUSSION QUESTIONS

1. Before the events of *The Returning*, Carrington and Remko must give up their daughter, Elise, leaving her behind in the Authority City and trusting that the Father will keep her safe. Have you ever sacrificed something important to you—your time, money, or goals—in order to serve God or help someone else? What was the outcome of that decision?

2. Lucy tells Carrington, "It happens in a flash, like a sneaky fox—suddenly the truth of your identity is replaced by the illusions of your mistakes." Why is it so easy for us to believe lies about ourselves? Can you think of a time you've been tempted to believe a lie about who you are or what you're capable of? What can we do to resist such lies?

3. At the beginning of *The Returning*, almost all the residents of the Authority City are controlled by the Genesis Serum—they are unable to make choices, have

no emotions, and have forgotten who they are. What is the main problem with the Genesis Serum—why is it so dangerous? Does it really make everyone equal?

4. In chapter 5, Carrington writes Elise, "Life, my sweet daughter, is a cycle of remembering and forgetting. But don't fret: the more often you practice remembering, the less often you forget." Do you agree with this assessment? In what ways have you noticed the importance of remembering in your own life? What things do you most often have to remember?

5. Several characters in the story, including Elise, Jesse, and Carrington, experience the voice of darkness and the voice of light. What are some of the main differences between these voices in *The Returning*? How does each of these characters decide whether to succumb to the darkness or to cling to the light?

6. Nicolas and his soldiers arrive at Trylin City in chapter 18, prepared to be met with violent resistance. Instead, Remko and the other Seers welcome them in, refusing to fight back. Why do they make that decision—and did you agree with it? Why does this response make Nicolas so angry?

7. In chapter 30, the voice of the Father reminds Elise, *Remember who you are. You are the light of the world.* The Bible tells Christians the same thing (see Matthew 5:14). What does it mean to be the light of

the world? What are the privileges and responsibilities of this identity?

8. In each book of the Seer series, a new corrupt leader exerts control over the Authority City—Isaac Knight in *The Choosing*, Damien Gold in *The Calling*, and the Scientist in *The Returning*. What do you think the people of the city should do to avoid the influence of a similar leader in the future? Throughout history, why have untrustworthy, self-serving leaders often been able to take over societies in turmoil?

9. Over the course of the series, several characters receive strength, encouragement, and insight in a place called "the Father's field." What does this field symbolize? What is its purpose? And why do you think the author chose a field, rather than some other location?

10. The story ends with hope, as Elise and Willis get married in the Capitol ballroom. What do you predict will happen in their future? In the future of the other characters, and in the society as a whole?

TYNDALE HOUSE PUBLISHERS IS CRAZY4FICTION!

Fiction that entertains and inspires

Get to know us! Become a member of the Crazy4Fiction community. Whether you read our blog, like us on Facebook, follow us on Twitter, or receive our e-newsletter, you're sure to get the latest news on the best in Christian fiction. You might even win something along the way!

JOIN IN THE FUN TODAY.

 www.crazy4fiction.com

 Crazy4Fiction

 @Crazy4Fiction